# "So...you're beginning to like me, aren't you?"

Unfortunately, yes. More than he could imagine. "Of course not," she replied, smiling impishly. "I just don't want your pain and suffering on my conscience, McCavett."

"Same for me, Perkins. Having you hurt when I'm supposed to be protecting you will make me look bad. Can't have you shot down and expect another prospective bride to feel secure. I'd get a reputation as a bad risk."

When he walked off, Pru stared after him, noting the way his trim-fitting breeches accentuated his lean hips and his muscular thighs. The man looked good coming and going. She wished she didn't enjoy having Jack underfoot quite so much. But...she did!

\* \* \*

***McCavett's Bride***
**Harlequin® Historical #852—June 2007**

## Praise for Carol Finch

"Carol Finch is known for her lightning-fast, roller-coaster-ride adventure romances that are brimming over with a large cast of characters and dozens of perilous escapades."
—*Romantic Times BOOKreviews*

### Praise for previous novels

### The Ranger's Woman

"Finch delivers her signature humor, along with a big dose of colorful Texas history, in a love and laughter romp."
—*Romantic Times BOOKreviews*

### Lone Wolf's Woman

"As always, Finch provides frying-pan-into-the-fire action that keeps the pages flying, then spices up her story with not one, but two romances, sensuality and strong emotions."
—*Romantic Times BOOKreviews*

# CAROL FINCH

## McCavett's Bride

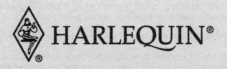
## HARLEQUIN®

TORONTO • NEW YORK • LONDON
AMSTERDAM • PARIS • SYDNEY • HAMBURG
STOCKHOLM • ATHENS • TOKYO • MILAN • MADRID
PRAGUE • WARSAW • BUDAPEST • AUCKLAND

ISBN-13: 978-0-373-29452-7
ISBN-10:      0-373-29452-2

McCAVETT'S BRIDE

This edition published by arrangement with Harlequin Books S.A.

www.eHarlequin.com

**Printed in U.S.A.**

# *Chapter One*

*Saint Louis, 1890*

Prudence Perkins paced the parlor of her home, mentally preparing for the inevitable clash with her father. Her grandmother, self-appointed ruler of the Perkins family, had been pressuring Pru's father to contract a marriage. Pru knew that her father had a history of bowing to Gram's wishes. It amazed Pru that Horatio Perkins, who was widely known for his tough business skills and his ability to steadily increase the profits of Perkins Fur Company, had never learned to stand up to his own mother.

Sighing heavily, Pru reversed direction to wear a few more ruts in the Aubusson carpet that Gram had ordered from Europe the previous year. She stopped short and glanced around the expensively furnished room, as if seeing it for the first time. It dawned on Pru that the furnishings and décor—right down to the grandfather clock in the corner, the original oil paintings on the walls and the ornately carved clock on the mantel—had all been selected and delivered at Gram's decree.

This wasn't Pru and her father's home. It certainly didn't reflect Pru's tastes. This was the proverbial castle that Gram had created to flaunt the Perkins wealth. Pru had become one of Gram's projects years ago and now she was to be thrust into a marriage she didn't want.

The thought caused Pru to halt abruptly, leaving her full skirts whirling about her legs. It suddenly occurred to her that her widowed grandmother had created this elaborately decorated dollhouse for her only son. Now she was railroading Pru into an unwanted marriage so she could assume the task of constructing a new dollhouse for Pru to live in. No doubt, Gram still intended to lord over Pru as she had for a dozen years.

A surging sense of panic overcame Pru. Her thoughts whirring, she took up pacing again and nervously wrung her hands. For the twenty-three years of her existence, she had been dragged to social events and taught to behave with the decorum befitting the high and mighty Perkins family—Gram's perception, not Pru's. She had managed to ditch every suitor who bore Gram's stamp of approval, but time was running out. Gram was on a relentless mission to get Pru married so construction could begin on a new, life-size dollhouse.

The impulsive urge to flee provoked Pru to lurch toward the door. Unfortunately, she was too late. Her father strode through the arched entryway. His hands were clasped behind his back. His brown hair, which was showing signs of gray and receding a bit, was combed back from his forehead. His facial expression and the intensity of his blue eyes indicated that he was deep in thought. At fifty-two, Horatio, a widower, was still a fine figure of a man. He was also one of the most sought-after men in Saint Louis' high society.

Horatio halted in the middle of the room, adjusted his wire-rimmed spectacles and flicked a piece of lint from his custom-made jacket—one of the many Gram had ordered for him. Then he gestured toward the tufted sofa that Gram had purchased last Christmas.

"Pru, take a seat, please."

"I prefer to stand." She tilted her chin and met his gaze head-on. "Why have you summoned me, Papa?" As if she didn't know.

"Your grandmother thinks it's time to make the formal wedding arrangements so we can get your life squared away."

Pru tilted her chin up another notch, causing her curly blond hair to ripple over her rigid shoulders. "I haven't found a man interesting enough to spend the rest of my life with," she replied. "It would be premature to plan a wedding until I have selected a groom."

"Your grandmother has been using her connections to find a suitable match." Her father's gaze narrowed as he added pointedly. "She doesn't think you've put much effort into finding a husband. She says that all your noble causes occupy so much of your time that your social life has suffered."

"Noble causes have a way of doing that," she contended. "They are also more important than frivolous social parties."

Horatio flicked his wrist dismissively. "All the same, Pru, you are well past marriage age, as your grandmother keeps reminding me. I need to take command of the situation."

There it was again. The annoying fact that Gram ruled

this roost and her son had difficulty standing up to his mother, even in defense of his one and only daughter.

Honestly, there was a time when she was a child that she had wondered if her mother had died just to avoid Gram's domineering manner. Later, of course, she realized that illness was the contributing cause. But still!

"The fact that you have been single since Mama passed on thirteen years ago proves that a Perkins can survive alone," Pru pointed out.

Horatio shifted awkwardly from one well-shod foot to the other. "Just because I haven't remarried doesn't mean I have been entirely without a woman's attention." He cleared his throat and stared at the gold-plated clock on the mantel. "For you, however, there is the obligation of providing an heir."

Her obligation? Her family duty? "I resent the implication that it is my duty to become a broodmare in order to produce the next overseer for the family fur business. This is *my* life and I am entitled to my own choices of what to do with it. One of my callings is to see that women enjoy the same rights and privileges as men, you know. I fully intend to be the mistress of my own fate, Papa."

"It's that rebellious attitude that has made it difficult to find you a match, young lady." *Thump, thump, thump.*

Pru spun around to see Gram lurking in the hall. She was dressed in her usual black ensemble and she surged into the parlor to the rhythmic click of her elaborately carved cane. It was fitting that the ivory handle was carved in the likeness of a dragonhead. Pru had been the recipient of many a whack from that cane when she had stepped out of line in years past.

"You were eavesdropping, Gram?" Of course she was. It was a perfected skill that Gram relied on to keep abreast of everything that transpired around this house. The only busybody in town who ran a close second was Victoria Reams, who had set her sights on Horatio. But even she couldn't outmaneuver the seventy-four-year-old curmudgeon to land one of Saint Louis' wealthiest entrepreneurs.

The thought of having Victoria as her stepmother, while Gram continued to lord over her, made Pru grimace.

"I was not eavesdropping," Gram harrumphed. "I was simply on my way through the foyer and happened to overhear your conversation."

Likely story, thought Pru. Gram could sniff out conversations that were none of her business better than a bloodhound.

The familiar thump of the cane serenaded Gram as she crossed the room to sink onto the sofa. "I have made the necessary arrangements with the Donald family and Edwin will be around tomorrow evening to escort you to the Winstons' spring ball."

Pru's back went ramrod stiff. "Edwin is the last man I intend to marry. He is his father's puppet and mouthpiece. Heavens, I'm not certain Edwin entertains any of his own thoughts or opinions. I'd die of boredom if I married him."

"Don't be melodramatic," Gram said and sniffed. "I managed to stay married to Horatio's father for twenty years and, believe me, no one was as dull as Henry."

Pru darted a glance at her father to see the small flicker of irritation in his blue eyes. But as usual when it came to an outright clash with his overbearing mother, Horatio Perkins kept silent.

Prudence Elizabeth Perkins, however, did not. "That is an insensitive remark about Grandfather. I—"

Gram thumped Pru's toe with that infamous cane then

shook her finger in Pru's face—and not for the first time, of course. Pru had been on the receiving end of that wagging forefinger even more times than she'd felt the sting of the cane.

"Do not be disrespectful, young lady," Gram scolded. "You are testing my patience to the limits."

Nothing new there, thought Pru. She'd been doing that for thirteen years. All these years of defying Gram's decrees and machinations had taken their toll and tried Pru's patience to the extreme. It had reached the point that freedom of choice and independence had become something Pru craved above all else. So Pru did what her own father didn't have the gumption to do—she stood up to Gram.

"There will be no wedding to Edwin or anyone else until *I* make the choice," Pru said in no uncertain terms.

Gram gasped and then stared her down with those slate-gray eyes that shot sparks. But Pru had learned to hold her own while debating civic issues and women's rights with her father's associates on the city council. They thought she was too young and too female to have an informed opinion but she let it be known that she was knowledgeable and determined.

When Gram couldn't glare Pru into submission, she turned to Horatio for reinforcement. Pru's greatest disappointment came when her father didn't rise to her defense.

"Your grandmother has gone to great lengths to secure a fine match to Edwin and the Donald family," her father chimed in. "And the merger will benefit our family business since the Donalds deal in priceless gems."

"Ah, yes, the merger of diamonds and furs," Pru said caustically. "What else could a woman possibly want?"

"Do not take that tone again," Gram's thin gray brows formed a sharp *V* over her eyes. "Sometimes I wonder if I made a critical error when I insisted Horatio name you after me."

And there was the rub. Prudence Elizabeth Perkins carried Prudence Meriwether Perkins' given name. If Gram had her way—and she usually did—Pru's firstborn daughter would be known as Prudence Meriwether Perkins Whoever.

Pru drew herself up to full stature. "Papa, I am hereby declaring that I am not marrying Edwin Donald because not only do I not love him—"

"What has love got to do with anything, you silly ninny?" This from Gram who was glaring poison darts at Pru.

"Nor do I even like Edwin very much. He is a stuffed shirt," Pru went on to say, ignoring Gram—which was no small feat. "Furthermore, I have decided to strike off to make a life for myself."

"Then you'll do it without the financial backing of the Perkins' fortune. Tell her so, Horatio."

Pru gritted her teeth and felt disappointment bombard her when her father kowtowed to Gram's wishes for the millionth time. He chose obligation to his mother over love for his daughter.

"Mother is quite right, Pru. It's time you learned that you are a product of your privileged upbringing. If you choose to strike off on your own, then you can finance the endeavor, which I must tell you would be an unwise adventure that will land you in trouble."

"If you think withholding funds will bring me to heel, you are both mistaken," Pru replied heatedly.

"I'm willing to bet that you will come crawling back to

the luxuries your father and I have provided for you in less than a month," Gram challenged. "You aren't trained for manual labor and I refuse to bear the shame of watching you become a nanny for an upper-class family. We will not be embarrassed because you have become disrespectful and rebellious."

Pru stuck out her chin—and her neck—and said, "I will take that bet. I'm sure there's something I'm good at and I intend to explore my options. Obviously, I have no life here, only unreasonable expectations. I will begin my search for gainful employment immediately."

"Come back here, you insolent brat! How dare you!" Gram snapped as Pru sailed past her father, who simply gaped at her then stared bewilderedly at his mother.

Pru didn't break stride, just snatched up the daily newspaper from the credenza in the marble-tiled foyer. She glanced at her reflection in the gilded mirror. Her face was flushed with angry red blotches. Her eyes—the exact same shade of cobalt blue as her father's—narrowed in indignation. Her chest rose and fell with every agitated breath. She looked exactly as she felt—furious, disappointed and belligerent.

"By damned, there is a position somewhere that will pay for my room and board," she told her reflection. Her private tutors claimed she had a bright, inquisitive mind and quick wit. Now was the perfect time to test her talents.

"Prudence Elizabeth Perkins, get back in here this instant!" Gram yowled. Her cane thumped the floor, as if that would bring her contrary granddaughter to heel. "Tell her, Horatio, for God's sake! You have no control whatsoever over that girl. She has become the bane of my existence!"

"Pru! Come back here!" Horatio demanded in response to Gram's direct order.

But Pru, with newspaper clenched in one fist and her cumbersome gown held aside with the other, bounded up the steps two at a time to reach her room.

"Hang dignity and decorum," she muttered. "Being a Perkins isn't worth the trouble."

Pru slammed and locked the door. A moment later, her father pounded on it.

"Pru, be reasonable."

"I am." She flounced on her four-poster bed—the one Gram had picked out for her without the slightest consideration for Pru's taste and sense of style.

She opened the paper and hurriedly searched the ads for employment. Her gaze settled on an advertisement for a mail-order bride. While her father tried to talk to her through the door, Pru reread the ad.

Wanted. A woman of average means who wishes to make a new start in Oklahoma Territory. Have a modest ranch house. Need a wife to share homestead. Will send traveling money.

"Jack McCavett." She read the man's name aloud and studied his address. "Paradise, Oklahoma Territory."

It sounded like the perfect place for a woman who was aching to unfurl her independent wings. A place in frontier society where a woman's position might not yet be so entrenched and defined. A place where the idea of equal rights for equal pay might catch hold and become a wave for the future. Heaven knew she'd been fighting conventional expectations in structured society for years.

A sense of hope and anticipation rose inside Pru while she continued to ignore her father's entreaty to open the door. She knew she would likely be in competition for the position as Jack McCavett's wife. There were probably dozens of women like Pru who were looking for a new start, for an adventure and opportunity to pursue her own dreams.

Pensively, she reread the advertisement. McCavett wanted a hardworking, unassuming, average woman who obviously didn't have high romantic expectations. He just wanted a woman willing to become a rancher's wife and share daily duties.

Pru bounded to her feet to fetch pen and paper. She glanced at the mirror above her desk and mentally composed her application to Jack McCavett. The tone of her telegram would be plain and simple, she mused. With that in mind she described her appearance and personality as modestly as she knew how. She would worry about the actual marriage ceremony later, she decided. Right now, she had to present herself in such a way that she might become McCavett's top selection for his prospective bride.

Since her grandmother had challenged her to make her way without the luxury of the Perkins fortune, Pru definitely needed the traveling money McCavett promised. With telegram in hand, Pru changed into the boyish clothing she kept on hand for tramping about in disguise after dark. A smile quirked her lips, wondering if her father and Gram would have a stroke if they saw her dressed as a ragamuffin. Probably. Gram would pitch a royal fit then get Horatio up in arms to back her up.

Pru breezed out the gallery door and scurried down the back steps. "Whoever you are, Jack McCavett," she murmured, "you're my ticket to freedom and to a life of my own. If you can get me where I want to go I'll take it from there. You'll be repaid for your trouble. I promise."

Jack McCavett pulled his timepiece from the pocket of his jacket then stared at the empty railroad track. The train carrying Miss Prudence Elizabeth Perkins from Saint Louis was due to arrive in a quarter of an hour. Anticipation and apprehension mounted and he tugged nervously at the sleeve of his new suit. The prospect of a mail-order bride had sounded practical and sensible at the time he placed the ad. Now, Jack was having second thoughts.

What the hell was he getting himself into?

"I still don't understand why you did this," Stony Mason, the town marshal said from behind him.

"No, you wouldn't understand," Jack murmured.

"But maybe if this works out for you I'll try your approach for selecting a wife," Stony remarked.

Jack toyed with the stylish cravat that felt like a noose around his neck. Then he glanced at his longtime friend. "Don't you have something else to do besides stand around, waiting to catch a glimpse of Miss Perkins?" He tried to shoo Stony on his way. "Go find someone to arrest."

Stony grinned, making his mustache turn up at the corners of his mouth. "I left my deputy in charge so I could be here with you for this monumental occasion." He hitched his thumb over his shoulder. "Looks like your neighbors and local acquaintances are suffering the same curiosity that's eating me alive."

Jack groaned aloud when he saw the Dawson brothers, Chester and Leroy, lumbering down the street. Behind them, several new acquaintances tagged along. Plus, a few folks he couldn't call by name but had seen around town had joined the procession. He felt awkward enough without half the townsfolk showing up to take a gander at Miss Perkins.

Stony must have spread the word about the mail-order bride and Jack was suddenly on display. That's the last thing he wanted here in Paradise.

So much for trying to lead an ordinary life and keep a low profile after seven years of riding herd over one of the rowdiest cow towns in Kansas. At the time, Stony had been *his* deputy. Then last year he had followed Jack south to make the Land Run to claim one-hundred-sixty acres for a homestead or town lot.

It seemed Stony was still following him around after all these years. In fact, Jack couldn't remember a memory that didn't have Stony and their friend Davy Freeman stuck right smack-dab in the middle of it.

His thoughts derailed when the train whistle pierced the late afternoon air. Black smoke rose above the grove of cottonwood trees where the tracks crossed the river. Anticipation spiked inside him as the sound of the approaching train became louder.

When Chester Dawson, a bulky, rawboned neighbor, tapped him on the shoulder, Jack jerked to attention.

"Me and Leroy brought you something to give your future bride." He thrust a handful of wildflowers at Jack. "Women like that sort of thing, I'm told."

Jack felt foolish for overlooking that courteous gesture.

But then, he had lived a hardscrabble life and his party manners had never been up to snuff.

"Thanks, Chester, I owe you one," Jack murmured as he surveyed the array of colorful flowers.

Chester and Leroy beamed and Leroy, who was the spitting image of his older brother, said, "Maybe your new bride will invite us over to dinner sometime. No one has fixed us a home cooked meal since we left Iowa to make the Run last year."

Jack watched the train approach the white clapboard depot and drew himself up into a military-like stance. Although he tried, it was difficult to maintain a low profile when he stood six foot two inches and towered over his friends like a giraffe in a herd of horses.

He wondered if Miss Perkins would feel as if she were on display the instant she stepped onto the landing and saw the gathering crowd staring curiously at her. According to her telegram, which had prompted Jack to select her, Pru had average looks, average intelligence and an average personality but strong character and stamina. She claimed she preferred the simple life to the hustle and bustle of the big city.

Nothing like getting off to a bad start because of this well-attended reception, thought Jack. Hell, he was surprised Stony hadn't hired the local band to strike up a tune—

"Good Lord!" Jack croaked when Stretch Newcomb, the banjo player from Wild Horse Saloon, burst into a song about coming around the mountain when she comes. Pru would think Jack had misrepresented himself when she encountered this large reception.

"That's it, Stony. I'll never share another piece of information with you in confidence," he muttered. "You can't keep your trap shut."

"Here now! That's no way to talk to your best friend in the whole wide world and the town marshal to boot. We all wanted to make this a memorable occasion for you and your fiancée."

Grimly, Jack stood with the wildflowers clenched tightly in his fist, waiting for the train to screech to a halt, listening to the banjo player belt out the chorus of his song and watching his acquaintances tighten the semicircle around him to have their first look-see at Prudence Perkins.

Apprehension shot through him when the conductor stepped onto the platform. Behind him, a middle-aged man with thick spectacles appeared. Jack held his breath and waited for his plain, common-looking, unassuming bride-to-be to step forward. He sucked in his breath when a young woman, who was clearly with child, waddled onto the platform.

All eyes flew to Jack who swallowed hard and nearly squeezed the blooms off the flower bouquet in his fist. The woman fit the description Pru had sent in her follow-up letter. Eyes spaced a bit too far apart, pert nose and wide mouth. He couldn't see the color of her hair because she had it tucked beneath a wide-brimmed straw hat.

If she had misled him about carrying another man's child, he wasn't going to be pleased. Not that he wouldn't agree to accept the child, for he intended to have a family one day, but he'd expected her to be honest with him—

His thoughts broke off abruptly when the woman broke into a grin, squealed in delight then waved excitedly to someone behind him.

"Emma!" the greeter called as he shouldered his way past Jack, Stony and the Dawson brothers.

"Howard!" Emma shrieked as she toddled down the steps.

"Guess that's not Prudence, huh?" said Stony.

"Guess not." A sinking feeling settled in the pit of Jack's belly when the last two male passengers disembarked and the conductor shouted, "All aboard!"

Again, his friends and acquaintances fixed their gazes on him—this time with blatant sympathy that made him feel self-conscious and awkward. He wondered which would be worse, being stood up at the altar or being stood up at the train depot by his mail-order bride. He figured one was as bad as the other—and not the least bit flattering.

# Chapter Two

"I guess she got cold feet," Stony said quietly. "Either that or she lured you in then exchanged the train ticket for money."

"Must've changed her mind at the last minute," Chester Dawson said in Jack's other ear. "Really sorry about this, Jack, I truly am. You got all dressed up in your Sunday best for nothing."

"Thanks for making me feel better," Jack muttered caustically as he wedged past Chester and Leroy, only to face the raft of bystanders who were also gazing sympathetically at him. Damn it, if he ever met Prudence Perkins he'd wring her neck for thrusting him into this awkward situation. He didn't want anyone's pity, didn't need it. Life's hard knocks had taught him to be mentally and physically tough years ago.

"Marshal!"

The alarmed shout pierced the air and Jack glanced up reflexively. He'd been a law officer so long that it was second nature to answer the summons. A half-second later, he reminded himself that Stony was now the man in charge of handling a town crisis.

"What's wrong?" Stony demanded as his overweight deputy jogged forward.

"The stagecoach was held up two miles from town," the deputy panted. "One of the passengers was dragged from the coach and got into a shouting match over a bracelet that a bandit stole from her. The two male passengers were roughed up a bit and the driver was told to head west without the female passenger…or else."

Jack wheeled toward his horse. "Stony, swear in a posse. If we don't track down the woman quickly she'll lose more than her bracelet."

While Stony deputized the Dawson brothers, Jack crammed the wildflowers in his saddlebag then bounded onto his horse. He was the first rider in pursuit. A quarter of a mile later he reminded himself that hapless victims, holdups and bandits were no longer his problem. He had served his time protecting other folks. He had faced down dozens of drunken sons of bitches who had chips on their shoulders and obsessions for making names for themselves by challenging Jack to showdowns.

Yet, here he was, haring off to chase bandits and rescue an innocent victim. He supposed it would take time to break the long-held habit, especially when Stony constantly asked for advice and assistance in handling a crisis.

"How dare you drag me off like this!" Pru yelped as she kicked and bucked to escape the two men who'd abducted her.

The burly bandit, who wore a hood over his face to disguise his features and muffle his voice, gave her arm a rough jerk that nearly dislodged it from its socket. He hoisted her onto his horse, leaving her jackknifed over the saddle like a feed sack. Pru tried to launch herself backward, but a loaded pistol jammed her in the ribs and discouraged her escape attempt.

"Hold still or I'll put a hole clean through you," the man snarled. "It's time you found out where a woman's place is, you little spitfire."

"You need to learn some respect for your betters and how to take orders, too," the second bandit scowled at her through his concealing hood.

"Two petty thieves are not my betters. And you obviously don't know the meaning of respect, you big oafs!" Pru clamped her mouth shut, wishing she'd had the good sense to do it *before* she antagonized her captors, not *after*.

The man riding behind her swatted her on the fanny. "Close your yap, gal." He glanced at his partner. "Can you believe her nerve?"

The second bandit didn't comment, just led the way into the thicket of trees that lined the road.

"Well hell!" Her captor grumbled sourly. "That was fast. A posse is already on our trail."

Pru grunted uncomfortably when her abductor gouged his heels into his horse's flanks and they plunged forward. The jarring gait forced the air from her lungs in spurts.

"Damn it, they're catching up!" the second outlaw growled. "Get rid of her."

"Get rid of her? I've got plans for her."

"Won't do you any good if we're caught and thrown in jail!"

Pru's breath burst from her chest in a pained grunt when the horse beneath her scrabbled up the steep embankment of the creek. She wailed in pain when the bandit suddenly shoved her backward. She hit the ground hard. Her plumed hat shifted sideways when her head collided with the tree trunk behind her. The pins holding her hat in place nearly yanked out her hair by the roots when the hat snagged on the bark.

The bandits thundered off while Pru's head spun furiously and she struggled to catch her breath. She muttered a foul curse at the two men who had left her penniless and without the heirloom bracelet her mother had given to her for her sixth birthday.

Pru tried to focus on details about the two men so she could give a good description to the local law-enforcement officer. The bandits were riding plain brown horses with unadorned saddles. Hats and hoods covered their heads. She squinted to get a look at their scuffed boots and spurs but they were too far away for her to pick up telling details.

"Damn you scoundrels!" she grumbled as she popped the side of her head with the heel of her hand, trying to stop the ringing in her ears.

It would be difficult to live without the money they stole from her since she'd been short on funds to begin with. But that bracelet was a keepsake representing fond memories of her departed mother. Fond memories of Perkins family members were too few and far between to let them go lightly, she mused.

The thrashing in the underbrush and the thud of horses' hooves drew her attention away from the fleeing bandits. Pru propped herself up on her skinned elbow and modestly jerked down her high-riding gown. When four riders arrived on the scene, she breathed a sigh of relief. She owed her life and her virtue to this rescue brigade.

She smiled gratefully as she peered at the tall, muscular man who sat his black gelding with the graceful ease that indicated he'd spent much of his life on the back of the horse. He looked to be in his early thirties. Windblown black hair framed his clean-shaven, suntanned face. Intense amber-colored eyes, surrounded by thick lashes, bore down on her, as if silently assessing the damage to her person.

"You okay, ma'am?" His deep voice was as rich and mellow as fine whiskey.

Pru nodded, astounded that she was still in an unlady-like sprawl, still staring at her rescuer in feminine admiration. The blow to her skull must have left her dazed and immobilized, she decided.

When she managed to drag her gaze off the powerfully built man who looked out of place in his stylish three-piece black suit, her attention settled on the man with the badge pinned to his leather vest. He had sandy-blond hair, a thick mustache and alert green eyes that assessed her frazzled condition.

Her gaze shifted to the two men who were obviously brothers of Nordic descent. She'd bet the Perkins fortune there was Viking blood spurting through their veins. They were stout, rugged and rawboned. Despite their broad shoulders and thick necks, they wore pleasant smiles.

Pru couldn't say the same for the man who led the rescue brigade. Despite his civilized veneer, he looked hard. Tough. The scar on the back of his left hand suggested someone had come after him with a knife. Pru was pretty certain, though, that he had been the victor of that battle because he had a dominating presence that was impossible to ignore.

"Poor Edwin Donald," she mused aloud. "All his money couldn't make him look this capable and masculine."

"Pardon, ma'am?" said the warrior in the citified suit.

"Nothing important." Pru pushed herself into a sitting position and forced a wobbly smile. "I am ever so glad to make your acquaintance, kind sir."

"You're damn lucky to be alive, lady," the dark-haired warrior said gruffly. "Rule number one. Never contest a thief who wants your valuables and backs it up with a loaded gun."

His brusque tone triggered her annoyance in one second flat. "Thank you so much for the pointer. I'll try to remember that the next time some burly heathen manhandles me and steals my heirloom bracelet."

While she was putting the lead rider in his place, the other three men dismounted and rushed forward to stand her up on her noodly legs. They brushed the grass and leaves from her clothing and she allowed the familiar contact because they had hoisted her upright so quickly that her head was spinning and stars winked before her eyes.

"Easy, ma'am," the marshal cooed when she swayed unsteadily. "I'm gonna set you on the horse with McCavett and we'll get you into town where you'll be more comfortable."

Pru froze. Her eyes shot open wide and her gaze locked on the angular face and hypnotic golden eyes of the man who had asked about her condition in one breath and then chastised her the next. She frowned in disapproval as she reappraised the muscular rider who looked about eight feet tall while he sat upon his shiny black horse.

Jack McCavett had tried to pass himself off as a simple, average man. Ha! There was nothing average about his appearance or the powerful aura that radiated from him.

"McCavett? Good gad!"

A moment too late Pru realized she'd spoken aloud and had drawn all four men's curious attention. Then golden-brown eyes locked on her in an accusing stare. She knew the exact moment when McCavett figured out who she was.

"Prudence Perkins?" he chirped in incredulous disbelief.

The other three men gaped at her as if she had vines sprouting from her ears. She glanced down to make sure she was properly covered, for all four men stared as if they had never seen a woman before.

"This is Miss Perkins?" Stony croaked frog-eyed, as his attention leaped back and forth between Pru and Jack.

Jack swore under his breath while he reevaluated the woman whose feathered hat sat askew on her silver-blond head. The most incredible blue eyes he'd ever had the pleasure of staring into were looking back at him. The detailed description Pru had given of herself in her second correspondence led him to believe that she was a mild-mannered plain Jane who was a little on the plump side.

Plump? Hell! She was so shapely and well-endowed that looking so tantalizing and appealing should be against the law. For sure and certain, staring at her provoked several *arresting* thoughts.

Did she really see herself as dowdy and common? Or had she purposely misled him on that count, too? And the burning question was, why would a woman with a body made for sin and the face of an angel—a woman who had the refined look of aristocratic breeding—want to take up residence in a newly formed territory? Why would she agree to marry a man who wasn't looking for love or romance, just mutual respect and companionship?

Jack would bet his left arm that this woman came with a complicated past that he didn't want to get tangled up in. Like Emma Whoever-she-was who arrived on the train, Pru might even be pregnant and looking for a new start, away from the humiliating scandal of Saint Louis society.

Stony snickered then grinned wryly. "Well, all's well that ends well, I guess. Up you go, Miss Perkins." He and the Dawson brothers lifted her up and placed her in front of Jack on the saddle, forcing him to scoot back to accommodate her. "Not the welcoming reception we planned, but you're here in one piece and that's what counts."

*Say something!* Stony's glance said. But Jack just sat there, feeling Prudence's rounded rump wedged familiarly between his thighs and her back meshed against his chest. Stony's next pointed stare prompted Jack to reach into the saddlebag to retrieve the wildflowers. Some of which had been beheaded. Others were limp and wilted, after being crammed carelessly into the pouch.

"These are for you," Jack said more gruffly than he intended. But damn it, he'd gotten a lot more than he bargained for when he chose Prudence as his mail-order bride.

And he was *not* pleased, believe you him. She had surpassed his expectations in ways that spelled trouble and complications.

"Thank you. How considerate," she murmured from beneath the cockeyed hat. The broken feather tickled his nose every time she moved her head.

"I didn't think of it by myself. It was Chester and Leroy Dawson's idea." He gestured to the two burly men then directed her attention to his longtime friend. "And by the way, the town marshal is Stony Mason," he introduced offhandedly.

When she turned her dazzling smile on the Dawsons and Stony, they practically melted like lard in a hot skillet. Jack rolled his eyes at his friends' sappy reaction to his would-be, completely-misrepresented-herself mail-order bride-to-be. She sure as hell wasn't going to bring him to heel with that blinding smile, so she had better not even start trying to work her wiles on him.

He was peeved at her. Plus, he had heard every line and seen every fraudulent scheme imaginable during his stint as a gunfighter and law officer. He was immune in ways the average man couldn't fathom and he sure as hell wasn't going to turn mush-headed and sappy just because a strikingly attractive female blessed him with a smile.

Jack reined his black gelding in the direction he'd come, setting a casual pace. His friends scurried to their horses to follow in his wake.

"What was so damn important—"

"—Language," she interrupted.

Jack defied her attempt to correct him and stared at the back of her blond head. "What was so damn important that you dared hand-to-hand combat with not *one* but *two* armed robbers?"

"What little money I had was stolen, along with a diamond bracelet my deceased mother gave me for a gift when I was a child. It was a sentimental memento of happier times."

So her life wasn't all good cheer and roses. Neither was his. He'd learned early on to accept his fate and get on with it. He wasn't going to let a sad story get to him. Especially one spouted by a woman who was nothing like he wanted or expected. She had trouble written all over her in bold letters.

"You could be dead—or worse—right now," he told her. "And what the hell were you doing on the stagecoach when I sent you a train ticket? The train wasn't robbed." There. Let her think about that for a moment.

"The train was more expensive so I redeemed the ticket and pocketed the extra money for miscellaneous expenses." She huffed out a breath and popped the wildflowers against the pommel in annoyance. A few more floral heads dropped off. "Now the bracelet is gone and I don't have a penny to my name."

He leaned close to her ear to ask the question in confidence so their companions wouldn't overhear. "And money is that important to you?"

Pru stiffened at the pointed question then shivered helplessly when Jack's warm breath whispered against the side of her neck. It was bad enough that she felt surrounded by his powerful body. And yes, even comforted by it, reluctant though she was to admit it. But being physically attracted to him was the last thing she'd expected to deal with.

In addition, the harrowing episode with the bandits had rattled her and she felt exposed and vulnerable. She'd looked upon this journey as an escape from structured society and the beginning of a grand adventure. But the robbery had unsettled her because she wasn't accustomed to dealing with danger on a regular basis. Not yet anyway.

Pru had the unmistakable feeling that wasn't the case with Jack McCavett. He was rough around the edges and not easily upset or flustered. Well, except for that half second when it dawned on him who she was, she amended. That had stunned him momentarily.

"I asked you a question, Pru."

She grimaced when his quiet words invaded her thoughts and the whisper of his breath stirred alien sensations again. She mentally scrambled, trying to recall what he'd asked. Ah, yes, the importance of money.

"It is said that money is the root of all evil," she remarked. "I disagree with that."

"So do I."

"Those who obsess after money, like those bandits, are the root of evil. I'll settle for enough cash to put food in my mouth and a roof over my head."

"No harm in that attitude. But what's your story, Miss Perkins? A woman who looks as good as you do shouldn't need to become a mail-order bride."

The comment rankled. "And what do you know of my background, Mr. McCavett? Nothing, that's what."

"It's Jack," he corrected. "So tell me what prompted you to answer my ad?"

He annoyed her with his prying questions and disconcerted her with the unexpected pleasure of sitting within the circle of his brawny arms and muscular thighs.

"I killed a man and I'm on the run," she countered, just for shock value.

He didn't so much as flinch. "Why'd you kill him?"

"Because he asked too many personal questions."

Jack chuckled in amusement. "Sassy little thing, aren't you, Miss Perkins? Did you give the bandits this much lip?"

"Yes, and it's Pru. You should know that pushy, domineering men bring out the worst in me."

"One last question. For now." He wasn't going to let her think he was finished interrogating her. She was just getting a temporary reprieve.

"Fire away," she invited.

"Did you leave Saint Louis because you are pregnant?"

"No." Her reply was abrupt, indicating that he'd made her uncomfortable with the intimate question. Plus, her face went up in flames. "I left because my life had been mapped out for me against my wishes. I want the same opportunity the men of the world enjoy. I want to be my own person and chase my own dreams, not dragged along on the coattails of a man who believes he has the right to think and speak for me."

He grinned wryly as he watched her fidget with the decapitated wildflowers. "You're going to have a problem being a dutiful wife, aren't you?"

"Yes," she assured him without hesitation.

"Thought so."

Jack dropped the interrogation when they rode into town. He gaped in disbelief when he saw the banner strung above the marshal's office. He half twisted to stare accusingly at Stony and the Dawsons who were grinning from ear to ear.

"We thought your wedding would be the perfect excuse for a celebration," said Stony. "Besides, it coincides with the first-year anniversary of the Land Run and the founding of Paradise."

"There will be a feast later," Chester informed him.

"And a street dance," Leroy added. "The restaurant owners and shopkeepers agreed to contribute to the celebration."

"How thoughtful," Pru mumbled without enthusiasm.

Her arrival had been a disaster, as well as her first meeting with Jack. She had planned to tell him there would be no marriage and that she would repay him the money she owed him after she found employment in town.

And now this! A celebration planned by Jack's friends would ensure everyone in Paradise knew about the mail-order bride and upcoming wedding. Curse it, this was snowballing into an even bigger disaster!

She nudged Jack in the ribs to gain his attention. "I need to speak privately with you at the earliest possible convenience," she murmured confidentially.

"We'll grab your luggage from the stagecoach station and find a back alley where we can speak freely."

Pru manufactured a smile when dozens of unfamiliar faces lifted then nodded, as if offering a silent welcome to their town. She felt like a fraud. Which of course she was. She had used Jack as a means to an end in her desperation to flee the arranged marriage Gram had planned. Jack didn't deserve her deception, but she'd been upset with Gram and disappointed in her father's lack of support. She'd latched onto the first opportunity to skip town.

She wondered how her father and grandmother had reacted when they found the letter she'd left on her pillow in the gilded cage that was her bedroom. *I'm taking your bet and striking off on my own,* it said. *I can make my own life without the Perkins fortune in furs to support me.*

She had assumed a false name and concealed her appearance as best she could when she boarded the first stagecoach from Saint Louis. She had covered her trail well, even if she said so herself. She planned to be estab-

lished in Paradise and living on her own salary by the time
her father tracked her down.

"Wait here," Jack requested as he dismounted.

She watched him walk purposefully toward the stage
depot and noticed the graceful economy of movement in
his long-legged stride. She thought of Edwin Donald, heir
apparent to the precious jewel dynasty and she wondered
if she could look at another sophisticated gentleman
without comparing him to Jack's brawny physique. In her
opinion, all other men sadly lacked Jack's air of arresting
masculinity.

Pru recalled her first impression of Jack. A tough and
capable warrior. Her opinion hadn't changed. Jack
McCavett was the kind of man you could count on in an
emergency and he would make an intimidating enemy.
She grimaced, wondering if he would go for her throat
when she told him that she didn't plan to marry him—or
anyone else—until she established her independence from
her family. Furthermore, it would be…

Her thoughts trailed off when Jack reappeared with her
two satchels. He lifted a thick brow then glanced speculatively at the bulging bags. She shrugged evasively. She
wasn't making excuses for bringing along a dozen changes
of clothes, plus her men's garb for prowling after dark
when the mood struck.

The boyish disguise provided her with the opportunity to
view life from a perspective she wasn't granted when traips-
ing around in a dress. In fact, she had trailed several prospective suitors to discover their less-than-proper habits on the
unseemly side of Saint Louis in years past. Talk about mis-
representing themselves! Pru had nothing on them.

Pru leaned sideways when Jack lifted his arms to draw her from his horse. When he set her to her feet, her legs nearly folded up beneath her. Apparently, the bump on her skull had done more damage than simply leaving her with a throbbing headache.

"You okay?" he asked as he slipped a supportive arm around her.

She took the pins from her hat, shook out her curly hair then drew in a steadying breath. "Okay enough," she replied as he escorted her toward the alley separating the stage depot from Harper's Restaurant.

"Don't be too long," Stony called after them. "The feast is scheduled to get under way soon."

Pru mentally rehearsed what she wanted to say as Jack guided her around wooden crates and trash bins. Then he drew her to a halt and stared at her expectantly.

"What big secret do you plan to spring on me now? That you're not really Prudence Perkins and that you disposed of the poor woman you've been impersonating while you were on the run from the other murder you mentioned?"

He was half jesting and half serious and guilt broadsided her. "The thing is…" Pru paused to draw in a bolstering breath before she met Jack's unblinking stare. "I really am Pru Perkins. I didn't kill anyone. I've wanted to a time or two, but I've restrained myself." She grabbed another breath and blurted out, "I have no intention of marrying. I'm a horrible person because I used your ad and your generosity to resolve my personal problems. I'm terribly sorry."

Jack stared down at her with those intense amber eyes that reminded her of a panther's. He said nothing, which made her feel as if she should fill in the stilted silence with more explanation.

"I was without funds and your ticket provided me with the chance to come West and make a new start," she hurried on. "But I'm the last person you would want to marry, believe me. I don't like myself very much right now because of my deception so I'm not surprised that you don't either."

"No one likes to be used or misled, Pru," he said harshly. "You lied about your intentions, your personality and your appearance." He glared at her. "By the way, there's absolutely nothing average about you. One look in the mirror tells you that you're stunningly attractive. That is *not* what I requested in a bride, but you led me to believe you were exactly what I was looking for."

She should have been flattered by his backhanded compliment, but his clipped tone inflamed her temper—which was short-fused on a good day. This had not been a good day.

"And what of you, Jack?" she fired back accusingly. "You claimed to be a simple rancher looking for a woman to share his common life on a modest-size farm. Look at you." She indicated his towering height and broad chest. "You aren't plain. You're ruggedly handsome and built like a Greek god. You're also tough as nails and not easily rattled. Whatever you were before you came to this new territory, I vow you weren't a hapless farmer."

He fisted his hands at his sides and stared her down. "That's true, but sometimes life offers few choices and you become what it makes of you. I rode the orphan train from Chicago to Texas. A widowed rancher named William Carter decided that I looked like I could pull my weight in work so he snatched me up. I learned to fend off rustlers, ride like a Comanche and shoot like a soldier. On one of the countless trail drives to Kansas railheads, I broke up a street fight between Stony and a drunken ruffian in which the sheriff was shot and disabled. I was instantly offered a job as his deputy. He became my mentor, and when he retired soon after I took his place. Stony became my deputy."

Pru listened, noting the drastic difference between his difficult existence and her pampered-but-restricted life under Gram's thumb. No wondered he'd turned out tough.

"I didn't keep track of how many drunken brutes I had to shoot in the line of duty or in self-defense," he went on bluntly. "Nor did I count the number of outlaws I tracked down and hauled to jail. My life has been one battle following on the heels of another. I might as well have pinned a bull's-eye on my back for all the would-be gunmen who wanted to use my reputation with a gun to make a name for themselves."

"So you are exceptionally handy with a pistol?" she inserted.

"Deadly." It didn't sound like a boast, just a simple statement of fact. "But I resigned to make the Land Run and I staked my claim so I could lead a normal life on my own homestead where the most danger I'll face is getting pecked by the rooster or kicked by a contrary milk cow. I wanted out of the limelight. Out of the public eye. I wanted a simple, average woman with average looks and docile personality to share my life."

Jack looked her up and down then smirked. "Instead I get you, a walking contradiction. You look like the picture of refined beauty, but you have enough gumption to take on two bandits over a bracelet and pocket change." His voice became an agitated growl. "Then I find out that you not only misrepresented yourself to me but now you refuse to uphold your end of our bargain. That's breach of contract."

He flung his arm in the general direction of the street. "And worse, we're caught up in your lie. We are the honored guests of a town-wide celebration organized by my well-meaning friends and acquaintances. I have to become as pretentious as you are in order to prevent hurting my friends and letting them down by announcing there will be no wedding today or any other day."

"If you're trying to make me feel worse than I do already then you've succeeded."

"Good." Jack noted her contrite expression. "At least you have a conscience, even if you are a fraud and a liar."

She jerked up her head and those luminous eyes flashed like blue flames. "So says the pot to the kettle," she countered sharply. "You also misrepresented yourself. Maybe I take offense to the prospect of marrying a man who has lived a life of violence and has blood on his hands. Spiteful outlaws might be looking for the chance to get even by gunning you or me down. In addition, I don't know if you will resort to violence when provoked to anger."

She raised her chin and stared directly at him. "Are you planning to shoot me because I deceived you? If you are, then by all means go ahead and get it over with."

"Don't tempt me," he said darkly.

She met his gaze as she flipped her long, curly mane of silver-gold hair over her shoulder. Jack had the insane urge to comb his fingers through those silky strands.

*That would be a big mistake*, he told himself quickly.

"I am truly sorry that I misled you, but *you* aren't what *I* expected, either. Yet, that doesn't excuse what I did."

"No, it doesn't and saying you're sorry doesn't make us square," he replied. "I'm out a considerable amount of money. Plus, I have to fumble through this celebration to appease my friends and acquaintances. You wasted my time and that's going to cost you."

"This is not going as well as I'd hoped," she mumbled, looking away.

"Did you expect to charm me into being be a gracious loser? Like you do the proper gentleman from your usual social circle?" he asked sardonically.

She scoffed at that. "Those so-called gentlemen are known to go behind a person's back to start rumors to get even. At least you are straightforward. I prefer the direct approach."

He watched her draw herself up to full stature—all five foot five inches of her. "I vow to repay you for the train ticket as soon as I find employment," she assured him. "I will even help you find a suitable replacement bride-to-be."

He snorted at that. "I can find my own wife, thank you very much."

"Obviously not," she retorted. "You placed an ad in a newspaper. And why in Saint Louis of all places?"

He shrugged nonchalantly. "Too far north and you get Yankees. Too far south and you get rebels. I was looking for middle of the road, like the woman I was expecting."

"And why a mail-order bride?" she questioned. "Is it because of your surly disposition and the fact that your former occupation might repel potential brides? Sight unseen works best for you, no doubt."

"It's because I don't have the time or inclination for

lengthy courtships." A hint of a smile quirked his lips.
"And although you have the most kissable mouth I've ever
laid eyes on, your tongue is as sharp as a dagger. I can see
why *you* aren't married. How old are you anyway?"

"Twenty-three, but a gentleman isn't supposed to ask
that." Her irritation fizzled beneath his engaging grin. "But
you're right, I'm afraid. I omitted in my correspondence
that I have fangs and I bite. Another misrepresentation in
your book, right?"

"Precisely."

"Jack!" Stony's voice echoed down the alley. "Everyone
wants to toast you and your bride-to-be. Get out here so
we can get this shindig under way."

Jack glanced back at Pru. "We haven't hammered out
who owes whom what yet. However, for the duration of the
evening, we're going to give folks the chance to enjoy what
they went to all the trouble to arrange: a celebration. I'm
going to pretend things between us are fine and dandy and
that I'm pleased with this match." He stared at her somberly.
"Can you do the same or are you too uncomfortable in my
presence to act like I'd make a suitable husband?"

She met his challenging gaze with a firm nod—and he
wondered if accepting challenges was one of her character traits. Who knew? After all, that trait might be what
launched her from her privileged life to the back alley of
this frontier town.

"You can count on me to be the charming would-be bride,"
she insisted. "Main Street will be my stage, Mr. McCav—"

"Jack." He took her arm to escort her down the alley.

"Of course, my dear Jack." She flashed her brightest
smile then patted his forearm. "Tonight will be good

practice, in case I take a job at a local dance hall. No one will know whether I'm actually having a good time or not."

"Same goes for me." He tossed her a charismatic grin and she had to remind herself that he didn't like her very much.

Obviously, he was good at hiding his emotions. She was no novice herself. She could endure Gram's lectures without changing expression, if necessary, and she'd tolerated her suitors' boring company without giving away her true feelings. She could play her role during the town-wide celebration and by damned, she'd do it better than Jack McCavett!

# *Chapter Three*

Pru sat at the head table, which was constructed of planks and sawhorses. Dozens of people filed past her to introduce themselves and wish her well. When she finally had the chance to taste the smoked beef, sourdough biscuits, boiled potatoes and cherry cobbler she realized she was famished.

"Tell me what it was like to make the Run," she requested of the Dawson brothers.

Chester blotted his lips with his napkin and his eyes lit up with remembered excitement. "It was the adventure of a lifetime," he recalled. "People lined up as far as the eye could see, waiting for the signal to race off to claim the surplus land the government acquired from Indian tribes."

"We felt bad about that," Leroy murmured. "The government gave each tribe member in the central part of Indian Territory one-hundred-sixty acres, even though they started with a lot more property. The rest was put up for homesteaders."

The Indian tribes had been shortchanged again, Pru mused. No matter how the government tried to sugarcoat it, they had reneged on their treaties and had taken away tribal land. So much for the promise that Indian Territory would belong to the Indians until the rivers dried up and grass ceased to grow.

The Indians didn't seem to have any more luck fighting for equal rights than women did.

Pru cut the brawny Dawson brothers, who bookended her, discreet glances then looked across the table at Jack. She was in no position to complain about shortchanges. After all, she'd misled Jack to gain independence from the Perkins' decrees and restrictions.

The thought caused her conscience to nag her again.

"There were people in wagons and buggies. There were men on horseback and on foot," Chester went on to say.

"Some rode the worst looking mounts you could possibly imagine and others rode the best money could buy," Jack added between bites.

Stony elbowed Jack and grinned. "Jack's being one of the best. He trained that black gelding and he can flat-out run as if the devil is hot on his heels. Jack could've sold his horse for ten times its value the day of the Run."

"Chester and I were lucky to keep up on our nags. We sailed along in Jack's wake and managed to drive our stakes in the ground before two gun-toting claim jumpers came calling."

"If not for Jack, we wouldn't be alive to enjoy our good fortune," Chester said, smiling appreciatively at Jack.

Pru watched Jack shrug modestly before taking another bite of smoked beef.

"Jack knocked sense into both men then sent them stag-gering off to the creek to wipe off the blood." Leroy reached across the table to pat Jack on the shoulder. "Nice to have a competent neighbor when trouble breaks out."

"I would imagine so," Pru agreed.

"Not to worry about your safety," Stony assured her. "Jack will take mighty good care of you. The best, in fact."

Pru smiled for the men's benefit then placed her hand over Jack's in an affectionate manner. At close range, she noticed the deep indentation of the knife wound. She wondered how many other souvenirs of battle he sported.

"Jack already saved me from those bandits and I am eternally grateful."

His inconspicuous glance silently assured her that her praise wasn't going to let her off the hook for her flimflammery. She really hadn't thought it would.

When the four-piece band—consisting of Stretch the banjo player, two fiddlers and a harmonica player—struck up a lively tune, Stony came to his feet. With a gallant flair, he bowed over Pru. "Miss Perkins, I would be honored to have this dance."

"My pleasure."

Several other couples joined them in the cordoned area of the street. Stony didn't dance the waltz as expertly as the men in Saint Louis, who attended elegant balls on a regular basis. But he wasn't as pretentious as his counterparts so that was a point in his favor. She liked the marshal's pleasant disposition and his easy smiles.

"I was a bit worried about Jack's method of finding a wife, but I assure you that you have done exceptionally well for yourself," said Stony.

She bit her tongue to prevent blurting out the truth while guilt hounded her mercilessly. But Jack had insisted that

the celebration would be pleasurable for one and all so she
kept the secret.

"Jack seems to be a fine man. Have you known him long?"

Stony chuckled. "Since I was six," he replied as he accidentally sideswiped another couple. "We came from the
orphanage together and ended up in Texas. All three of us.
Jack, Davy Freeman and me."

"Yes, he mentioned he was taken in by a gruff, no-
nonsense rancher named William Carter."

Stony's thick brows shot up. "He did? Jack's usually
tight-lipped as a clam about his past." He shrugged. "But
you being his bride-to-be, I reckon he opened up."

Again, guilt niggled her. She compressed her lips and
told herself to keep quiet.

"Carter was only planning to take Jack because he was
big and strong for his age. But Jack pleaded with him not to
split up the threesome. Davy was sickly and Jack promised
to make up the difference and Carter finally agreed."

"Where is Davy now?"

Stony's smile faltered. "He went to meet his Maker four
years later. We were on a cattle drive, crossing a swift-moving
river when Davy's horse went under with him on it. The
horse resurfaced downstream, but we never found Davy."

"Jack also told me that a ruffian picked a fight with you
in a Kansas cow town and the sheriff got shot."

Stony stopped short then swiveled his head around to
glance at the table where Jack watched the dancers. Then
Stony returned his attention to Pru. "Dang, did you pry this
information from him or did he volunteer all of it?"

"We were swapping past history," she replied as she
waved and smiled at Jack for appearance's sake. "I was

hoping you could supply the details since he only gave me the boiled-down version."

"Not really much more to tell." Stony took her hand and waltzed off again. "The drunken galoot shot Sheriff Lemke in the knee when he tried to get between us. Jack used the butt of his pistol on the back of the man's head. He was facedown in the dirt before he knew what hit him. The rest of us were still standing there in stunned fascination, watching the sheriff bleed all over himself. But Jack reacted immediately. Just like he did when word came about the stagecoach holdup today." Stony grinned. "I was just about to *think* of racing off to save the day but Jack was doing it already."

"Is that what made him a legendary sheriff in Kansas?"

Stony bobbed his head and his green eyes twinkled. "Quick reflexes, quick thinker. A tough survivalist who's as logical and practical as the day is long. Which is why this mail-order bride business stunned me," he admitted.

Pru thought about that for a moment, wondering why he imported a bride and wondering why he'd selected her. "Perhaps when he took a new lease on life after making the Land Run, he decided to be more impulsive and less practical."

"Could be. But I think there's more to it than that." He smiled and winked. "But my old friend got lucky when he found you. Hell, I'd send off for a bride myself if I could guarantee I ended up with a woman as delightful and attractive as you."

"Believe me, Stony, he didn't get that much of a bargain." She paused momentarily then prompted. "Now, you were telling me about your heydays in the cow town."

Stony circled back to the previous topic as they waltzed around the dance area. "Those were the wild days of rowdy cowboys riding into town in swarms to wash down trail dust and kick up their boot heels. They drank hard, chased women and shot out windows for the sport of it. The gamblers and shysters were there to prey on the cowboys and to separate them from their hard-earned salary."

"Wild and violent times," she summarized.

Stony nodded. "But Jack's reputation spread like wildfire and he became legendary. Sensible men chose not to cross him and eventually things settled down. Except for the gunmen who tried to cut their teeth on Jack McCavett."

He shook his head and sighed ruefully. "There's a long list of arrogant fools who tried to beat Jack to the draw. But he has something none of them possessed. He's fearless. Brave to the bone. I try to be the lawman he was, but I doubt I can pull it off. I'm not as fast on my feet or as quick with a pistol."

"You seem to have a handle on this town," she noted.

"This ain't Hell's Fringe," Stony replied. "I deal with the occasional bank robbery, dishonest gambler and property disputes. It's nothing like the old days in Kansas."

"Mind if I cut in?"

Pru missed a step, unaware that Jack had come up behind her.

"Of course not. She's your fiancée, after all," Stony said as he stepped away, bowed politely then left.

Pru pivoted to smile at Jack, but he continued to stare somberly at her. "If this is your idea of pretending to have a good time your expression falls well short of the mark."

"I doubt you'll be smiling when I inform you that the

mayor and the justice of the peace just asked me if we wanted to hold the ceremony here and now, since the whole town is on hand to serve as our wedding guests."

Pru swallowed hard as Jack gestured toward the fortyish mayor who had long legs, thin brown hair and a bird belly. She smiled feebly at him and then nodded to the short, squatty justice of the peace.

She hadn't expected to be railroaded into a whirlwind wedding. Her alarmed gaze flew up to Jack. She didn't know him well enough to interpret the expression in his whiskey-colored eyes. But she had the feeling her reaction insulted him. As if she had rejected him somehow.

Confound it, didn't he understand that she wasn't rejecting him personally? She was objecting to leaving her *father's* home to take up residence in *Jack's* home. She craved freedom of choice, longed to be on her own. She had been deprived of independence and freedom of choice her entire life and she *craved* it like an addiction.

"I told them we need time to get to know each other before we speak our vows," he said belatedly.

Pru sagged in relief—another reaction that didn't go unnoticed. Those whiskey-colored eyes missed nothing.

"At the very least, we are asked to take the dance area as the couple of the hour."

"Of course," she said cheerily. "Looking forward to it."

"You shouldn't be. I'm not very good at dancing. Haven't done much of it."

Jack didn't know why he felt insulted that Pru practically collapsed at his feet when he informed her that he'd refused to hold the wedding ceremony tonight. He ought to marry this woman, just to foil her deceptive plans. But that would have been spiteful. Still, her expression reminded him of the looks he'd seen on the faces of people who had passed over the clumsy, oversized orphan he'd been in favor of taking toddlers into their homes and their hearts.

The word that came quickly to mind from his childhood was *rejection*. He wondered if Pru had taken one look at him and his unpolished manners then decided to call off the wedding. Or had she really come to Oklahoma Territory with no intention of marrying anyone, as she claimed?

*Doesn't matter*, Jack assured himself. When he hatched the idea of a mail-order bride, he hadn't intended for the marriage to be a love match. It was a business arrangement. He would provide certain services to make life comfortable and safe and so would his wife. After all, he could find physical satisfaction for a price in town if it came to that.

Too bad he'd taken one look at this feisty female and decided he could find all the pleasure he wanted with her. But that wasn't going to happen, he reminded himself. Nor did he want it to. Prudence Elizabeth Perkins was everything he *didn't* want in a wife and he better not let himself forget that by staring too long into that enchanting face and those mesmerizing blue eyes.

When Pru clutched his hand and headed for Tom Jenkins and Richard Wilhelm, the mayor and justice of peace, who had introduced themselves to her earlier, Jack discarded his pensive thoughts. This was a charade and he had a role to play for the evening. He sure as hell wasn't going to force a woman to marry him if she weren't inclined. He was sure Pru considered him too rough around the edges to suit her refined tastes. She was right, of course, but it still hurt his feelings a smidgen to know that she probably didn't think he was good enough for her.

*Stop doing so much thinking or you'll give yourself a headache,* said the scolding voice inside him.

"It's so very kind of you to suggest a ceremony this evening," Pru told Tom and Richard, who bowed politely over her. "But the harrowing holdup, the bump on my head and the lengthy overland trip has been exhausting."

"We understand," Tom said.

"We just thought it would top off our town-wide celebration," Richard added. "Nonetheless, we want to feature you and Jack for a waltz." He whistled loudly to gain the crowd's attention. "May I present to you, Jack McCavett and his fiancée, Prudence Perkins. The floor is yours." He made an expansive gesture with his arm as the band burst into another melody.

Jack slid his arm around her trim waist and stared down into these hypnotic blue eyes. A jolt of desire came out of nowhere and hit him hard and fast. He really hated that he was fiercely attracted to Pru. First off, he didn't approve of her underhanded tactics. Secondly, she'd all but rejected him as a prospective husband. Thirdly, she was too outspoken and independent to make a cooperative and obedient wife. Put simply, Pru would be too much trouble. Jack had had more than his fair share of it the past thirty-two years.

"You're still peeved at me, aren't you?" she asked perceptively.

"Don't know why I should be." He smiled pretentiously

for the onlookers who lined the perimeters of the dance area. "Let's see now, you came here under false pretenses, traded in the train ticket to make profit by taking the stage-coach. Then, after I came to your rescue when you faced down two thieves and nearly got yourself killed, you informed me that I wouldn't suffice as a husband."

"I told you," she said through her own exaggerated smile, "this isn't personal. I'll do all I can to find you a suitable wife and I'll repay you. I don't know what else I'm supposed to do to make amends."

He had a few ideas, but they included being as close and intimate as two people could get—naked. Clearly, that wasn't on the bargaining table.

"How about this," he suggested. "You repay me by hiring on at my ranch. The barn still needs to be con-structed. Meals need to be prepared, laundry washed and crops planted. I'll deduct what you owe me until we're square. Plus, you'll have free room and board."

"A hired hand?" she chirped. "But I had planned to take a job in town to repay you."

"You've got yourself a real beauty, Jack!" one of his acquaintances called out, lifting his cup in toast as the couple waltzed past. "To wedded bliss!"

"Here, here!" someone else chimed in.

Jack smiled, as if delighted with his bride-to-be. In truth, he'd like to strangle her swan-like neck for making him play this charade so he wouldn't disappoint the whole damn town. After all, he'd known disappointment by being turned down as an orphan. He didn't want to subject anyone to the feeling if he didn't have to. At least not on the night of the celebration.

\* \* \*

"This is gonna cost you extra," he said through his fake smile. "I'll be explaining what happened to our supposed betrothal for weeks. Maybe months."

Guilt bombarded Pru again. "I've made a mess of things."

He didn't let her off the hook. He said, "Damn right."

"But I'm truly sorry. I was desperate to leave town and I didn't stop to consider what it would be like for you, didn't know I was walking into this celebration." She glanced sideways, seeing the smiling faces of Jack's friends and acquaintances. "I want you to tell everyone that I don't suit you and that you're the one who broke off the engagement."

He arched a thick brow. "You're willing to accept criticism in order to help me save face?"

"This is your community. It's only fair that your friends side with you," she contended. "It will be up to me to make my own favorable impression on your neighbors."

He didn't say anything for a long moment, while he waltzed her in another wide circle. But the look on his face suggested that he was reevaluating his opinion of her.

Only God knew why she didn't want Jack to think the worst about her. She hadn't given a fig about men's opinions because she had refused to live her life trying to win men's approval and acceptance. Plus, her vast wealth made it impossible to tell if men liked her for who she was inside or if they were after the Perkins fur fortune.

"If you don't want to be a farmhand then I'll put you up at the hotel for a few days," he surprised her by offering out of the blue. "Otherwise, there will be speculation about our sleeping arrangement. That might damage your reputation and future betrothals."

Pru mentally tabulated the extra expenses. Ah well, she would just be indebted to Jack a little longer than she had originally planned. "Thank you for your generosity and consideration. Just put it on my tab."

"Count on it," he replied. "I still expect your labor at my farm during the day."

Pru sighed audibly. It looked as if she was destined to become a field hand. On that issue, Jack refused to budge. She didn't blame him for being a mite spiteful. He would probably enjoy seeing her with dirt smudges on her face and calluses on her hands.

"Fine," she agreed. "We have a deal. A hard day's work for an honest day's pay. I'll ride into town at night—" Her voice broke off and she frowned.

"Need to rent a horse?" he asked with a wry grin.

"Curse it. I'll be your indentured servant for months," she grumbled. "But yes, I'll need a horse."

"And tack? Do you plan to come and go riding bareback?"

She huffed out her breath, exasperated. When she noticed the ornery grin twitching his lips, she cocked her head to study him closely. "You're enjoying this immensely, aren't you? You can tack on fees for everything and I'm forced to pay because I'm over the proverbial barrel. Are you going to charge me for breathing the air on your ranch, too?"

He chuckled as the music stopped, leaving them standing in the middle of the dance area—the torchlights and attention fixed on them. He tapped her on the tip of her upturned nose with his forefinger and winked, for her benefit as well as the bystanders'. "Everything has a price, Pru. Except breathing. That you can do for free. But everything else is gonna cost you."

"Ah, my own private banker and moneylender." She eyed him warily as he led her toward the table to retrieve their drinks of punch.

For the life of her, she didn't know why the broad smile that encompassed his rugged features sent warm tingles down her spine. Blast it, where was her usual indifference to the attentions of men? She was immune to the practiced charm of gentlemen in Saint Louis society. But Jack was another matter entirely. She didn't want to be affected by him, attracted to him…but she was.

"Tell me something, Jack. I'm curious as to why you chose me from the other women who undoubtedly responded to your ad."

He cast her a sideways glance. "It was your clever turn of phrase and the spirit vibrating through your correspondence, I suppose. The others didn't show much imagination."

"And yet you claim that *obedient* and *average* is what you're looking for in a woman," she reminded him teasingly. "Seems to me that you asked for it when you picked me."

Jack muttered under his breath. "I did, didn't I? What the hell was I thinking?"

"Give your bride-to-be a kiss to seal the deal!" Stony called out.

Laughter, cheers and wolfish whistles erupted from the crowd. Oh damn, thought Pru. She had tested her reaction to Jack one too many times today. She had felt the stirring of desire while sitting within his encircling arms and muscular thighs during their horseback ride into town. She had felt the arousing pleasure of his breath whispering against her neck. Then she had danced in his arms, her body brushing suggestively against his masculine physique enough times that heightened awareness was jumping alive inside her.

This kissing business was only going to make things worse. No doubt about that.

# *Chapter Four*

"At least act like you're enjoying our kiss," Jack murmured as he angled his head toward hers.

That wasn't going to be a problem. Enjoying his kiss too much was, Pru realized immediately. The feel of his sensuous lips moving over hers with such gentleness made her weak in the knees—and the head. It made her wonder if she should marry Jack. For sure and certain, she was attracted to him. Furthermore, the marriage would prevent her father from dragging her home. Yet, that would be another way of using Jack for her purposes and she'd done that already. But then, it would provide her with the opportunity to explore these unexplained sensations that buzzed through her while they kissed.

Pru was already aware of how tantalizing it was to have his power-packed body brushing familiarly against hers while on horseback and while dancing. She not only knew how appealing his masculine scent was to her, but she also knew how delicious he tasted—and he tasted warm and sweet and addictive. That was something else she didn't need to know if she had any hope of battling this fierce attraction.

Before she realized what she'd done, her hands glided over his chest then she looped her arms around his neck. She stretched up on tiptoe to compensate for the difference in their height and kissed him back. Cheers went up around them, but Pru was far more aware of her pulse pounding like a drum in her ears and the rush of pleasure surging through her body.

Hungry need lambasted Jack when he felt Pru's arms on his shoulders and heard the soft sigh that caused her full breasts to brush enticingly against his chest. He had to remind himself, repeatedly, that this was an act and that he should keep his hands to himself. He and Pru were on display again, damn it. And the lie they were living was getting worse every arousing second. Hell! So much for keeping a low profile in his new life in Paradise.

The alarming thought of how fiercely this spirited female affected him and how much attention they were receiving prompted Jack to break the kiss. His male body objected, but Jack held his ground instead of moving toward her again. He waved to the crowd then offered Pru his arm so they could continue on their way to the table.

He felt a little better when he noticed she swayed slightly on her feet. Good. He didn't want to be the only one hot and bothered by their embrace. He might not be prime marriage material for Pru, but her reaction indicated that she wasn't immune to him completely. That soothed his pride a bit.

Chester Dawson doubled over at the waist in an exaggerated bow as the couple approached him. "Shall we have a go at it, Pru?"

"Of course," she said graciously.

Jack watched Chester lead Pru back in the direction they'd come then he glanced disparagingly at his mischievous friend, Stony. "Requesting that public kiss was a bit much. What did I ever do to you, except help you avoid a few dangerous scrapes through the years?"

"It was all in good fun," Stony replied, undaunted. "And before you get bent out of shape, resign yourself to a charivari after your wedding ceremony."

Jack clamped his mouth shut and kept quiet. Eventually he'd have to confide in Stony that there wouldn't be a marriage ceremony or playful charivari afterward. Jack decided to tell Stony later. At the very last minute. Until then Stony could have his teasing amusement.

His focus of attention shifted back to Pru who smiled and chatted easily with Chester while they danced. When the music ended, three male partygoers rushed forward to take Chester's place. A minute later a half-dozen men formed a line, waiting their turn to dance with Pru.

Maybe it was a good thing Pru called off the wedding, he mused. The woman, too spirited by nature and too much the dazzling beauty, would be extremely high profile. Jack craved a simple, uneventful life that was far removed from the hassles of long trail drives and keeping the lid on wild cow towns.

The instant Jack noticed Pru's smile looking strained and caught sight of the dark circles forming around her eyes he snapped to attention. What the hell was the matter with him? The woman had endured a long stage ride, encountered a holdup, been captured and injured. Then he'd forced her to participate in the celebration held partially in their honor. Pru was probably dead on her feet and was sticking it out because he had demanded it.

Jack detached himself from the small group of men who had gathered around him. He was ready to make a beeline toward Pru when Stony called out to him.

"Hold up, Jack. With all the goings-on, I didn't ask Pru for a statement about the robbery or get descriptions of the thieves."

"That will have to wait. She's exhausted and I should have put her up at the hotel an hour ago."

"A hotel?" Stony echoed. "But I thought—"

Jack turned toward his friend. "At least until she has a chance to rest up and we plan the ceremony. Plus, no need for unflattering speculations," he added in explanation.

"Right. Of course, protect her reputation." Stony nodded thoughtfully. "Good thinking. I guess I was putting the cart before the horse."

"You can interview Pru when she's rested," Jack said before he pivoted on his heels and walked away. "She can come see you when she feels up to it."

A moment later, he tapped the mayor on the shoulder. "Sorry to cut in, Tom, but Pru has had an exhausting day."

"Certainly. The holdup and all." Tom Jenkins bowed politely to Pru. "It's a pleasure to welcome you to our town, Miss Perkins. If I can be of help don't hesitate to ask."

Jack frowned speculatively, wondering if the tall, gangly bachelor who owned the dry-goods store would leap at the chance to court Pru when word spread that the wedding had been canceled. Undoubtedly.

"Thank you," Pru murmured as she leaned heavily on

Jack's arm. "I'm so tired that I'm ready to drop in my tracks. This headache from hell seems to be getting worse by the minute."

Which explained her pinched features and the dark circles around her eyes, Jack mused. "Shall I introduce you to Dr. Quinn so he can give you something to relieve your pain?"

"No, I just want to crawl into bed and sleep."

Jack headed toward Paradise Hotel, the best accommodations in town. He rented a room then escorted Pru upstairs. "I'll be back in a few minutes with your luggage."

Sighing heavily, Pru closed the door and flounced back on the bed. It didn't compare to the soft, luxurious bed in her room at home. But that was one of the prices she'd gladly pay for her freedom.

A quiet rap at the door brought her back to her feet. "That was quick—"

Her voice dried up when the two masked men she'd encountered earlier barged inside. One of them clamped his gloved hand over her mouth to keep her quiet. The other one rammed the barrel of his pistol into her chest.

"Okay, lady, here's the deal," the first bandit growled gruffly. "You keep your trap shut about us and we'll let you live. You start trying to give our descriptions to the marshal and you'll be dead before you're hitched. Then we'll ambush your husband-to-be. You got that?"

Unable to do anything else, Pru nodded her head.

"Smart lady," the second outlaw mumbled. "We'll be watching and waiting so don't think you can pull a fast one on us. You only get one mistake. *Your last mistake.*"

And then they were gone as quickly as they had pounced. Pru poked her head around the door to see the men scurrying toward the fire escape at the far end of the hall.

Damnation, she detested being threatened and manipulated. It reminded her too much of Gram's tactics. This time, however, Pru faced deadly consequences, not just the whack of Gram's dragonhead cane. Plus, Jack would be in jeopardy if she didn't watch her step. Confound it, his life was already in a tangle because of her. She didn't think her conscience could handle the prospect of being the reason for his death.

Of course, she would be dead already so battling her conscience would be a moot point, she mused. She'd have to await Jack's arrival at the pearly gates to apologize for ruining his life.

No telling what he'd charge her for that!

When she heard footfalls in the hall, she glanced to the right. The dim lantern light sprayed over Jack's impressive physique and angular features. Fear and exhaustion put her in motion. She flung herself at him impulsively while he had his hands full carrying her heavy satchels. An instant later, she asked herself how she was going to explain her unexpected behavior.

Sure enough, he asked, "What was that for?" His warm breath caressed her neck and heightened her awareness of him. As if she wasn't aware of him already. "No one is watching now and we don't have to keep up appearances," he reminded her.

Annoyed with herself for feeling needy, insecure and unsettled after the second encounter with the bandits, Pru forced herself to let him go and step back a pace. "Sorry. All the events of the day just caught up with me."

Jack grabbed the two satchels in one hand then patted her shoulder comfortingly—and a little awkwardly, she noted. "You'll feel better tomorrow, I'm sure. Stony wants to take your statement and get a description of the outlaws when you feel up to it."

Pru inwardly winced. She wondered if those bandits would be watching and waiting when she traipsed over to the marshal's office. Who were they? Why hadn't they trotted off to another town to pawn the jewelry they'd stolen?

For a half second, she considered telling Jack about her intimidating visitors, but she didn't want to put him in danger. Besides, the bandits were her problem. Not his. He had dealt with his share of vicious scoundrels in Kansas and he insisted that he wanted to lead a quiet, uneventful life.

"I'll go see Stony soon," she murmured.

"Only when you feel up to it and not a minute before," he emphasized. "I told Stony not to push."

"Thank you, Jack."

She peered into his golden eyes and felt regret hammer at her again. She had royally fouled up his plans of finding a wife and quite possibly had placed him in danger. She hadn't intended for *her* quest for freedom to complicate *his* life.

"I'll give myself a day to recuperate, if that meets with your approval."

"Make it two," he insisted generously.

"Thank you. Then I'll walk out to your ranch to begin my employment," she assured him.

Jack reached into the pocket of his breeches then placed money in her hand. "This will buy you two days of three square meals—"

Her groan of frustration interrupted him. "And that's gonna cost me, right?"

He chuckled. "Right. Now get a good night's sleep."

She couldn't imagine how that was going to happen, when her dealings with those mean-spirited outlaws would likely be there to fuel her nightmares.

"I'll see you in a couple of days, Pru," he said before he strode off.

Pru closed and locked the door. She peeled off her clothes and left a trail behind her. She was fast asleep in five minutes. But sure enough, a nightmare awakened her a few hours later and it was a long time before she dozed off again.

Horatio Perkins glanced up from his desk, surprised to see his mother at his downtown office. His bad day was getting worse. First, he'd endured a visit from Theodore Porter, a local competitor who delighted in annoying him every chance he got. Now his mother was here to spoil what was left of his disposition.

"Now see what you've done!"

"What did I do?" he asked, dumbfounded.

His mother stamped toward him, her cane playing a rapid staccato that indicated the heightened degree of her irritation. She thrust a letter at him. "This is from your contrary daughter," she muttered sourly. "Turns out she hasn't been staying with friends in the country the past few days. I just found the note she left for us. She ran away from home. Permanently."

"What!" Horatio choked out as he grabbed the letter his mother waved under his nose.

"She accepted the dare you issued two weeks ago and

now she has struck off on her own when we least expected it," his mother reported.

"The dare *I* issued?" he countered.

His mother flicked her wrist dismissively. "The point is that your headstrong daughter rebelled against our expectations. She went haring off to only-God-knows-where to do only-God-knows-what!"

Horatio scanned the letter his daughter had penned. "She plans to make a life of her own without relying on Perkins money," he mused aloud.

"How absurd," his mother said and snorted. "She insists on finding a job, but there is no need for her to work when we have accumulated more money than she can possibly spend in her lifetime." She gave him the evil eye. "If you had ruled with a firm hand this wouldn't have happened. Good thing I've been here all these years to help corral that headstrong child of yours. She might have been more rebellious than she is now… Where did she get that annoying independent streak anyway?"

Horatio looked at his mother and thought, *you ought to know*.

"Don't dawdle, Horatio. Get up and get moving." She grabbed his shirt collar and tugged, demanding that he stand. "Hire the best detective money can buy and put him on her trail before disaster befalls that harebrained daughter of yours. Her virtue is at stake. Edwin Donald might back out of the wedding contract if…well, you know what I mean."

She pelted toward the door. "While you're speaking to a detective I'll spread the word that we sent Pru on tour to visit our relatives back East." She halted to stare deliberately at Horatio. "When Pru returns you can bet I will have a thing or two to say to her about the turmoil she's putting me through."

"I'm not *betting* anyone anything ever again," he muttered as he read the note a second time.

Scowling at the unexpected turn of events, Horatio sped off to hire a private detective. He knew he was doomed to listen to his mother rant and rave until Pru turned up. And blast it, Pru had better be all right. He could endure his mother's tirades if it guaranteed he'd get his daughter back in the same condition she'd left.

Pru felt refreshed—somewhat—after a full day of relaxation and two nights of rest. She still had a bump on the back of her skull, a mild headache and the lingering memory of a nightmare in which the bandits had spirited her away, never to be seen or heard from again.

Famished from skipping meals while she recuperated, she retrieved the money Jack had given her. She descended the steps to enter the café attached to the lobby of the Paradise Hotel, Miller Restaurant.

She smiled cordially at the pregnant waitress who approached to take her order. "I'll be looking for a job in a few weeks," Pru commented. "Do you think your employer might hire me to fill in while you're home with your newborn? Just temporarily," she added to reassure the red-haired waitress. "Just until you're ready to return to work."

The waitress stuck out her hand. "You're Prudence Perkins," she acknowledged. "I saw you and Jack at the town-wide party. I'm Gracie Witham." She hitched her thumb toward the other waitress. "That's Myrna Bates. She is green with envy that you're marrying Jack. She's had a crush on him since he first showed up in town." She barked a laugh. "Of course, she had to stand in line because most of the single women around here have set their caps for him, too."

Pru made a mental note to put Myrna Bates on her list of prospective brides to parade past Jack. Myrna looked to be a few years younger than Pru. She had a thick head of raven hair, dark eyes and a wide smile. She was built sturdily and stood a few inches short than Pru's five foot five inch frame.

"I'll take you back to the kitchen to meet Terrence Miller, the proprietor," Gracie offered.

Pru gave Gracie her order then approached the round-bellied, balding owner who labored over a skillet of ham, grits and eggs. "I'm interested in replacing Gracie while she's caring for her newborn. I'm—"

"Prudence Perkins, yes, I know," he said. "And so does everybody else in town. Jack plans to let you work after you're married? That's surprising."

"*Let* me?" Pru settled her ruffled feathers quickly. "Er…yes. He thought temporary employment might be a good way for me to get acquainted with everyone."

"Smart thinking on his part," said Terrence. "Hadn't thought of it that way. Good man, Jack. Honest, hardworking. Just the man you want around when trouble breaks out." Terrence smiled, displaying the gap between his two front teeth. "'Course you found that out after the stagecoach holdup."

"Yes, he's quite competent and reliable."

"You're lucky to have him."

"Lucky indeed," Pru agreed. "Now, about the temporary employment?"

Terrence bobbed his bald head. "Fine by me. Come around in a couple of weeks and let Gracie train you. Ever waitress before?"

"No, but I'm eager to learn," she enthused.

"Wha'd you do before coming here?" he asked curiously.

Pru had been in charge of the family budget. "Accounting," she informed him.

"Yeah? Maybe you could help with my books." He frowned sternly. "But it's confidential. Don't want my customers knowing how much I make and what things cost. That's private information."

"Mum's the word," Pru promised before she pivoted around to nod a greeting to the scrawny lad who was washing dishes.

After a hearty breakfast, Pru strode toward the newspaper office, inspired by Jack's comment that she was clever with a turn of phrase. In addition, working at the newspaper office would help her with her cause to promote women's suffrage and improve salaries and working conditions. Although she planned to apply at several other businesses, nothing would make her happier than writing editorials that called attention to her other noble causes of city beautification and literacy.

Pru pasted on her best smile as she breezed into the newspaper office. She stopped short when she saw a thin-chested man crouched over flyers that had flown off the table when the draft followed her through the door. She noticed a hand-printing press beside a desk filled with paper and notes.

"Sorry about the mess," she apologized as she knelt down to help the editor gather the flyers.

"Happens all the time."

"Then perhaps you should move this table to the far corner where the gushing air doesn't reach," she suggested.

"Not a bad idea. You're Miss Perkins, aren't you?"

*I really wish people would quit telling me who I am. I know who I am,* she mused. "You must be the editor of the *Paradise Times Star.*"

"Yes, ma'am. Oscar Epperson at your service." He came to his feet then dropped into a polite bow. "How may I help you, Miss Perkins?"

"Please call me Pru," she insisted. "I'm interested in a job and I wondered if you could use help."

"Jack is in favor of this?"

Pru gnashed her teeth. Why, she wondered, did everyone around here think she needed Jack's permission? Curse it, this was as bad as being expected to filter all her ideas through Gram and her father. She didn't want to have to answer to anyone. That was the whole point of making a new start in Oklahoma Territory.

"Jack thinks it's a good way to get acquainted," she said, noting the comment pacified Oscar much as it had Terrence at Miller Restaurant.

Oscar's frizzy blond hair fell over his forehead and he raked his hand through it to comb it back in place. He gestured toward the flyers that still littered the floor like casualties of battle. "I could use help with the typesetting, the job printing I do for the land office, Wanted posters for the marshal's office and printing for local stores that want to advertise."

Pru would have preferred to write thought-provoking articles, but if she could get her foot in the door, she would be on her way. "I accept," she declared. "Problem is, I might have a few weeks—" She paused, mentally scrambling to explain her arrangement with Jack, "of household changes to make at Jack's ranch before the…um…wedding. I'm not sure yet how much time the tasks with require."

"I understand," Oscar said. "But I'm surprised that Jack has agreed to this when you have so many changes and arrangements to make at the ranch."

Pru bit down on her tongue. One of her new goals was to change the male attitude that a woman needed a man's permission to do whatever she decided to do, whenever she decided to do it.

"Jack is a very progressive thinker," she said, crossing her fingers behind her back. "He agrees that I have my own life to lead and my own objectives to achieve. He doesn't expect me to be an extension of his will or his life."

Oscar's thin blond brows rose on his wide forehead. "I had no idea Jack felt that way."

Pru had no idea if he did, but she projected her philosophy on Jack to get her point across. Curse it, she was using him again, she realized guiltily.

"I'm lucky to have found someone so understanding and considerate of my need for independence." She squatted down to pick up the rest of the flyers, which advertised a land sale. Apparently, several folks had made the Run the previous year, built a few outbuildings as the government had stipulated and then decided to make a profit after the appointed amount of time had passed. Either that or a family had run onto hard times and decided to pull up stakes. Whatever the case, the flyers notified interested citizens that property was for sale.

When she came to her feet, she noticed Oscar was apprais-

ing her. "I'd like to interview you and write a story about the
holdup and your ordeal." He smiled wryly. "I might even let
you write the article yourself if you'll give me exclusive
rights that the other newspaper in town can't have it."

Pru inwardly cringed. She would have to guard her
words carefully in the article or those thieving brutes would
be back with more threats that might endanger Oscar. But
this was an opportunity too good to pass up.

She thrust out her hand. "We have a deal. I'll come
around later this afternoon to discuss the article."

Oscar beamed. "Perfect. I'll be waiting."

Pru detoured into the hotel before marching off to Stony
Mason's office. Just to be on the safe side, she planned to
change rooms so the bandits couldn't find her so easily.

"Something wrong with the room?" the clerk questioned.

"No, I want a room where the window faces the street."
She smiled cheerily. "Being new in town, I want to famil-
iarize myself with all the stores and get a feel for the
goings-on. What better way than with a bird's-eye view?"

The clerk nodded then pushed his drooping spectacles
back to the bridge of his nose. "Very clever of you. I'll see
what we have available."

"It was Jack's idea," she heard herself say and realized
she was categorically giving him credit for all her ideas so
she wouldn't cause waves. For now.

While he rooted around for a room key, Pru scanned the
lobby. There were several scruffy-looking men lounging
about. Some were reading the two competitive newspapers.
Some just stared off into space. Some appeared to be
gamblers who were wearing colorful vests and gaudy rings.
Others looked as if they hadn't been near a razor or bathtub

in weeks. Drifters, she supposed. The vultures of frontier society were circling, hoping to make easing pickings from a hapless victim.

Were two of these men the ones who had robbed her on the stagecoach? She appraised the men's faces then glanced at their boots and spurs, hoping to make an identification. One man might have been the right size and stature to be her captor, but she couldn't swear to it.

*The people you have contacted today might be in danger because of you*, came that niggling voice inside her head.

Frustrated by the threat hanging over her, as well as Jack and her new acquaintances, she retrieved her satchels and moved into the new room. Then she trooped to the marshal's office. Her footsteps halted in front of Madame Rozalie Pitman's Boutique. A hat, adorned with delicate feathers and lace called out to her. Of course, she was living on borrowed money so she couldn't possibly afford the eye-catching hat.

"Come in, Miss Perkins!" the proprietor insisted as she poked her curly dark head out the door. "That hat would look positively stunning on you. I noticed that the hat you were wearing at the celebration had been damaged. Was it because of that dreadful holdup?"

Pru nodded as she stared covetously at the hat. She loved hats and she had since childhood. It was one of her weaknesses. According to Gram, Pru was lousy with them.

Madame Rozalie clucked her tongue. "Blasted bandits have no idea how fond women are of their hats. It should be a criminal offense to damage one as fine as the one you had on when you arrived in town."

Pru glanced past the outgoing woman who looked to be

in her early thirties. She focused her attention on a younger woman working industriously on an emerald-green gown.

Rozalie followed Pru's gaze. "That's Samantha Graham." She leaned close to say, "Sweet little thing, but her husband is an overbearing bore. Every time she comes to work with a bruise on her arm or cheek I want to take after Phil with the pointed end of my parasol. Molly Palmer, who works at the bakery, has the same sort of husband. The same goes for Amelia Thorton who's a waitress at Harper's Café. I'd like to whale on Henry Palmer and Earl Thorton, too."

Pru silently seconded the notion. She had met her share of women who had been knocked around in Saint Louis. In her opinion, abusive husbands should be whipped to see how they enjoyed the pain. If she were allowed the freedom to write other articles for Oscar's paper she would address the issue, she decided.

"Sam!" Rozalie called out. "Come here and meet Prudence Perkins. I'm trying to persuade her to buy that marvelous hat you created."

"You designed the hat?" Pru asked. "It's lovely."

Sam moved forward, head downcast humbly. "Thank you."

"The woman is bursting with creativity," Rozalie praised. "I remind her of it daily, too."

Pru rather thought it was Rozalie's way of trying to coax Samantha from her shell. She predicted this Phil person spent his time degrading his wife to keep her submissive. She hadn't met Phil but she disliked him sight unseen. She felt the same way about Molly Palmer's husband, too.

Pru impulsively retrieved the generous amount of

money Jack had given her for meals. "I do believe I'll take that fine hat and a parasol." She checked the rack, looking for the one with the sharpest point. "That one."

She definitely needed some sort of makeshift weapon if those bandits kept popping up periodically to intimidate her.

While Pru handed over almost every cent that Jack loaned her, she made a mental note to ask him to teach her to handle a pistol. He was an expert, after all. If she had to face down those outlaws, she wanted to know how to defend herself with something besides the sharp tip of a parasol.

Pru wondered how Jack would react if worse came to worst and she had to engage in a shoot-out with those bandits. Any association with *her* would reflect unfavorably on him. He craved a quiet life, free of scandal and gossip. It would be best if Jack called off the wedding quickly so he could detach himself from whatever trouble awaited in her future.

For sure and certain, Pru was going to take on the Phil Grahams, Henry Palmers and Earl Thortons of the world who victimized their wives, daughters or children. If her crusade invited more trouble then so be it. Someone had to speak out for oppressed kindred spirits.

Yes, indeed, Pru thought as she strode toward the marshal's office. There was work to be done to raise awareness of a woman's plight in Paradise. Destiny had sent her here to make a difference. She just hoped Jack didn't get sucked up into the melee. Jack was...

An arousing tingle skittered across her skin when the memory of their kiss bombarded her. *Enough of that*, she told herself. Jack had assured her that she wasn't what he wanted and she had insisted that she didn't want to marry anyone. She was here to spread her independent wings. Just because Jack's tantalizing scent, gentle touch and delicious kiss melted her resolve momentarily didn't mean she was giving up her long-awaited dreams and her noble crusades.

With that in mind, Pru sailed into the marshal's office to make her statement without revealing so much as to get her killed before she could achieve her worthwhile missions in life.

# Chapter Five

Jack glanced up from feeding the livestock to see the heavily loaded wagon from the lumberyard approaching. He'd spent the past two days doing odd jobs and wondering if Pru had recovered from her exhaustion. Honestly, he didn't know why he was sparing her a single thought. The feisty female had complicated his life six ways to Sunday and she'd only been in town for three days.

He grinned when he saw Chester and Leroy trotting their horses toward the new barn site. Apparently, they had decided to repay him for helping them construct their barns by showing up to unload his stack of lumber.

Thirty minutes later, he and the Dawsons were stacking wood with the help of two employees from the lumber company.

"Do you think Pru got rested up?" Chester asked as he scooped up the canteen to take a drink.

"All things considered, she held up well," Leroy commented as he took the canteen from his brother. "She must be much tougher than she looks."

Jack made a neutral sound that could have meant anything. He'd given Pru too much thought already. *He* didn't want to discuss her. His friends and neighbors, however, did.

"Prettiest thing I ever saw," Harry Morton, one of the lumberyard employees said as he mopped sweat from his brow with his handkerchief. "You're one lucky rascal, Jack."

"I'd keep close tabs on her," Virgil Sparks advised. "I heard several men fantasizing about her at the party. If I were you, I'd have her tucked in at your ranch, not left in town. Rumors be damned. That's too much beautiful woman to be running around without a chaperone."

"Stony will look after her," Jack insisted, wondering why this odd sensation was spiraling through him. Hell! Was this what possessiveness felt like?

"I gotta agree with Virgil," Chester spoke up. "At the very least you should ride into town tonight to check on her. Take her out to supper."

"After all, women like to be courted," Leroy remarked. "Mail-order bride aside, a woman likes to feel special."

Chester elbowed his brother and grinned. "When did you get to be such an authority on women?"

Everyone looked at Leroy and waited expectantly.

"Ma gave me pointers while I was courting Kathleen Emery back in Iowa."

Chester snorted. "She wasn't good enough for you, little brother. Good thing you left her behind to make the Run."

Jack went back to work. He had no interest in courting a woman who didn't want him. It was a waste of time. Besides, Stony had promised to keep his eye on Pru.

Nevertheless, two hours later Jack had bathed at the

spring-fed creek and was on his way to town to invite Pru to supper. He shook his head in dismay. One minute he was telling himself to disregard the stunning, blue-eyed blonde. The next moment he was calculating how long it would take to get into town to see her. He must be going crazy from spending so much time alone on his ranch the past year.

Or at least he hoped that was the cause of this maddening preoccupation with Pru.

"So you don't remember a single thing about either of the bandits?" Stony asked dubiously. "Surely you remember *something*."

When his green eyes focused intently on her from across the scarred office desk, Pru forced herself not to fidget under the marshal's scrutiny. She wanted desperately to tell him what the bandits had said when they showed up unexpectedly in her room. But she didn't want to drag Stony into potential disaster. He was Jack's longtime friend and companion.

"Pru?" Stony prompted. "I get the feeling there's something you're not telling me."

She sighed heavily then slumped in her chair. "Forgive me. It seems that I'm just now dealing with the terror of the robbery. Jack told me that I was crazy to battle those men for possession of my heirloom bracelet. It has finally soaked in that resisting the criminals was dangerous and foolish."

He smiled slightly. "Not the smartest thing you could have done, I agree."

Pru surged to her feet. "Perhaps after this lingering headache fades some details about the men will occur to me. Right now, it's like a hazy dream. I was too busy fighting them to pay attention to details."

"You come see me immediately if you recall something, hear?" Stony encouraged.

Pru bobbed her head, grabbed her parasol then strode off. Her stomach growled, but she ignored it. She'd been skipping meals to compensate for her shortage of funds. She glanced wistfully at the new hat atop her head then at the parasol.

Too bad they weren't edible.

The hair on the back of her neck stood up suddenly and Pru glanced around, feeling as if she were being watched. Blast it, she detested being intimidated and terrorized. She was in an unfamiliar town surrounded by dozens of unfamiliar faces. Everyone knew who she was—the thieves included—and she had only a few acquaintances.

Her stomach growled repeatedly as she mounted the hotel steps. If she could survive the rest of the day, she could hike to Jack's ranch and find something to eat. Room and board, he'd said—

Pru gasped in pain when her two personal demons burst from the supply closet and slammed her against the wall. Their pistols bit into her ribs and a gloved hand clamped over her mouth again. To her dismay they bustled her down the hall then dug into the pocket of her skirt to retrieve the key to her new room. Obviously she should have told the desk clerk not to divulge her room number to anyone.

"Wha'd you tell the newspaper editor, bitch?" the first bandit snarled as he closed the door of her room. He laid a knife to her throat. "Answer me!"

"Nothing," she croaked as she stared at the black hood that concealed the man's identity. "I swear it."

"What about the marshal?" the second outlaw sneered

as he crammed his pistol barrel a little deeper into her ribs. "He'll get shot in the back if we see a Wanted poster with our descriptions on it."

"As for you," the first bandit growled as he pricked her neck with the dagger, drawing a drop of blood, "I'll slit your throat and carve up that pretty face if you don't keep your yap shut."

Rage surged through her and she realized that she had a serious personality flaw. When threatened she got angry instead of scared. The same thing had happened during the holdup.

She didn't realize she had uplifted her parasol to gouge the point into the bandit's groin so he'd back off with his knife. He doubled over and howled when she reflexively skewered him. Unfortunately, her attack provoked the second bandit to backhand her before she could let loose with a scream for help.

Her tender head smacked against the wall and her legs wobbled unsteadily. Worse, the second bandit kicked her feet out from under her. She landed in an unceremonious heap on the floor but she lashed out with her parasol to stab him in the groin, too. He leaped backward to avoid a direct hit. Then he followed his cohort through the doorway.

"Keep your mouth shut, bitch," he sneered venomously. "We know where you are and we'll be back."

When the door clicked shut, Pru trailed her hand over her stinging cheek. Her head was throbbing again. Her eye felt as if it had exploded after the backhanded blow. Pain pulsated in her ankle where the bully had kicked her with his boot.

Shaking, she climbed to her knees then to her feet. She

opened the door to note the hall was empty. Damn it! How'd they get away so quickly?

Muffling a sniff, Pru limped over to wash her face and check for damage in the mirror that hung above the washstand. There was a red welt on her cheek and a bloody prick on her neck.

"Pru?"

She blinked in surprise when she heard Jack's voice in the hall. She opened the door and waved to him while he stood in front of the original room he had rented for her.

Frowning, Jack strode toward her. "Why are you—?" His voice became a muffled curse as he focused on her face. "What the hell happened?"

Jack stared at the trickle of blood she had yet to wipe away. When she clamped her hand over her neck to stop the bleeding, he removed her hand to inspect the puncture. Then he closely surveyed the red welt on her cheek.

"Who did this?" he growled ferociously.

She shook her head and refused to meet his intense gaze. "It's nothing."

"It's something," he countered as he curled his forefinger beneath her chin, forcing her to meet his grim stare. "I was in law enforcement too long not to want justice for this kind of abuse. Stony is sensitive to it, too, because his mother died from a severe beating. That's what landed him in the orphanage…. *Now who did this to you?*"

"It's not worth your getting hurt over," she insisted.

*"Me?"* he hooted. "Someone is obviously terrorizing you and I want to know who it is. He and I need to have a little chat."

Despite her vow to keep silent so Jack wouldn't become

involved, this second assault and deadly threat had gotten to her. She trembled uncontrollably and tears clouded her eyes. She flung herself at Jack before she had time to think it through. She told herself that it was because she was alone in this unfamiliar town and had nowhere else to turn for comfort and moral support. She refused to let herself think there was more to it than a terrified victim needing a sturdy shoulder to lean on.

Well, so much for her self-reliance and independence, she thought with a self-deprecating sniff.

She might have recovered her composure if Jack hadn't shown up so soon after the attack. But she was in his sinewy arms and he tucked her head against his shoulder so she savored the feeling of being protected.

"Now tell me what happened," he murmured as he kissed away the sting in her cheek.

She tried to keep her mouth shut, but her crackly voice erupted. "The bandits showed up to threaten me again."

*"Again?"* He cupped her chin in his hand and forced her to meet his gaze. "You mean again after the holdup?"

She shook her silver-blond head and her eyes glistened with tears. Jack disliked the fact that he was enormously affected by Pru and he was attuned to her woes. The welt on her cheek infuriated him. The prick of a dagger on her neck made him see red. The tears in those luminous blue eyes got to him—to the extreme.

"No, the bandits showed up the night of the celebration while you were retrieving my luggage."

Irritation roiled through him when he recalled that he'd questioned Pru about why she'd flown into him arms in front of her hotel room that night. "And you didn't tell me immediately after it happened? Why the hell not?"

"Because they swore they'd bushwhack you if you started asking questions. Same for Stony. If he tacks up Wanted Posters using descriptions of the stagecoach robbers, he's destined to have a bullet lodged in his back."

Jack muttered under his breath, but he didn't interrupt because he wanted to keep Pru talking instead of remaining close-lipped about the two incidents.

"I shouldn't be telling you this." Her breath hitched.

"Of course you should," he insisted.

She stared apologetically at him. "No, because I don't want you in danger. You deserve to live a simple life after what you've endured. I'm complicating it every which way."

That was the God's honest truth. Nevertheless, it didn't change the fact that he felt responsible for Pru being in the territory. He was concerned about her safety and outraged by the threats and assaults.

"I changed rooms in hopes those brutish cretins couldn't locate me, but they must have asked the desk clerk for my new room number," Pru elaborated. "They burst in to find out what I'd told Stony and the newspaper editor I'd talked to."

She inhaled deeply and squared her shoulders. "I was afraid to tell Stony what little I know about these bandits, for fear he'd suffer the consequences, too. The same for Oscar Epperson. They swore he'd bite the bullet if the story about the robbery was too detailed and incriminating."

Jack cursed foully. "That does it. You're moving to the ranch right now."

"But—"

"No buts, Pru. I want you where I can protect you. Those bastards will have to come through me to get to you."

She shook her head adamantly and curly ringlets of blond hair danced around her bruised face. Roughed up though she was, she was still the most fetching female he'd ever met.

"I'm staying here and you're going to act as if you know nothing," she demanded. "Oscar offered me a job at the newspaper office. I was going to wait until I had repaid you by working for you, but—"

"A deal's a deal," he interrupted as he strode over to scoop up her carpetbags. "We'll eat at Miller Restaurant then head home."

"Eat in public while sporting this?" She called his attention to her discolored cheek. "What if rumors spread that *you* struck me?"

He flung his arm dismissively. "Leave it to me. I'll think of something." He had no idea what yet.

Before she could object—and she looked as if she intended to—Jack whisked her out the door and down the hall. He heard her stomach growl and raised an eyebrow.

She gestured toward her stylish hat that had suffered minor damage during the scuffle and then pointed at the parasol she had clamped in her fist. "I bought the hat to make Samantha Graham feel better about herself and the parasol for my protection. It took all the money you gave me. But the praise I heaped on Samantha fortified her self-confidence and this makeshift weapon already paid for itself. I did bodily harm when those brutes attacked me today."

It impressed Jack that Pru placed Samantha's needs above her own. Admirable, he mused, and then glanced at the sharp-tipped umbrella. He couldn't help but grin at her ingenuity when it came to self-defense. "Hit them where it hurts the worst, did you?"

She nodded and managed a faint smile. "Unfortunately one bandit backhanded me then kicked my feet out from under me. My aim was off the mark and I only gouged him in the thigh. I wish I could have run him through... Jack, I'd like to ask a favor."

"Name it."

She stared at him so earnestly that he would have promised her anything if it would erase her tormented expression and dry her tears. Damn it, he shouldn't be letting Pru get to him so easily. What was it about her that made him so vulnerable?

It wasn't just her arresting good looks and her shapely physique. And it wasn't that in the time it took to blink he could get lost in those intelligent blue eyes, surrounded by those thick curly lashes. She was everything he hadn't wanted in a woman. She attracted trouble. She was too spirited, too daring...too everything. He'd wanted plain, low-key and average.

He got Prudence Elizabeth Perkins instead.

"I want you to teach me how to handle a pistol. I know it's going to cost me and I'm far too indebted to you already, but I despise being victimized. I want to learn to stand up for myself the way you can."

"Okay. We'll start first thing tomorrow."

*See there?* mocked the sensible voice inside him. *Wha'd I tell you? You're giving into her. Who knows where it will end?*

A moment later he knew why he'd granted her request without the slightest objection. She smiled at him so radiantly that the world seemed a brighter place. Plus, that welt on her cheek and the knife puncture made him feel even more sympathetic and vulnerable to her. She turned him into a soft touch with so little effort that it alarmed him.

*A word to the wise, Jack, never let this woman know how vulnerable you are to her,* said the cautious voice as he escorted Pru downstairs to the restaurant.

Pru smiled when the pregnant waitress approached the table. When Gracie's considering gaze darted from her injured cheek to Jack, Pru waved away her suspicions before Jack concocted his explanation.

"This is not Jack's doing," she said quickly. "If there is one thing I have learned about Jack in our short acquaintance it is that he is a protector not an abuser."

"And I intend to repay the brute who left his mark," Jack insisted. "A woman should be able to walk down the street without being set upon. I'll see that it doesn't happen again." He smiled at Gracie. "I had planned to settle Pru at the ranch *after* the wedding, but her safety is more important than rumors and speculation."

"That is so sweet and considerate." Gracie glanced from Jack to Pru. "You are so lucky."

"Don't I know it," Pru replied—and realized that all these unforeseen complications were going to make it even more difficult to break off the engagement without inciting gossip. "Jack is a prize catch and I'll have to beat off competition with a stick, I'm sure."

Gracie grinned as she glanced pointedly at Myrna Bates, the dark-haired waitress who was infatuated with Jack. "So…what can I get for you good folks?"

After Gracie took their order and waddled away, Pru discreetly called Jack's attention to the buxom brunette. "As a potential wife, what do you think of Myrna? She's interested in you. She's hardworking, attractive and available."

Jack scowled. "Save the matchmaking for later. Let's deal with your assailants first, shall we?"

"Okay, but place Myrna on your list," she advised. "I'll let you know more about her while I'm filling in for Gracie after she's had her baby."

He frowned, confused. "I thought you said you were going to work for Oscar Epperson at the *Paradise Times Star*."

"I am. The waitress job is part-time and temporary."

His brows flattened. "You aren't starting either job until we flush out the bandits, Pru."

"Then we better be quick about it because I want to take those jobs and pad my savings account. Not to mention that I want to repay you for your trouble and allow you to get on with your search for a suitable wife."

"Suitable wife? I'm wondering if that isn't a contradiction in terms. Besides, I've managed thirty-two years without a wife. I can wait a little longer." He stared meaningfully at her. "You, on the other hand, won't have the chance to begin the career you obviously crave if those bandits dispose of you. You sure as hell won't get your heirloom bracelet back if you're buried six feet under."

Pru didn't debate the issue. Couldn't. The instant Gracie set the heaping plate in front of her she dug right in. She was so famished that she ate like a field hand.

Jack's soft chuckle brought her head up. "Skipping meals definitely doesn't agree with you."

"Fending off criminals demands a lot of energy, as you

well know," she said between bites. "I didn't engage in hand-to-hand combat in Saint Louis. My fath—" She pretended to choke to cover her blunder then touched the napkin to her lips.

"What about your father?" he guessed correctly. "Tell me about your family."

Pru guarded her words carefully. First off, she didn't want her father to locate her too quickly. She wanted to settle into her new life so that he could see for himself that she could survive without him paving the way for her. Plus, she didn't want anyone to know—Jack included— that she had great wealth at her disposal. For once in her life, she was going to know for sure and certain if she was appreciated for herself and not for the fortune attached to the Perkins name.

"Not much to tell," she replied. "I lost my mother to serious illness when I was ten. Then my grandmother came to live with my father and me."

"What does your father do for a living?"

Curse it, he would have to ask that. "He's in transportation of goods and products," she hedged.

It was just a little white lie. Her father did deal with delivering furs—here and abroad. She just omitted the part about owning and operating the company.

"You mean he's a wagon driver?"

Pru smiled wryly. Her father did drive a wagon occasionally when he was shorthanded. "Yes."

"And what's the real reason you answered my ad?" he questioned before he took a sip of water.

"So I could afford a trip to this new territory where a woman's restrictions are less defined. Plus, Gram was pressing me to wed a man who didn't interest me. He allows his position in society to dictate his behavior and he permits his father to do all his thinking for him. I'm too unconventional to settle into his expected lifestyle."

Jack snickered. "He isn't open-minded enough to accept your free spirit, huh? Why doesn't that surprise me? I wonder if any man can."

He noticed Myrna staring and he flashed her a smile.

"There, you see? There are potential brides right under your nose. Why did you think you needed to import one?"

His smile faded and he turned his attention back to his plate. "I thought I'd give someone else a chance to make a fresh new start." Plus, his grateful bride might not care that he was an extra person in the world who had no idea of his family history.

"That isn't the least bit romantic. But then, I think romance is overrated myself," said Pru. "Marriage is an arrangement that benefits men far more than it does women,"

"How so?" he teased, wagging his eyebrows.

Her face turned the same color as the welt on her cheek. But, Pru being Pru, she plowed ahead, refusing to be intimidated by the intimate innuendo. "The benefit of convenient lust, of course." She grabbed a quick breath, cleared her throat and continued. "In addition, a live-in housekeeper, cook, laundress and field hand. Which, incidentally, are the exact positions you wanted to fill when you placed your ad in the newspaper."

True. She had him there. But that didn't stop him from pointing out, "The arrangement works to a woman's advantage, too, you know."

"She gets to cook and clean and appease a man's

passions at his whim?" She smirked. "Doesn't sound so great to me."

"She gets protection from danger," he replied. "She gets a roof over her head. A companion." He grinned rakishly. "Plus, all the passion she wants, whenever she wants it."

Pru wrinkled her nose and pursed her lips. "I'll be sure to list all those advantages while I'm selecting prospective brides for you."

Jack tossed money on the table as he came to his feet. He drew Pru up beside him then said, "I don't need women lined up for me. I'll contact the ones I passed over or place another ad when I'm ready to repeat the process."

"Careful, Jack," she teased playfully. "You might end up with someone else like me."

"There is no one else like you," he insisted as he escorted her onto the street. He gestured toward his black gelding tied at the hitching post. "We'll have to ride double to the ranch. Do you mind?"

"Certainly not. Why should I?" She drew herself up and marched determinedly down the boardwalk. "I'd much rather have you crowding my space than those two brutish heathens."

"Gee, thanks," he said as he trailed behind her. "Nice to know that I rate a step above a couple of vicious outlaws."

# Chapter Six

It didn't take long to make the two-mile jaunt from town, but sitting in Jack's lap was a vivid reminder that Pru found him too attractive for her own peace of mind. She was entirely too aware of the man. It was bad enough that she'd cried on his shoulder and had run to him as if he were her port in the storm. An emotional attachment and physical attraction was ill-advised. Marriage was not what she wanted and she wouldn't make the kind of wife he was looking for.

Her thoughts trailed off when Jack halted his horse on the rise of ground that overlooked the gentle slopes of a valley bisected by a rock-rimmed, tree-lined stream. It rippled with a series of small rapids that tumbled into one clear pool after another. A small clapboard home was silhouetted against the golden rays of sunset. A henhouse, shed, jolt-wagon and corrals sat a short distance from the home.

"When I rode over this hill on the day of the Run this place called out to me," he said quietly.

"I can understand that," she murmured as she surveyed the panoramic valley.

"For the first time in my life I have a place to call my own. A place I built with my own hands and furnished to my tastes. I'm no longer a hapless transplant subjected to someone else's sense of style."

Pru couldn't have said it better herself. She understood how Jack felt about adding his personal touch to the place he called home. She'd never had the luxury, not with Gram ruling the roost and objecting when Pru tried to incorporate her own ideas into what was supposed to be her and her father's home.

"This place is spectacular," she said in awe. "I envy the challenge of racing off into the unknown to find your own destiny and discover a place that calls to you. Gram always…"

When her voice trailed off, he nudged her gently, prompting her to continue. "Gram always what?"

She smiled dryly. "Our house is a tribute to Gram's likes and my dislikes. Our tastes have never been the same."

"I know my house isn't much—"

"It's perfect," she interrupted as she glanced back at him. "It's also yours and you've made something of nothing. In my book, that counts for everything."

She noticed the pleased expression on his rugged features and realized that he'd wanted her approval of his home. It was touching really. And a little amazing that a self-reliant, self-sufficient and independent man would care what she thought.

How refreshing, she mused with a jolt of pleasure. Someone cared about her opinion for a change. The hidebound gentlemen she encountered in her former social circle didn't give a whit what she thought, how she felt, what she believed in. But Jack was honestly interested in her first impression of his home.

Impulsively, she reached back to hook her elbow around Jack's neck and give him a one-armed hug. He stared at her curiously, making her feel self-conscious. It was unlike her to initiate physical contact with men. She'd done it several times with Jack. How out of character for her! Why did she feel so at ease with him? Only God knew.

"Wha'd I do to deserve that?" he asked as he trotted toward the stacks of lumber she presumed would soon become his new barn.

"I'm obviously an emotional wreck. The incidents of the past few days put me in a tailspin and kept me there. I'll try to contain myself in the future."

He chuckled in amusement. "I'm afraid I have bad news for you. You have entirely too much spunk and spirit to contain yourself."

She smiled, thinking that most men made that remark as if she had flaws that needed correcting. Jack said it as if he accepted her for what and who she was.

Before she gave him another spontaneous hug, she clamped her fists on the pommel and waited for Jack to dismount. When he reached up for her, she leaned out to brace her hands on his sturdy shoulders. Her gaze locked with those intriguing amber eyes and she had the wild urge to kiss him.

Sweet mercy! She *was* an emotional disaster.

Jack swallowed hard as her lush body glided erotically against his. He set her to her feet and felt the aftershock of pleasure undulate through him. Need scorched every inch of his sensitized body. Hell! Riding double had been another exercise in self-control, another test that he was on the verge of failing. The willpower he'd spent years culti- vating didn't hold up well against his attraction to a woman who was everything he hadn't wanted in a companion.

He should've asked Stony to place Pru under his protec- tion and left her in town, as she preferred. Instead, like some overprotective knight in shining armor, Jack had toted her to his home. If he had a lick of sense he'd take her back to town, let her begin her new jobs and repay her debt rather than work it off at the ranch. Unfortunately, those two bandits kept harassing her and he felt responsible for her safety.

Stepping away, while he still had the willpower to do so, Jack gestured toward the house, which sported a wide covered porch. "We'll put your things in the spare bedroom." His voice crackled and he cursed the side effects of too much physical contact with a woman who aroused him without even trying.

She followed him inside and he found himself waiting anxiously for her initial impression of his home. It was absurd. Why should he care what she thought? She wasn't staying permanently. He told himself it was only a rehear- sal for the day he brought his next prospective bride home.

Not Pru, of course, but someone else in his future.

"This is charming," she exclaimed as she surveyed the stone hearth, planked table and two rocking chairs. She walked over to trail her fingertips over the ornately carved mantel clock that had caught his fancy at a store in town.

Damn if he knew why her praise pleased him so much. He couldn't think of one good reason why a woman who caused unexpected complications should matter to him.

She spun in a circle, her arms uplifted, a dazzling smile on her heart-shaped lips—and that nearly brought him to his knees. "And it's all yours, Jack. *Your* belongings in *your* home that *you* built to *your* specifications. How wonderful and liberating and gratifying that must feel!"

Only now did he fully understand what she meant when she said a woman was planted in her husband's home. Yes, she had a roof over head—in a man's domain. Surrounded by his possessions and only a few of her own. That's exactly what it would be if they married. In order for an independent woman like Pru to live and breathe, she would need to carve out her own space to feel fulfilled. As he had.

"Arrange the spare room however you want and add whatever touches and decorations that will make you comfortable during your stay," he offered.

She blinked up at him, as if he had handed her the moon. "Thank you for such a kind and generous offer."

Feeling sappy and ill-at-ease, Jack wheeled away. "I'll bring in more wood for the stove while you get settled."

And off he went, wondering how he was going to get any sleep with Pru in the next room. Suddenly he wanted much more than to have her nearby for her protection.

He wanted her…under him. Beside him. On top of him….

The arousing thought sent him down to the creek to cool off.


Pru woke up the next morning feeling safe, secure and entirely too content. She swung her legs over the edge of the bed, stretched leisurely then inhaled a deep breath that was thick with the scent of bacon and eggs cooking on the stove.

"Oh, damn." She bounded to her feet to dress hurriedly.

*She* was supposed to do the cooking. First she'd have to learn, but she was determined to repay Jack.

She surged through the doorway to see Jack setting two plates on the table. "I'm sorry I overslept," she murmured.

"You'll get a reprieve today." He ambled over to brush his finger over her bruised cheek. "Tomorrow we'll begin full-steam ahead."

"I have a confession," she said, enjoying his gentle touch too much. "I don't know how to cook or do laundry but I'm eager to learn."

He frowned at her. "How is that possible?"

"Gram put herself in charge of our household," she explained evasively, hoping to give very little about her background away. "I wasn't allowed in the kitchen and I wasn't permitted to mingle with anyone who was hired help. I was to be a lady not a servant. Gram's words. Gram's philosophy. Not mine."

"I don't think I like Gram very much," Jack said. "Sounds too domineering for my tastes."

"Mine, too," she murmured. "She has her saving graces." Pru just couldn't think what they were at the moment.

Jack made quick work of showing Pru how to adjust the stove temperature and instructed her on the timetables for cooking various foods. She listened attentively, hoping to be a quick study. She'd be satisfied if she became *half* as capable and self-reliant as Jack McCavett.

While Pru gobbled the tasty meal, Jack studied her curiously. "It amazes me that you can pack away so much food and still be so slim and trim."

She grinned impishly. "Got more than you bargained for when you offered room and board, didn't you, McCavett?"

"I'll say." He glanced the other way then said, "I'll leave you to wash the dishes while I set up target practice. I assume you still want to learn to handle a weapon."

She nodded eagerly then gathered up the empty plates. "I won't be satisfied until I'm a sharpshooter and handy with a knife. The next time those big galoots try to intimidate me, I want to be able to match them shot for shot and blow for blow."

He clutched her arm to detain her. She glanced up at his solemn expression and felt the corner of her heart melt.

"I don't want there to be a next time with those bastards, Pru. Before the day is out, I want every detail that you remember about the thieves. Their manner of dress, of speech, their horses and saddles. Anything that might help me identify them and put them out of commission. My ad brought you here. I'm responsible for keeping you safe."

"No," she contradicted. "*Your* safety is *my* responsibility. Those scoundrels wouldn't be breathing down my neck if I hadn't challenged them. I don't want you hurt," she repeated emphatically.

He grinned teasingly at her. "So…you're beginning to like me, aren't you?"

Unfortunately yes, more than he could imagine. "Of course not," she replied, smiling impishly. "I just don't want your pain and suffering on my conscience, McCavett."

"Same for me, Perkins. Having you hurt when I'm supposed to be protecting you will make me look bad. Can't have you shot down and expect another prospective bride to feel secure. I'd get a reputation as a bad risk."

When he walked off Pru stared after him, noting the way his trim-fitting breeches accentuated his lean hips and his muscular thighs. The man looked good coming and going. She wished she didn't enjoy having Jack underfoot quite so much. But she did. He was a refreshing change from her other male acquaintances. Plus, he could teach her to become the self-reliant individual she longed to be. She'd love to become the female version of Jack McCavett. She'd be very satisfied with herself if she were.

Pru scrubbed the dishes industriously and vowed to find just the right woman to become Jack's future bride. After all, she wanted him to be happy with his wife…. The thought caused her to frown disconcertedly. The prospect of another woman sharing Jack's home, his attention and lively conversation disturbed her more than it should. Why?

She had come west to enjoy her independence and freedom of choice. She didn't want to be tied down and dominated by a man. She didn't want to live up to anyone's expectations. Not after years of Gram's constant criticism and decrees and her father chiming in to side against her. She wanted to be the mistress of her own fate for the first time in her life.

Pru hurried to her room to change into her breeches and shirt—though minus the oversized vest and clunky boots she usually added to her disguise when she took to the streets at night. Eager to begin her instruction with firearms, she strode off to find Jack.

Jack nearly dropped his pistol when Pru walked outside to join him. She was dressed in clinging breeches and a cream-colored shirt that called attention to every feminine curve and swell she possessed. She wasn't wearing a chemise—and it showed. Her blond hair tumbled around her shoulders and curled alluringly over the rise of her full breasts. He was bombarded by the insane urge to run his fingers through those thick, curly strands and hold her head just so when he kissed and caressed her....

Holy hell! How was he supposed to concentrate on giving instructions on handling weapons? His every thought was wrapped around Pru's shapely physique and bewitching face—even when she was sporting a noticeable bruise, which should have detracted from her stunning beauty but didn't.

She stopped in front of him and grinned. "Don't tell me, let me guess. You don't approve of women wearing breeches and a shirt. I'm encroaching on your masculinity, right?"

Jack slapped the peacemaker in her hand. "No, I don't approve. You're too damn appealing in a dress. In breeches it's worse and I end up looking my fill—" He snapped his mouth shut, wishing he'd done it *before* he'd blurted out that revealing confession.

Pru's delicately arched brows rose in surprise. "You find me attractive? I thought you said I wasn't the kind of woman you expected or wanted."

She seemed amazed by that.

"Hell yes." *Damn it, shut up!* "Let's get on with this, shall we? We have chores to do and livestock to feed when we're finished with your firearms lesson."

He grabbed her arm and positioned it beside her hip then indicated the paper-sack target he'd nailed to a tree. "Cock the hammer on the pistol and squeeze the trigger gently."

"This weapon is heavy," she commented.

"Grow some muscles if you wanna be a hard-as-nails gunslinger. Shootin' ain't for sissies, darlin'," he drawled.

She flashed him a challenging grin. "You can't possibly be referring to me. I am not a sissy."

"Of course not. You've got a loaded pistol in your hand."

"Smart man. Always cater to the whims of a pistol-packing woman."

She pulled the trigger and a small branch five feet above the target dropped to the ground. Her shoulders slumped in disappointment. "Looks like you're much safer than I anticipated. I missed by a mile."

"It's your first lesson. You'll make the adjustments. You aren't going to become a crack shot by tonight." He positioned himself behind her to press her elbow closer to her ribs. "Hold your arm parallel to the ground. Space your feet farther apart and balance your weight."

When she shifted, her hip brushed his crotch. Jack sucked air. He was too close to her already. The incidental touch heightened his awareness of her. He could feel the warmth of her body spreading through him. He inhaled her appealing scent and his senses clogged. When need coiled tightly inside him Jack sighed in frustration. This wasn't shooting practice; it was erotic torture.

She glanced over her shoulder. "What did I do wrong?"

His gaze dropped to her petal-soft lips and her thick-lashed blue eyes. She lived. She breathed. She aroused him in two seconds flat. She was leaving her memory all over his ranch, all over *him*. He was going to recall how it felt to have her around, to have her close enough to touch. Then this place would feel empty—*he* would feel empty—without her. Bringing her home was a mistake of gigantic proportions, he realized.

"Jack?"

He gave himself a mental kick in the head then clamped his hand over her shooting arm. "Steady." Another word to the wise, he thought. "Focus absolute concentration on the target."

When she fired a shot, she shifted her weight to counter the buck of the Colt. Her rump collided with his crotch again. He stepped back before she realized that he was hard and aching.

"That's much better. At least you hit the paper target this time."

She beamed proudly and a corner of his heart caved in. And hell, he thought he'd built a wall of rock around his heart. *Do not get attached to her*, he cautioned himself for the umpteenth time in three days. *She is only a temporary part of your life.*

"Aim and fire again, a little faster this time," he instructed, his voice on the husky side.

The shot hit an inch closer to the center of the target. "You have a natural eye for shooting," he noted, "but you need a lightweight weapon. You have to work too hard to keep the pistol steady and parallel to the ground."

"How much is a weapon going to cost me?"

"I'll put it on your tab and you can pay me back while you're working those two jobs in town."

She aimed and fired and he chuckled when she whooped and hollered excitedly over her success in hitting the bull's-eye. She lurched around to hug him and the pistol barrel clanked against his skull. He angled it away and frowned in disapproval.

"Watch what the hell you're doing with that thing. If you blow my head off you won't get lesson number two—"

His voice evaporated when she pushed up on tiptoe and kissed him right smack-dab on the mouth. Need pounded in rhythm with his hammering pulse as he pressed her against his aching contours. He knew this was a mistake, but at the moment he couldn't remember why. So he kissed the breath out of her—and himself—until they both gasped for air.

She stared at him strangely as her pistol tumbled over his shoulder and thudded on the ground. To his amazement, she cradled his face in her hands and took his lips beneath hers in another enticing kiss. Suddenly he was right back were he started—wanting her like crazy, longing to map her supple body with his hands and devour the honeyed taste of her until he'd taken his fill.

As if his hands possessed a will of their own, they drifted over her shapely bottom. He hauled her against his arousal and she moaned softly. Then she wiggled seductively against him and he nearly blacked out. His left hand skimmed over the trim indentation of her waist then uplifted to trace her rib cage. His hand settled over her breast and he caressed her, learning the feel of her luscious body while he kissed her deeply and thoroughly.

The report of a rifle rang through the air. A bullet whistled past his ear and he reacted instinctively. He pulled Pru to the ground and covered her body protectively with his own while he reached for the discarded pistol. Although there were only three bullets left in the chamber Jack vowed to make each one count. He fired at the telltale trickle of smoke that rose from the underbrush beside the stream.

He heard a yelp and figured he'd hit the bushwhacker. Then another shot erupted from a nearby bush, indicating there were two men lurking by the creek.

Jack fired when he saw the flash of color partially concealed by the leaves. He didn't know if he'd found his mark, but, if nothing else, he'd succeeded in discouraging the bastards from taking potshots at him.

He heard the ambushers thrashing in the bushes in an attempt to escape. He was on his feet in a single bound. Although he had only one shot left, he hoped to slow down one of the culprits and make identification.

Jack plunged into the underbrush, only to hear the thud of hooves beating a hasty retreat. Then he heard thrashing behind him and he wheeled, prepared to shoot. He scowled and dropped the pistol to his side when he saw Pru. Her eyes were wide and her curly blond hair was in a tangle. Her breasts heaved with each panted breath she took.

"Did you get a look at them?" she wheezed.

He shook his head. "Didn't even get a look at their horses."

"That's it then."

She lurched around and strode off before he could chastise her for chasing after him and taking the risk of getting herself shot.

"What's it then?" he asked, hot on her heels.

"I'm leaving. You were nearly shot because of me. I'm destroying your peaceful existence, putting you in jeopardy."

Pru was rattled to the extreme. It was bad enough that Jack had come dangerously close to getting his head blown off. Plus, they had kissed each other as if there was no tomorrow—which there almost wasn't. She had discovered what irrational, uncontrollable desire felt like and it stunned her. Jack had touched her familiarly…and she had wanted more, wanted to caress him just as familiarly.

She had spent years repelling men's advances and today she had *invited* it. Who knew where she and Jack might have ended up if that bullet hadn't zinged by their ears to jolt them back to their senses.

Moving at a fast clip, Pru jogged past the spot where Jack could have breathed his last breath. She shuddered at the prospect of crouching over him, seeing him sprawled in a pool of his own blood and apologizing for ruining his life before he flew off to the pearly gates.

"Pru, hold up."

"No."

He caught up with her in three long strides and tugged on her arm until she tumbled off balance. "You are not leaving here," he said in no uncertain terms.

"Yes, I am," she said in the same uncompromising tone. "I intend to look up Dr. Quinn and see if he treats anyone with a gunshot wound. At least I'll have a potential suspect. It's infuriating that these men are terrorizing me to ensure my silence. They seem to think I know something incriminating about them when I can't figure out what it might be."

She wrenched her arm from his grasp. "I'm not involving you or anyone else in danger," she said as she stormed off. "I'm going into town to publicly announce that *you* have called off our wedding. I'll begin working at the newspaper office immediately."

"Damn it, Pru. I can take care of myself. I'm not some helpless greenhorn," he called after her.

"Are you implying that I am?" she challenged, insulted.

"Yes, as a matter of fact," he said flat out. "You hit a stationary target—barely. Now you think you can stand up against two men who are determined to keep you quiet by terrorizing you. You already have a bruise on your cheek, a stab wound on your neck, a tender ankle and a couple of bumps on your head. A bullet through your heart is really going to make it hard for you to enjoy the independent life you keep yammering about."

It was more than wanting freedom, she realized as she stepped onto the porch to open the front door. It was all these alien feelings for Jack that frightened her as much as being ambushed. How was she going to enjoy her freedom if it came at his expense, if *he* became too important to her? When her life was threatened, it made her angry enough to fight back. When his life was threatened it scared her spitless.

How was it possible for a man to matter this much in only a few days? Now *that* was disturbing!

She felt Jack's presence behind her as she breezed into the spare bedroom to scoop up her satchels. She rooted into one bag to retrieve the pale yellow gown she had carefully rolled up to avoid wrinkles. She spread it out on the bed and used her hand to smooth the garment.

"I'm going to change clothes now," she declared.

He crossed his brawny arms over his chest and propped himself against the doorjamb. "Fine, go right ahead. No one's stopping you."

She cut him an annoyed glance. He didn't think she'd disrobe while he watched. But he'd find out quickly that it went against her nature to back down from a challenge.

She unbuttoned the top two buttons of her grass-stained shirt.

Still, he didn't budge from the spot. The irritating rascal. He was testing her. She refused to back down now.

Boldly, she unfastened another button.

Their gazes locked and clashed. Then those smoldering golden eyes riveted on her gaping shirt that partially revealed the swells of her breasts. His gaze burned over her as surely as his caresses had made her skin sizzle before unexpected gunfire erupted a few minutes earlier.

Pru discovered that she *liked* the way he stared at her. She should be self-conscious…but she wasn't. At the very least, she should be embarrassed. What made her respond so uncharacteristically to this one man and to no other?

She unfastened another button. Then another. When there were no more buttons left, she turned her back and drew her arms from the shirt. She reached for the gown on the bed then glanced over her shoulder.

Jack had bailed out without making a sound.

A triumphant smile quirked her lips as she pulled on her chemise and then her gown. She heard the front door slam a moment later and she snickered at the thought of making the hard-nosed ex-marshal who'd become a legend in Kansas back down. He might be hell on outlaws, but he didn't know how to handle a woman.

Pru shed her breeches and stuffed her belongings in her satchels. Then she pulled her long hair atop her head, pinned the thick mass in place and grabbed her sharp-pointed parasol. She glanced around the modestly furnished room, comparing it to her palatial bedroom at home. Then she compared the past week of facing one misadventure after another to her sheltered, structured life in Saint Louis.

Her grandmother and her father never would believe that she preferred new challenges to a pampered life. She supposed that's how people reacted to years of restraint.

Whatever the cause, she was making her own way without Gram or her father pulling strings and making plans for her.

When she exited the house, Jack stood beside a sorrel mare equipped with a saddle and bridle. Although Gram frowned on riding, Pru had sneaked off to ride sidesaddle occasionally. She was by no means a skilled rider, but she wasn't quite a novice either. Thank goodness.

"Here, you'll need this to purchase a pistol and buy meals." He slapped several banknotes in her hand then extended the reins. "Pay attention to your surroundings, in case those bastards are lurking around."

She nodded agreeably. "You can fetch your horse from the livery next time you're in town. You can add—"

"—the rented horse to your tab," he finished for her. "I'll tally your debt to the very last penny. Tell Stony you're back in town so he can check on you."

She didn't respond because she wasn't about to burden Jack's good friend with the dangerous task of protecting her from cutthroats, either.

"Buy yourself a lightweight handgun," he insisted. "Something small enough to conceal in your clothing. A knife tucked in your garter might be a good idea, too."

Pru smiled impishly. "Or I could disrobe and send my would-be attackers running scared. It worked with you." She studied him curiously. "Why did you turn tail and run, Jack?"

He angled his head and looked up at her after she settled in the saddle. "I left because if I'd stayed you would have been flat on your back on the bed and we would have been as close as two people could get."

Heat suffused her cheeks as his gaze moved deliberately from the peaks of her breasts to her waist and her thighs. The frightening part was that she wouldn't have objected if he had seduced her. She'd like to see his masculine body naked, to feel the muscular contours beneath her exploring hands.

"What? No clever retort?" he taunted as she reined the horse toward town.

She glanced over her shoulder and smiled wryly. "I could have used the instruction. Same as with the pistol. If you had asked, my answer would have been yes. But then you would have expected me to marry you to make an honest man of you. That isn't part of my plan because you deserve better."

When his jaw dropped open and his eyes nearly popped out of his head, Pru chuckled then nudged the mare into a trot. She delighted in shocking Jack and getting his goat. She certainly couldn't compete with him in other arenas, but she could match wits with him. She thoroughly enjoyed the banter that was so unlike her previous encounters with gentlemen in sophisticated society.

"Be careful," he called out as she rounded the bend of the road.

"Where's the fun in that?" Pru spurred on the mare and raced the wind, hoping to outrun the unwanted attraction.

# Chapter Seven

Jack reined his horse into the cover of the trees to monitor Pru's trek to town. Since she valued her independence, he had allowed her to ride off alone. But that didn't mean he wouldn't be nearby in case of trouble. Furthermore, he knew her well enough to realize she did not intend to alert Stony of her return—unless they crossed paths. Jack intended to report the attempted ambush to his friend.

Old habits kept needling him. It felt strange not to be chasing down leads in hopes of capturing Pru's mysterious assailants. He speculated the bandits planned to keep working the area. Otherwise, they would have lit out to prey on another stretch of the stage route and forget about Pru. Either that or the thieves wanted to torment her because she'd defied them.

As he followed Pru from a distance, he recalled her impish comment about delighting in adventure—or something to that effect. With each passing day, she was becoming more self-assured and uninhibited. She had confided that her grandmother had restrained her. Clearly,

Pru craved the freedom to make her own choices. She was thriving in her new environment, even if it was a backward frontier society.

He shook his head, remembering how she'd met his challenge by peeling off her shirt. He'd left the room because he'd been too tempted to do what he'd claimed. The prospect of lying naked with Pru had left him burning—and he hadn't cooled down yet. The woman fired him up too easily. Maybe it was a good thing she had gone back to town. Jack wasn't sure he could trust himself alone with her indefinitely.

As soon as Pru dismounted at Dr. Quinn's office to pose her questions, Jack made a beeline for the marshal's office. The deputy informed him that Stony had hiked off for lunch at Harper's Café. His footsteps stalled when he glanced through the pane-glass window of the bakery to see Molly Palmer tending the counter.

There was a welt on her cheek similar to Pru's. Making a mental note of it, Jack strode off to find Stony seated with his back to the wall—a lawman's rule of thumb. Jack dropped into a chair beside Stony so he would have a clear view of the door, too. His gaze shifted to the waitress, Amelia Thorton, who sported fingerprint-size bruises on her right forearm. Jack gnashed his teeth, certain the timid, petite brunette dealt repeatedly with rough manhandling.

"Where's Pru?"

"Hello to you, too," Jack replied. "I've called off the wedding. It isn't going to work between Pru and me. She's back in town. I'm hoping you'll keep a watchful eye on her."

Stony's green eyes bulged from their sockets. "What the hell went wrong? I thought you two were getting along fine."

"She can't cook. She's never done laundry before and she's too headstrong and sassy to conform to the conventional role of a wife."

Stony slumped back in his chair. "You are out of your mind to give that appealing woman her walking papers. You know that, don't you?"

"Thanks for the insult." He smirked.

Stony waved his arms in expansive gestures. "She's every man's fantasy come true…" He frowned pensively. "Unless she revealed something about her past that gave you cause for concern. Did she?"

"You mean did she kill somebody and skip town? Doubt it. She's just too independent minded and free-spirited to settle into the quiet life I've designed for myself in Paradise. Plus, she attracts too much attention and trouble. This morning, while I was giving her target practice, two men took potshots at us."

Stony blinked like a startled owl. "The hell you say."

"So, if you see anyone around town sporting a gunshot wound, you should check it out. I think I winged one of them. Pru went to question Dr. Quinn before renting a room at Paradise Hotel again."

Stony stared somberly at Jack. "You realize, of course, that there will be a stampede of bachelors heading to the hotel when word spreads that you aren't marrying Pru."

Possessive jealousy tried to grab hold of him but Jack shrugged it away. "That's not my problem."

"So, if I invite her out to dinner you won't care?"

Of course he would. He'd also shoot himself in the foot before he admitted it. "No. Do what you want, Stony."

Jack surged to his feet and strode off. He didn't make a

habit of lying to his best friend, but this was different. His association with Pru was one big charade. What was one more white lie? Right?

Pru entered the doctor's office to survey the empty padded chairs that lined the wall. She had to commend the physician for his consideration. Patients didn't have to sit on hard wooden benches while they suffered. Windows provided light and a welcoming atmosphere. Pru liked Dr. Quinn's attention to details.

When she heard the murmur of voices coming from what she presumed to be the examination room, she lurched toward the door. If the bandit was being tended, she didn't want to risk having him panic and take the doctor hostage. The thought of Jack being targeted because of his association with her played hell with her conscience already. No need to put the doctor at risk.

She exited the office and tucked herself from sight before the burly patient, his left arm in a sling, lumbered outside. Pru studied the man carefully, trying to decide if he might be one of the scoundrels who accosted her. To her dismay, she couldn't positively identify the man, except to say that he was of average height, with brown hair, hazel eyes, stubbly beard and a stocky build. His boots didn't look the same as the ones she'd noticed either of the two men wearing, but that didn't mean thieves didn't have a spare set of footwear.

When the coast was clear, Pru ducked into the office. Dr. Quinn, who looked to be fortyish, glanced at her. He wore dark trousers, a crisp white linen shirt and suspenders. His greeting smile put her at ease instantly.

"Miss Perkins. It's nice to make your acquaintance. I'm Dr. Quinn."

She knew the instant she stepped into the light spearing through the windows that he noticed the unsightly bruise and puncture wound. He frowned disconcertedly as he approached to take a closer look.

"That had better not be the work of Jack McCavett, for if it is—"

"It isn't," she insisted, waving him off. "Jack is a perfect gentleman and competent protector. I was attacked on my way back to my hotel room yesterday. I managed to fend off the two men with the sharp tip of my parasol." She held it up for his inspection. "But I didn't escape unscathed."

"I have some ointment that will relieve the soreness and swelling on your cheek," the doctor said as he pivoted toward the examination room.

"That isn't necessary." It would also cost money she didn't have to spare. "I came by to ask you about the patient who just left. What kind of injury did you treat?"

The doctor frowned, bemused.

"I think the two men who accosted me tried to ambush Jack and me this morning."

"Good gad!" he chirped.

"My sentiments exactly. Jack managed to return fire and we thought perhaps he might have winged one of the men."

"My patient was Dexter Hanes," the doctor informed her. "He sweeps up at a local saloon and does odd jobs for folks who need help constructing homes and businesses. Dexter said a bullet grazed his arm when he broke up a brawl at the saloon this morning."

"This morning?" Pru snorted in disgust. "Gaming halls are open in the morning?"

The doctor smiled at her offended expression. "They're open twenty-four hours. Where else are gamblers and card sharks supposed to congregate?"

"Where I come from there are city ordinances barring the opening of such establishments until after noon."

Doctor Quinn chuckled. "Good luck getting the founding fathers of Paradise to pass that ordinance. Three city council members own either a saloon or a brothel. But rest assured that my wife, Anna, feels the same way you do. Unfortunately, our fledgling town is only beginning to become civilized."

"I think it's dangerous to have drunks stumbling around the streets at all hours," Pru declared. "Their mental faculties are impaired and they could be dangerous."

"I couldn't agree more."

"Where does this Dexter character work?" she questioned, circling back to the previous topic of a potential assailant.

"Wild Horse Saloon."

"Then that shall be my next stop."

"Not without a chaperone," the doctor insisted. "West Side isn't the best side of town. Dignified ladies avoid the area as much as possible."

She smiled mischievously as she pivoted toward the door. "Then I'll be fine. I'm not dignified and have no aspirations in that direction."

"But—"

The doctor's warning fell on deaf ears. Pru shot through the door and marched off on her crusade to find her bushwhackers. She also intended to bring civilization and women's suffrage to this town. First things first, she reminded herself on the way down the boardwalk. She needed to purchase a handgun in case trouble broke out—as it had a habit of doing lately.

"Good morning," Tom Jenkins called out. "What can I do for you?"

Jack nodded a greeting at the mayor and owner of the dry-goods store who was fortyish with baby-fine brown hair and a thin physique. "I'm running low on supplies." He glanced around the stocked shelves. "Coffee, flour, lantern oil. The usual staples."

Tom retrieved the items then set them on the counter. "We had a fine time at the celebration, didn't we? Were you surprised?"

"Yes, and thanks for your effort. It made Pru feel welcome."

"She's a real beauty, Jack."

Jack shrugged nonchalantly. "Unfortunately, things didn't work out as I'd hoped."

Tom blinked in surprise. "Why not?"

"Too spirited and independent," he explained for the second time that morning. "I was hoping for someone a bit more sedate. Plus, Pru prefers to live and work in town instead of camping out at the ranch."

"That's a shame."

Jack didn't think the mayor sounded particularly disappointed.

"I could use some help arranging and stacking new shipments of supplies. Do you think Pru might be interested?"

Judging by the hopeful expression on Tom's face, he'd

hire Pru on the spot and try his luck at courting her. Jack told himself he didn't care, then strode over to survey the rack of shirts that had arrived recently.

When another customer entered—a young woman with her head downcast who didn't glance in his direction—Jack gestured for Tom to wait on her first.

"Are you all right, Samantha?" Tom asked kindly.

"Fine, sir, just another clumsy accident," she murmured. "I need a few supplies."

Jack tuned out the conversation as he lifted a cream-colored shirt. He decided it was time to upgrade his faded and tattered wardrobe. He wanted to keep a low profile in his new life as a farmer and rancher, but he'd worn so many holey, patched garments at the orphanage and the Texas ranch that he vowed to improve his clothing when he could afford it.

*Now* he could afford it. He'd amassed a tidy nest egg from fees, bounty money and salary while serving as a Kansas law-enforcement officer. The thought prompted him to grab another shirt and an extra pair of breeches. He even tried on a new pair of boots. Since he wasn't paying for a wedding and reception, he might as well treat himself to needed items.

Not to impress Pru, of course, he quickly reminded himself. He had called off the engagement and he probably wouldn't see too much of her. His only concern was this cloud of doom hanging over her head. Hopefully, Stony would keep an eye on her so Jack wouldn't have to fret.

Yep, a clean break was what he needed. He was too attracted to that blue-eyed firebrand and she had taken the starring role in too many of his fantasies already. The sooner his life got back to normal the better.

\* \* \*

Pru watched Dexter Hanes step out the back exit of Wild Horse Saloon. She decided now was the time to confront him. Since he had one arm in a sling, she figured she had a sporting chance if they came to blows.

"Remember me, Dexter?" she called out as he tossed aside a crate of empty bottles and tin cans.

His hazel eyes widened as she emerged from the shadows of the alley. Shocked at her arrival and the implication that he might be one of the bandits, Dexter wasn't quick-minded enough to conceal his surprise.

"You have something that belongs to me and I want it back," she insisted as she approached.

Dexter scowled as he carelessly tossed aside another crate. "You were a pain in the ass, right from the start. Should've shut you up permanently…"

When he swore under his breath, realizing that he'd incriminated himself, Pru smiled triumphantly. However, she backed up a step when he stormed toward her. Even with his left arm in a sling, he looked menacing with his woolly brown beard, squinty eyes and the sneer on his thin lips.

Yet, she mustered her bravado and said, "I want my bracelet back. If you give it to me, I won't tell the marshal that you were involved in the robbery."

He snorted. Clearly, he didn't believe her—and he had no reason to because she could point an accusing finger at him the first chance she got.

"Don't know what you're talking about."

"Of course you do. Now *you* know *I* know," she countered as she thrust out her hand, palm up. "Give it back, Dexter."

"I guess you aren't too bright, bitch," he growled at her.

"I wasn't horsing around when I said you'd be sorry if you didn't keep your trap shut."

His right arm uplifted to backhand her on the same cheek that was still sporting a bruise. Pru yelped and leaped back, only to trip on the trailing hem of her dress. She landed with a gasp in a cloud of dust. Eyes wide with alarm she peered up at Dexter who was sneering maliciously at her. When he tried to swoop down on her, she stabbed him with the point of her parasol.

"Damn you," he muttered as he went for her throat.

Jack was on his way down the street on horseback, with his sack of supplies tied behind the saddle, when he heard a shot and a yelp that sounded all too familiar. He spurred his horse into a fast clip and saw the crowd gathering in the walkway beside Wild Horse Saloon. He was off the horse in a single bound and mumbled several "pardon me"s as he elbowed his way into the alley to see that Stony had already arrived on the scene. He was assisting Pru— whose hat was askew again, her yellow gown covered with powdery dust—to her feet. Jack instinctively strode forward to examine her for injuries. Seeing no new bloody wounds, he stared grimly at her.

"What happened this time?"

Pru brushed off her skirt then uprighted her cockeyed hat. "I believe I ferreted out one of the men who robbed the stage and tried to ambush us this morning," she said.

Jack was annoyed to no end that little miss independent had taken matters into her own hands after just one shooting lesson. The damn daredevil was trying to drive him crazy—and she was about to succeed! *"And?"*

"And Dexter Hanes shoved me down in the dirt and went for my throat."

"Gee, can't imagine why he'd do that," he muttered sarcastically. "You're getting too good at provoking people."

"I was accosted," she said, offended. "I was forced to grab my handgun to defend myself." She tapped the bulge in her upturned parasol.

Jack held his breath. "And you shot him?"

"Oh, hell." Stony gaped at her in amazement.

"I was discouraging him from doing more bodily harm," she explained. "I stabbed him with my parasol but he wouldn't back off so I shot his boot." She gestured west. "He limped off in that direction, after calling me a few names that I have no idea what they mean."

Jack stared in the direction she pointed. West Side wasn't known for its cleanliness or upstanding citizenry— which was why he wanted to strangle Pru for being there in the first place. Crates, broken glass and bottles littered the alley between the gaming halls and houses of ill repute. This was no place for a woman, even if she was packing her single-shot pistol.

"Stony, see if you can track this Dexter character while I accompany Pru back to the hotel."

"I thought you two—" Stony glanced speculatively at Jack and Pru. "Sure, unless you prefer to investigate so you don't have to...you know."

"This is fine, thanks."

Pru frowned, bemused, as Jack grabbed her arm and led her to the far side of the saloon so they could avoid the curious bystanders. "What was that all about?"

"I did as you asked and told Stony and Tom Jenkins at

the dry-goods store that I called off the wedding. Stony thought I might be uncomfortable in your company."

"Oh."

"And by the way, Tom is ready to offer you a job at his store," he informed her. "You know, after this little fiasco with Dexter, word will spread that you were on the wrong side of town, inviting trouble—"

"I wasn't inviting trouble," she protested as he tugged her along at such a swift pace that she had to jog to keep up.

"Call it want you want, Pru. But you should have sent Stony to confront Dexter Hanes."

"This is not Stony's problem," she maintained.

Jack stopped short, causing her to ram him broadside. She glanced up to see his amber eyes narrowed in annoyance. "The hell it isn't. It's his job. He's the city marshal, damn it."

She tilted her chin to a defiant angle that fascinated him and frustrated him at once. "Dexter wouldn't have admitted to anything if I hadn't come alone. I caught him completely off guard and he incriminated himself. Since he didn't see me as a threat he spoke freely."

"He confessed to the robbery?" Jack questioned.

"Of course." She surged forward. "I provoked him."

"Now there's a surprise," he muttered as he fell into step beside her.

"He blurted out that I was trouble in a skirt, or something to that effect. He said he should have disposed of me right off."

Jack shook his head in amazement. Pru had gotten results, even if her foolhardy actions could have gotten her killed. She was a daredevil, no doubt about it.

"Did Dexter mention his accomplice's name?"

"No," she muttered sourly. "But I did check with Dr. Quinn. He treated Dexter's gunshot wound, which Dexter claimed he received while trying to break up a fight at the saloon."

Jack veered into the hotel. After Pru rented a room, he accompanied her up the steps. "You are officially out of the investigation business now," he insisted. "Stony has a lead and he can pursue it. When he catches up with Dexter, you can press charges. In the meantime, do whatever it is you've been hired to do at the newspaper office and then at Miller Restaurant. Steer clear of more brawls and gunfights. *Please.*" He outstretched his hand. "Let me see your new pistol."

Pru retrieved the handgun from her parasol. He suppressed a snicker as he studied the piddly, snub-nosed derringer.

"The gunsmith claims it belonged to a down-on-his-luck gambler who pawned the weapon to pay his debts," she reported.

"Just don't square off with someone who has a Colt or a shotgun," he advised. "Your firing range is only a few feet."

"I'll keep that in mind next time I decide to shoot someone."

He frowned darkly. "That's not funny, Pru."

"Maybe I'm not kidding."

"That's what scares the hell out of me."

She waved off his concern with a dismissive flick of her wrist. Damn woman, now that she'd claimed her independence she seemed to think she was indestructible, too.

"Since you have called off our wedding publicly you are free and clear of me, Jack. I promise to give you every cent I can possibly spare of my wages until you are paid in full."

Pru was learning quickly how the other half lived when money was not easily accessible. Before now, she could afford whatever she wanted. Now, she couldn't be frivolous. When she splurged, it took food from her mouth. But if that was the price of freedom, so be it.

"I'll fetch your satchels." Jack wheeled around. "Where are they?"

"Still on the horse I borrowed from you. It's tethered in front of the gunsmith shop."

"Do not open this hotel door for anyone but me," he ordered gruffly. "I don't want to find you lying in a pool of blood after Dexter Hanes and his cohort decide to retaliate."

Pru bobbed her head. "For only you then. No matter what."

"No argument?" he teased as he poked his head back around the edge of the door.

She shrugged. "Rough morning. I could use a reprieve." She frowned thoughtfully. "Is this what your life was like as a law officer? One problem to resolve after another?"

He nodded his dark head. "Gets old quick."

Pru chastised herself for drawing Jack into her troubles again. He'd obviously already endured all the adventure and danger he wanted. Now here she was, turning his quiet life upside down—and sideways.

She plopped down on the edge of the bed and expelled a sigh. She needed to avoid Jack. Yet she'd been thrilled to see him racing to her rescue after her clash with that snarly brute, Dexter Hanes. She would follow Jack's advice and leave Dexter's capture and interrogation to Stony Mason. She would focus her efforts on her new job at the newspaper office and café. She would also take up her crusade to reduce the operating hours of the gaming halls and brothels and to bring awareness of women's rights to the community.

There was entirely too much gambling, thieving and prostitution going on in town. Pru vowed to become the voice of society—if Oscar Epperson agreed to let her pen articles that called public attention to the evils in Paradise.

Her crusade to civilize this town and give women a voice would help her keep her mind off Jack. She had to get past her obsessive attraction to him, she told herself resolutely. In addition, she had to find Jack the perfect wife. Which *she* obviously wasn't—and never would be.

Pru decided it had been a mistake to let it be known the wedding was off. Since Jack had broken the news the previous week, she'd been inundated with invitations for dining out and for evenings at the newly opened theater. Plus, she'd received a few rude requests that didn't bear mentioning. Her new boss, Oscar Epperson, even asked her to supper. Pru wanted to get a foothold in the newspaper business, but tolerating Oscar's doting attention after discovering the tantalizing pleasure of Jack's caresses—

She jerked to attention before her thoughts wandered in the wrong direction—for the forty-eleventh time.

"Something wrong, my dear?" Oscar questioned curiously.

She forced a smile then went back to creating a flyer for Tom Jenkins' dry-goods store. Also, Tom had offered her a job and invited her to accompany him to the school's box supper that weekend. She had declined as tactfully as she knew how.

"Nothing's wrong. I just thought of something I forgot

to do." Which was to forget Jack. It had been the first thing on her list all week and she still hadn't gotten it done.

"You mentioned wanting to write an article about limiting the operation of local gaming and dance halls?" he tempted her.

Pru smiled hopefully. She'd presumed he'd retracted the offer after she declined to see him socially. It wasn't that Oscar, who was only a few years older than Jack, wasn't charming and polite, for he was. *He just isn't Jack,* she mused.

"I've been mentally writing my first installment of articles since I started working here last week," she said.

"We could discuss your ideas over lunch," he baited.

Pru resigned herself to the fact that Oscar hadn't given up a romantic pursuit. She was going to have to be seen socially with him in order to get the article published. Might as well, she decided. She hadn't seen anything of Jack—and she didn't expect to. He'd gone back to his low-profile life at the ranch. Probably constructing his new barn, she presumed.

"Lunch sounds fine," Pru said with more enthusiasm than she felt.

An hour later, she set aside the half-finished flyer and took her stork-legged employer's arm. The only good thing she had to say about her upcoming meal was that it was free and that gaining Oscar's cooperation might be the break she was hoping for, the one that would launch her career in journalism.

# Chapter Eight

"Jack, you've got to do something about Pru!"

Jack glanced up from his chore of nailing two-by-four braces to the frame of his new barn. Stony stared grimly at him, but he shrugged nonchalantly.

"Pru isn't my concern since I called off the wedding." Now, if he could stop thinking about her all the damn time his life would return to normal.

"The mayor and several local citizens sent me out here to ask you to persuade her to back down from her crusades," Stony said as he dismounted. "They're blaming *you* for importing trouble that they suddenly have to deal with."

"What else has she done besides parade a few women out to my ranch as prospective brides?"

Stony thrust the latest newspaper at him. "She offended gaming hall and brothel owners by demanding they limit their hours of operation. She has suggested writing a city ordinance that forces the businesses to the outskirts of town." He tapped his forefinger on the second editorial. "In addition, she's rallying women to unite against domineering husbands so their voices can be heard. She's advocating reform and social change and who knows what will be next."

Jack grinned. "Ah, the modern version of Joan of Arc. Firing them up, is she?"

"Yeah, and I'd hate to see Pru fired up—literally," Stony muttered. "You wouldn't think this is amusing if you were city marshal and you had a steady stream of disgruntled men lining up to object to her putting independent ideas in women's heads." He threw up his hands in exasperation. "And don't get me started about the complaints from the patrons of brothels!"

"She's a progressive thinker, a social reformer," Jack remarked as he read the rousing article that called for women to protest the fact that they weren't allowed to vote, hold public office and enjoy equal salaries. "I never gave it much thought, but she's making valid points."

"*I'm* not voicing my opinion because it will only get me in trouble. I advise *you* to do the same in public," Stony said. "Nobody complained when Pru organized the Ladies Social and Literary Society or the City Beautification Committee. And they were probably fronts for women's suffrage rallies. Now she's stepping on men's toes. They don't like it."

Jack handed the paper back to Stony. "I have a barn to build and the Dawson brothers promised to come by this afternoon to help raise the rafters." He glanced curiously at his longtime friend. "What became of Dexter Hanes? Is he in jail for assaulting Pru?"

Stony shook his head. "The man vanished from sight without a trace. Pru told me that he all but admitted to being involved in the robbery but it's her word against his.

He lit out without giving a statement about their confrontation. And didn't stop in the doctor's office to treat his injured foot."

"Maybe he and his accomplice decided to focus their efforts on another stretch of stage line," Jack remarked. "Dexter could be casing a new town while working odd jobs."

"It's a possibility. I did receive word of a holdup north of Guthrie three days ago," he replied. "The thieves were wearing hoods to conceal their identity. There were two of them. Same as before."

Jack sincerely hoped the ruffians had moved on so he didn't have to worry about Pru clashing with them again. They had terrorized her too many times already. In addition, he had almost received a permanent part in his hair—compliments of a speeding bullet—because of his association with her.

"You should spare the time to talk some sense into Pru. As a favor to me," Stony requested.

"How can I keep a low profile and live an uneventful life if I associate with the infamous social and political reformer in town?"

"Funny, Jack. You're a laugh a minute," Stony grumbled. "I'm beginning to see why you walked away from law enforcement. This was a lot easier when I was just your deputy. Maybe I'll buy a homestead and leave all these headaches to someone else."

"Maybe you can hire Pru as your deputy or temporary replacement," Jack teased, taking a drink from his canteen.

"A lady city marshal?" he hooted. "The menfolk in Paradise would really be up in arms about that. Probably call for my head on a silver platter."

Jack watched Stony ride away and he praised himself for refusing to get involved in the conflict between Pru's social causes and the disgruntled men who didn't know how to deal with a spirited, independent-minded woman.

Not that he did, of course. What man did? Her ideas went against status quo and required making a conscious effort to change philosophy and long-held opinion.

He frowned curiously, wondering if Pru had been run out of Saint Louis on a rail for being a barnstorming rabble-rouser who advocated women's rights. He wouldn't be surprised.

Thankful that he wasn't in the midst of the turmoil, Jack returned to work. However, the vision of curly blond hair and vivid blue eyes popped to mind. Immediately followed by the stirring of desire that he'd been battling unsuccessfully for two weeks. Yet, he was damn proud of himself for not caving in and going to see her.

He'd accomplished the feat by working himself into exhaustion every day and taking cold baths in the creek every night. The treatment hadn't cured the ill-advised attraction to a woman who was all wrong for him, but it relieved the symptoms—temporarily, at least.

Wearily, Pru flounced on her bed. Working at the newspaper office and waiting tables the past two weeks after Gracie Witham had her baby daughter, kept Pru meeting herself coming and going. However, she was pleased to be assisting Oscar Epperson with the typesetting and writing articles and editorials that united women and encouraged them to speak out for reform.

Her campaign wasn't popular with the menfolk,

however. They sent her dour glances and grumbled as she passed them on the street. The dinner invitations had come to a screeching halt, too. Her boss was the only man delighted with the attention she was receiving. Newspaper sales had tripled, forcing the editor of the competitive newspaper to attempt to lure her away. Oscar had raised her salary when he found out.

Now that she had extra funds, Pru planned to make an installment on her debt, but she hadn't seen Jack.

Thoughts of Jack caused a pang of regret. He had backed so far away that he might as well have moved to Texas. She knew he hadn't, though, because she'd sent him one prospective bride after another. Reports came back that he was as handsome, appealing and eligible as ever.

She rolled to her side on the bed and stared out the window into the darkness. Things were going her way with her new career and her noble causes, but she missed Jack. Blast it, this wasn't supposed to be happening. He certainly wasn't hurting for female companionship. In fact, Myrna Bates was scheduled to visit him this very evening. Pru doubted Jack had time to miss her or the trouble she'd caused him. He was probably glad to be done with her.

Her thoughts trailed off and she frowned curiously when she heard a quiet rap at her door. Then she noticed the note lying on the floor.

Warily, she sat up on the bed. "Don't fall into a trap," she cautioned herself as she stared at the folded note.

Her first impulse was to jerk open the door to see who had delivered the note. But there was no telling who was lurking in the hall, waiting to pounce. It could be anyone— she wasn't the most popular personality in town these days. Her various crusades had drawn as much support as they had animosity from those who held opposing views.

Pru walked over to pick up the note. It read: *We have arrangements to discuss. Come to the back door of Wild Horse Saloon. Dexter.*

Pru reread the missive then frowned pensively. Stony Mason hadn't been able to locate Dexter after their confrontation. He'd vanished into thin air and hadn't shown up for work after the incident. Obviously, he'd gone on a drunken binge and had recently sobered up. She wondered if he planned to sell her bracelet back to her to compensate for his lack of salary at Wild Horse Saloon. Probably.

Tired though she was, Pru blotted her face with cold water then doffed her gown. She donned the breeches and shirt she used as a disguise. She crammed her blond hair beneath the oversized cap and shrugged on the tattered vest that concealed her feminine physique.

Soot from the lantern globe downplayed her refined features and gave her the look of an urchin. She stuffed her feet into her cloddish boots and appraised her reflection in the mirror. Her appearance had changed drastically— which was the whole point of this disguise, after all.

After several minutes, she checked the hall to find it empty. She crept quietly down the corridor to make use of the fire escape. If Dexter had stationed himself near the front exit of the hotel, hoping to ambush her or overtake her, then he was in for a long wait. In that case she'd reach the alley behind Wild Horse before he did.

Pru tapped her pocket to ensure her derringer was at the ready and hurried off into the darkness.

\* \* \*

Jack muttered under his breath when he heard a knock at his front door. If this was another prospective bride Pru had sent to him, he was going to have to look her up, despite his vow to avoid her.

Madam Rozalie Pitman had come bearing food the previous night. Jack had been cordial even though Roz had stared at him as if he were on the menu. Two days before that, Kathryn Sykes, a young farmer's daughter, and her father had shown up to invite him to supper. Jack had accepted the invitation, but he'd hem-hawed when Hubert Sykes took him aside later to inquire about a possible match.

Now he had another potential suitor, compliments of his former bride-to-be, standing on his stoop. Jack sighed inwardly before he opened the door for Myrna Bates, the dark-haired waitress from Miller Restaurant. Obviously she had gotten off work late and had come calling.

Myrna smiled brightly. "Pru suggested I drop in to see how you're doing. I brought dessert."

Jack stepped aside. "Nice to see you again, Myrna. How are things in town?"

As if he didn't know. Stony had dropped by the previous afternoon to update him on Pru's crusades and men's reactions.

The prompt got Myrna to talking. She was a whiz at conversation, he noted, and she was attractive. A damn shame Jack had recently acquired an exasperating fascination for blue-eyed blondes. But Myrna, Roz or the farmer's daughter would all make acceptable wives. He could live with any one of them, he supposed.

However, he could live without them just as easily.

"Would you like some apple pie?" Myrna said in a seductive voice.

"Love some."

He hadn't expected Myrna to plant herself in his lap when he sat down at the table. But suddenly there she was, offering herself for dessert—and insisting he should help himself…

Pru tiptoed along the alley, careful to remain within the shadows. She squinted, searching the area near the rear door of the saloon. Seeing no one lurking about, she hurried forward. She halted abruptly when light from the open doorway illuminated the object lying beside the back steps.

Warily, she crept closer. Her mouth dropped open when she recognized Dexter Hanes's body sprawled facedown in the dirt. There was a dagger buried in his back. Pru nudged him with the toe of her clunky boot to see if he was still alive. When he didn't move she used the heel of her boot to ease him onto his side and noticed the blood stain on his chest. He didn't budge or make a peep. She crouched beside him to check his pulse. He didn't have one.

Pru was in the process of rising to her feet when something hard clanked against the back of her skull. Stars exploded in front of her eyes and pain reverberated inside her head. She pitched forward and landed atop Dexter.

The world went black and silent.

"Jack! Stony said for you to come quick!" Chester Dawson hollered from the front porch.

Myrna Bates scrambled off Jack's lap, allowing him to surge to his feet. He was at the door in three strides.

"What's wrong?" Jack demanded.

Chester dragged in a deep breath then blurted out, "Pru Perkins stabbed Dexter Hanes out behind Wild Horse Saloon. Stony has her locked in jail. Unfortunately, the menfolk are in such an uproar over her radical ideas for liberating women that they want to string her up, just to show her that sometimes women *do* get the same rights as men."

He nodded a greeting to Myrna when he noticed her standing behind Jack. Then he added, "Stony said to tell you that he could use a skilled law officer to prevent a lynching."

Jack whirled around to fetch both pistols and his rifle. He stopped short when he realized Myrna was still there. Of course she was. She had been kissing the breath out of him and he had tried to convince himself that he liked it before Chester had interrupted them. And wham, the instant Pru's name was mentioned no other woman existed or seemed to matter.

That realization was enough to make Jack crazy.

"Go help Pru," Myrna insisted. "You men might not like it, but her newspaper editorials have given us pride and self-esteem and it feels good. I can tell you for sure that if something bad is about to happen to Pru, every woman in town will be there to protect her. Also, I can guarantee that we'll be withholding favors and services until men cry uncle."

Well hell, thought Jack. Trouble was brewing in Paradise.

He fastened his double holsters around his hips. He checked to make sure he had plenty of ammunition—and prayed he wouldn't need it.

"That goes for the harlots, too," she added as he lurched toward the door. "They don't care if they're shuffled into new buildings outside the city limits. They agree with what Pru has to say about unifying against abuse and disrespect from men."

Chester sent Jack a significant glance. "It's a town divided these days," he confirmed. "Men against women."

"Exactly right," Myrna spoke up. "If you hadn't been out here hiding your head in the sand—"

"Hey! I've been minding my own business," Jack interrupted indignantly.

"All the same, social reform is necessary and inevitable," she spouted. "Abigail Scott Duniway, the mother of women's suffrage in Oregon, has been promoting reform for years. According to Pru, women in Wyoming have been voting in elections for twenty years, thanks to the tireless efforts of Esther Morris, who was the first woman in America to hold judicial office. Then there is Emmeline Wells, the newspaper woman from Utah who is leading the way for women's rights. Suffrage is alive and well in Colorado, Washington and Idaho, too. We should have the same rights in Oklahoma Territory."

Jack knew those were direct quotes from the articles Stony had shown to him yesterday. Pru had definitely stirred up emotions in Paradise and the town was about to split in two. Jack was being blamed for importing the troublemaker who was about to incite a social riot. He and Pru both were becoming pariahs in Paradise.

Jack rushed off. He borrowed Chester's horse since it was saddled. He nudged the steed into its fastest gait. Long before he reached town, he could see the flare of torches lining the streets and hear shouts calling for Stony to step outside to face the irate mob who wanted vindication.

Out of habit, Jack plowed through the crowd to gain

control of the volatile situation. Packing pistols in both hands, guiding the horse with his knees, he cut a wide swath through the congested street.

"Well, if it ain't the root of the evil finally showing his face again," someone jeered.

"See what you caused when you placed an ad for a wife?" someone else sneered. "Had to go and invite a freewheeling hellion to town then turn her loose on us, didn't you?"

"Now it's a nightmare in Paradise. The crazed woman murdered Dexter for manhandling her a few weeks back. I say hang her since she demands equal rights for women!"

Shouts resounded in the streets while Jack slung his leg over the saddle and hopped to the ground. He grabbed his rifle then backed up the step to the boardwalk. Feet askance and armed to the teeth, he stationed himself in front of the marshal's office like a one-man police squad.

"Go home and let the marshal do his duty," Jack ordered.

"We want Pru Perkins released!"

Jack glanced west to see the congregation of women, armed with shovels and brooms, marching down the street. He inwardly cursed when the men ordered their wives and daughters to disband. The women proceeded to tell the men what they could do with their suggestion to disband.

There would be no peace in Paradise if he didn't get the potentially dangerous situation under control—quickly.

Lurching around, he burst into the office to see Stony hovering beside the window, his rifle at the ready. Even his oldest and dearest friend flashed him a glare that indicated this brouhaha was his fault.

Ignoring Stony's stony stare, Jack strode into the back room. Pru was locked in a cell. Her blond hair was in wild disarray beneath a grimy cap. Her features were smeared with soot. She was wearing breeches, a stained shirt and a shapeless vest that had seen better days years ago.

"Is it impossible for you to stay out of trouble? I left you alone for two weeks and look what's happened," he muttered, eager to take his frustration out on her.

"This is not my fault," she countered. "I did *not* kill Dexter Hanes."

"A bloody knife and the red stains on your shirt say otherwise," Stony contradicted as he appeared in the open doorway. "Word about the knife being the murder weapon spread like wildfire. Whether or not you killed the scoundrel—"

"—Which I most certainly did not," Pru erupted in offended dignity.

"—is irrelevant," Stony went on to say. "Every man in the street *wants* to believe you're guilty because he's mad at you for turning his wife, girlfriend, mistress or daughter against him."

Stony unlocked the cell door then quick-marched Pru into the front office to look out the window. "See that? That's your doing. Any minute now, this shouting match is going to turn into a street brawl. Men are going to be slapped upside the head with those brooms and shovels and women are liable to be backhanded or shoved to the ground. Thank you so much!"

Jack watched Pru jerk up her head and glare at Stony. "Blame me if you want, but all I did was reassure the women of this town that they count for something and they have a voice. They also have inalienable rights that they have been long denied. If you were the suppressed gender you'd want reform, too."

Stony looked to Jack for support and reinforcement. Hell, this was why Jack had resigned as a law officer. He was tired of making all the difficult decisions and backing them up, tired of resolving everyone's problems with force and violence and endangerment to his own life.

Nonetheless, here he was in the thick of things again. He was being blamed for Pru's presence in town and her barnstorming campaign for women's rights. Damn it, all he'd wanted was a docile bride and a quiet life in the country. Instead, he got a freewheeling hellion on crusade.

"Uh-oh," Stony groaned. "The fight's on."

Jack glanced over the top of Pru's tousled head to stare out the window. Sure enough, women pounded men's skulls when they tried to storm the marshal's office to retrieve Pru. Shrieks and curses turned the evening air black and blue.

"Time to get the hell out of here while there's a distraction outside," Jack decided instantly. He clutched Pru's elbow to place her protectively behind him then glanced at Stony. "We'll hide out by the creek until things in town cool down. I don't want this mob showing up at my doorstep looking for Pru."

Jack ducked out the door and darted off, dragging Pru behind him. He veered into the alley to prevent being spotted and jogged off in the darkness.

"I'm really sorry about this," she murmured.

"No, you aren't," he snorted. "I'm beginning to think you delight in inciting riots and provoking tempers…ouch!"

To his amazement she kicked him in the fanny to display her irritation. He glared at her over his shoulder. Not to be outdone she glared right back.

Jack grabbed her hand again and sprinted down the alley. When he'd placed some distance between them and the rioters he stepped onto the boardwalk and took off toward the livery stable rather than wading into the melee to retrieve his black gelding.

"Sweet mercy!" Pru chirped.

"That's one way to put it. All hell breaking loose says it best," Jack insisted as he viewed the battle at a distance. "It's a shameful sight to behold."

The torchlight cast flickering shadows over husbands and wives who were bickering and fussing until push came to shove. Even the harlots were out in full force to insist that Pru had the right to defend herself against the man who had physically attacked her previously.

"This is amazing," Pru said with a wondering shake of her head. "Even Amelia, Molly and Samantha are in the midst of battle and holding their ground. I'm thrilled to see them standing up for themselves."

"They are standing up for *you*," he corrected as he tugged her toward the livery stable. "They might have pulled the trigger in this battle but *you* put the guns in their hands."

"And you don't approve?" she challenged.

"Don't try to drag me into a debate over women's equality," he muttered as he entered into the stable to grab the first two horses he could get his hands on.

Jack slipped the bridles on the mounts in nothing flat. There wasn't time for saddles. He left money to pay the going rate for renting the horses for a couple of days on the counter by the door.

"Before I forget, stop sending would-be brides to my house," he demanded grouchily.

"That reminds me, where is Myrna? Did she come by your place tonight?" Pru asked.

"Yes, but I don't know where she is now. I ran out on her in my haste to save you from another disaster. Myrna is probably in the middle of that fracas."

"Myrna really is nice—"

Jack rounded on her and shook his finger in her startled face. He was mad at her. Also, he wanted to kiss her and that made him even madder. She tangled his emotions and she caused all sorts of trouble. People were aggravated with him because of his association with her and he still wanted to scoop her up and kiss her breathless.

He definitely was loco, he decided. Myrna had kissed him earlier and all he could think of was that she wasn't Pru. Pru was the woman he secretly desired—against his better judgment.

"I don't give a tinker's damn if Myrna would make the perfect bride, the model wife. Stop arranging my love life for me!" he yelled to relieve his torment and frustration.

When he realized how loudly he'd shouted he dragged in a calming breath and let it out slowly. He managed to gain some semblance of control but he couldn't quell the obsessive urge to kiss Pru. It had been almost three weeks—and there were just some things a man needed to survive.

It was as simple and as complicated as that.

The fact that she leaned into him and responded instantly didn't make it any easier to break the ravishing kiss. The whinny of a horse prompted him to reconnect with his surroundings and recall the problem brewing in the street. He glanced around, struck by the uneasy feeling they were being watched. Before trouble pounced, he scooped up Pru and set her on one of the horses.

"I'm glad they didn't hang you before I got here," he admitted as he swung onto the steed.

"I'm glad they didn't, too." She reached into her boot to retrieve a small leather pouch. "This is the first install- ment to repay my debt."

Jack tucked the pouch in his shirt pocket and wondered if she had earned it or lifted it from Dexter after she stabbed him. *In self-defense*, he added quickly. At least he *hoped* it was self-defense and not outright murder.

"Can you ride bareback?" he asked as he led the way from the stable.

"If it saves me from a lynching, I'll manage," she said as they trotted from town, watching the women of Paradise waging war on her behalf in the middle of the street.


"I find it positively outrageous that your overpaid private detectives can find neither hide nor hair of Prudence," Gram snorted as she entered the parlor, the thump of her cane indicating the intensity of her irritation.

Horatio winced. It had been a long day and he was tired. His mother had been on the rampage for more than three weeks and he was catching the brunt of it. Although he knew Pru was intelligent and could take care of herself rea- sonably well, the fact that she hadn't contacted him was wearing on the one good nerve he had left. Gram had trampled on the rest of them.

"Pru is clever and imaginative," he said in a calm tone that he hoped would settle Gram down. "Whether she left on horseback, stage or train or if she is simply hiding out with friends to prove her point, she obviously won't be found until she's ready."

"Never mind about when she's ready!" Gram yowled. "Edwin Donald's mother is badgering me to no end about Prudence's extended visit with family. She wants to set the nuptial date. I'm going to do it in her behalf."

"I wouldn't plan a wedding until you can produce the bride," he advised. "Or is this going to be by proxy?"

Gram scoffed. "Your feeble attempts at humor are just like your father's. *Feeble*."

"Sorry," he mumbled reflexively, even if he wasn't.

"I should hope so. Now then, you did give your incompetent detectives a description of Prudence, in case she's using an alias, didn't you?"

"Of course." Honestly, sometimes his mother didn't give him credit for having a lick of sense. "But she could have been in disguise, you know."

Gram's wrinkled face puckered in another scowl. "Confound that child. And curse you for pushing her so hard."

*"Me?"* he hooted before he could restrain himself.

"You practically dared her to defy us."

Horatio wanted to pull out his hair. He was beginning to understand why Pru had flown the coop. He was seriously considering resorting to the same tactic. If he knew where Pru was hiding out, he'd join her so he could get his mother off his back.

# Chapter Nine

Pru ducked beneath a low-hanging branch as they followed the meandering creek to avoid being detected by the vigilantes that might be following them. Despite the turmoil her life had become, the restlessness that had plagued her the past two weeks had eased up.

She knew why, of course. She had missed Jack McCavett. A lot. She enjoyed his company. She felt safe and secure and content when she was with him. The yearning deep inside her soul and the desire she had tried so hard to deny was back in full force.

This was not an encouraging revelation for a woman who had escaped the bondage of her ivory tower and craved the freedom to live as she pleased, while encouraging other women to demand the right to do the same.

"We'll camp here." Jack drew the borrowed horse to a halt. "We'll have to do without the comforts of home, but at least the lynch mob won't show up on our doorstep."

He dismounted then strode over to lift Pru from the horse. The moment her hands settled on his broad shoulders and his hands clamped around her waist awareness shot through her like a lightning bolt. Their previous kisses had instilled a craving that demanded more. Pru wanted a long, deep taste of this man. She wanted to wrap herself around him, to absorb his strength and forget the harrowing events that had left her jailed for a murder she hadn't committed.

One touch, one look into those fathomless amber eyes and forbidden hunger simmering beneath the surface bubbled up. Pru surrendered to the desire that had tormented her for days on end. She wrapped her legs around his hips, lowered her head and savored the addictive taste and scent that had the power to dissolve good sense into mush. She held nothing back, just kissed Jack thoroughly, while she raked her fingers through his hair and leaned into him.

When he clamped one arm around her bottom and brushed the thumb of his free hand over the rigid peaks of her breasts, need boiled through her, putting the last of her inhibitions to flight. She didn't recall how they'd come to be sprawled in the grass or how her shirt had come open. Nor did she remember tugging at the buttons of Jack's shirt so she could press her lips against the muscled wall of his chest. All she knew was that she wanted to appease the hungry need bursting inside her.

"I want you," she said brokenly. "I know it isn't fair—"

"—No, it damn well isn't," he murmured against the column of her throat.

"I'm trying to find you the perfect bride," she said breathlessly.

"Right, the perfect wife," he whispered as his lips skimmed her collarbone. "That's what I need."

"So this would be a mistake, I know, but—"

Her voice evaporated when he lowered his head to flick his tongue against her nipples. Pleasure seared every fiber of her being. She arched helplessly toward him, aching for more, needing to discover the meaning of complete intimacy with a man. With Jack. Only Jack.

Her breath came in ragged spurts as his hot lips and wandering hand trailed over her rib cage to swirl over her abdomen. He traced the band of her breeches and anticipation sizzled through her. A wave of fire crested over her as he dipped his fingertips beneath the fabric. His hand eased lower until he pressed his palm between her legs.

Erotic sensations burned through her. She moved instinctively toward his hand. She wanted his touch so badly that she was shaking with it. She also wanted his mouth on hers. Now.

Pru fisted her hands in his shirt collar and brought his face back to hers. "Teach me what passion feels like. All of it. I—"

He cupped her in his hand then slid his fingertip inside her. A knot of desire coiled so tightly inside her that it made her lightheaded. Pleasure rippled through her like waves on the sea as he stroked her gently, repeatedly. Her body moved on its own accord, rising to meet his caressing hand.

She offered not one protest as he eased her breeches over her hips. She shivered when the cool evening air skimmed her bare thigh, but heat quickly replaced the chill when his mouth drifted down her belly. She trembled helplessly, amazed by the fiery sensations he aroused, overwhelmed by the shock waves of pleasure shooting through her.

"Jack?" She didn't know what she was asking, just needed something she didn't understand.

All thought escaped her when he eased two fingers inside her. She gasped at the unfamiliar pressure and the pleasure shimmering inside her as he stroked her rhythmically. Mindless desire left her silently begging for more. When he flicked at her with his thumb then traced her moist flesh a wild cry burst from her lips. She could feel the fiery sensations recoiling on top of her, intensifying like a wildfire consuming all within its path.

At the exact moment when he brushed his lips over her secret flesh and withdrew his fingertips, incredible pleasure throbbed through her. She clutched desperately at him, demanding that he appease the empty ache that drove her mad with wanting.

"Come here," she panted hoarsely.

Jack fumbled with the placket of his breeches then braced himself above her on one arm. He hated that he hadn't taken time to undress completely, hated that he was so frantic and desperate to sink into Pru's soft flesh that finesse had fallen by the wayside. He wanted her the way he couldn't remember wanting anything in his life.

He nudged her legs farther apart then surged toward her. He tried to be gentle because he was pretty sure she'd never been intimate with a man. But she kept clutching at him impatiently and his self-restraint was no match for the breathless urgency that riddled him like bullets.

With a shaky sigh, he sank into her velvety heat and felt her body close hot and tight around him. He felt her stiffen momentarily, but she was still reeling from her climax and he wanted nothing more than to be inside her and have her caressing him in the most intimate way possible.

The innate feeling that she was necessary to his existence worried the hell out of him, but he was so deep in the throes of passion that nothing but rushing to wild completion and having Pru with him every step of the way seemed to matter.

He tried to slow his frenzied pace, to prolong the infinitesimal pleasure streaming through him, but his body was paying no attention to his brain. But then, it never did when it came to this blond-haired siren who lured him against his fierce will.

"Oh…my…" Her voice shattered.

He knew the exact instant she climaxed again. He could feel the spasms of her body surrounding him, holding him, caressing him. Another incredible sensation blossomed inside him, rushing upward to explode like fireworks in his bloodstream.

Jack swore the top of his head was about to blow off when she stiffened in his arms and sank her nails into his back. They strained against each other in wild desperation as wave upon wave of passion buffeted them.

Grasping for breath, feeling his body shudder in helpless release, Jack slumped against Pru. He was cradled between her thighs, his head tucked against the curve of her neck. He could feel her pounding pulse. He could feel *her* all the way to the bottom of his soul.

And that scared the bejesus out of him.

"No, please don't move yet," she murmured when he tried to ease away. He felt her smile against his chest. "This is far better than a lynching. I'm glad you came to get me."

How was he supposed to retreat physically and emotionally when the feel of her lush body and her playful comments hit him right where he lived?

"Is it always like this, Jack?" she asked as she combed her fingers through his tousled hair.

Now how was he supposed to answer *that* question without giving too much of himself away? No, it wasn't like this. Ever. He'd never felt this close to a woman before, during or after appeasing his needs. It was impossible not to be emotionally involved with a woman who was a dozen different passions bursting at the seams, a woman who possessed such a vibrant spirit that he got caught up in it, caught up in *her*.

Being with Pru was like being whisked up into the vortex of a cyclone. He was trying damn hard to skirt the edges of life and to adopt a peaceful existence. But he couldn't resist her, even when he knew she was trouble and turmoil and high profile. Hell!

"Jack?" she prompted when he took so long to respond.

"No, it isn't always like this," he admitted reluctantly.

She cocked her head and tangled blond curls fell across his hands. He impulsively brushed the silky mane with his fingertips.

"It must have been the excitement of a near-hanging that got to us. Danger enhances the senses and the emotions," he insisted—and wished that's all there was to it.

"I think I'm going to like living dangerously...."

To his amazement, she wriggled seductively beneath him and his body roused instantly. Discovering that he was extremely sensitive and susceptible to Pru disturbed him—apparently not enough to encourage him to move away from the flame before he got scorched, though. It didn't stop him from kissing those honeyed lips and letting common sense whirl in the wind, either.

He remembered how Myrna Bates had tried to seduce him earlier that evening and he'd experienced a lukewarm reaction. This is what had been missing, what he craved to obsession. This insatiable fire that constantly demanded to be fed only applied to Pru.

Tomorrow he'd work on getting his head back on straight, he promised himself. But not now. Not tonight. If Pru wanted him again then he was all hers.

Jack rolled to his back and taught Pru how to ride him to wild, breathless completion before they collapsed in exhaustion and he fell asleep with a smile on his face.

The next morning Pru came awake and reached over to find an empty space beside her. She pried open one eye to survey the pastel colors of dawn spreading across the horizon. A sleepy smile pursed her lips, recalling the unbelievable night of passion she had shared with Jack.

It was as if they both had developed unquenchable needs that demanded they make the most of their private moment. She'd discovered things about herself that amazed her. First and foremost, she had reveled in passion, though Gram had always claimed that a woman had to fulfill unpleasant duties to her husband in the bedroom. Sleeping in Jack's arms was anything but a hardship.

Pru's eyes shot open wide and she jerked upright when a disturbing thought lambasted her. She had been parading potential wives past Jack and then she had slept with him.

What kind of matchmaker was she? The kind that tried out the merchandise so she could recommend it to interested women? Dear God! What had she done?

And what did Jack think of her character and moral

fiber? That he wasn't good enough to marry but good enough to sleep with one reckless night when her world had gone all to hell? And would he think that once she'd tasted the forbidden fruit of passion she'd become addicted? True, she had wanted him so many times during the night that they'd barely gotten a wink of sleep.

Pru groaned in dismay then scraped her hand through the mop of tangled hair that cascaded over her shoulders. She had behaved outlandishly. Even for her. Jack probably thought she belonged in a brothel, given her eagerness to be with him. Repeatedly. Yet, as much as he had pleasured her, she felt deprived because she had wanted to become as familiar with his masculine body as he had become with hers.

Pru scrambled to cover herself with her discarded clothes when she heard a rustling in the underbrush. She sagged in relief when she saw Jack's raven head appear above the tall weeds. When he refused to look directly at her, she felt her heart sink. She was certain that he regretted giving into his lust—he thought she had committed murder and now he must be wishing he could rewind time and skip over the reckless passion he'd shared with Paradise's most scandalous criminal.

Curse it, she'd made a mess of Jack's life. She'd dragged him into the quagmire, unintentionally turning his friends and neighbors against him. Then she'd gone to him for comfort and passion after setting him up with potential wives.

The men in Paradise disliked her politics and the women had joined her crusade for social reform. Jack was caught right smack-dab in the middle of the conflict because of his association with her. He didn't deserve to suffer.

"Breakfast is coming right up," he said as he sidestepped down the creek bank to gather driftwood.

"I'd like a bath," she murmured, clutching self-consciously at her clothes.

*A little late for modesty, isn't it, Pru?* came the mocking voice in her head.

Jack hitched his thumb over his shoulder. "There's a shallow cove about fifty yards upstream. When you've finished bathing, we need to talk."

She mumbled in agreement as she walked away. She had the unshakable feeling Jack expected her to *listen* while *he* did all the talking. He would tell her that he'd come to his senses and now she was on her own. He'd saved her neck several times and he was finished playing the role of a gallant knight rushing to her rescue.

Jack watched Pru disappear from sight then expelled the breath he hadn't even realized he'd been holding. It was damn hard to face Pru in the light of day after he had crawled all over her like a rutting schoolboy half the night. She probably thought he didn't have one ounce of self-control when it came to lust. Which he didn't, obviously.

He swiped his hand over his face, cursed himself about a half-dozen times, then got the small campfire going so he could cook the rabbit he'd snared. Damn, what must Pru think of him? And how was he supposed to behave toward her this morning? Like nothing had happened—about a half-dozen times? And they had a serious topic to discuss— her involvement in Dexter Hanes's death. He needed to get past this morning-after awkwardness and focus on acquiring all the facts in this case.

He shook his head in disbelief, remembering that less than a month ago he and Pru had been the sweethearts of Paradise. Now they were outcasts. He was being ridiculed for bringing the barnstorming reformer to town. Her arrest for murder had incited a rebellion pitting men against women.

Jack had untangled some volatile situations in his day, but resolving this mess had him stumped. If Pru's case went to trial, she would never find twelve impartial male jurors within a hundred miles. No doubt, she would proclaim the law needed to be rewritten so that half the jurors were women.

He glanced up when Pru reappeared. She looked as self-conscious and unsure of herself as he felt. Resolutely, Jack cast aside his confused emotions and gestured for Pru to sit down beside him. It didn't help that she smelled fresh and clean and—

*Stop it*, the voice of reason snapped at him. *Focus, Jack. Behave like a former lawman, not a randy adolescent.*

"I need to know exactly what happened last night at Wild Horse Saloon." He stared at the curl of smoke drifting in the breeze—stared anywhere except at the intriguing woman beside him. "Every detail."

"I finished my shift at Miller Restaurant and I went back to my hotel room. I was exhausted from working both jobs all week," she reported.

There was nothing wrong with her work ethic, he mused. Also, he admired the fact that she'd paid an installment of her debt promptly. He wasn't strapped for money, but he appreciated her integrity.

*Well, except maybe when she crossed the line and murdered Dexter Hanes*, he tacked on sourly.

"Someone tapped on my hotel door, but refused to identify himself," she continued. "Since the articles I wrote for the newspaper were published, I've received rude comments. Twice this week, someone hid in the shadows and hurled eggs at me to show his displeasure. First, outlaws tried to intimidate me and now disgruntled men are trying to run me out of town. Naturally, I was cautious about opening the hotel door."

"Smart lady. Start a lot of riots in your old life, did you?" he teased.

She smiled good-naturedly. "Nothing like the Paradise rebellion. A few peaceful protests, is all." Her expression sobered. "Someone slipped a note under my door."

Jack perked up. "Hallelujah. Evidence. Let's see it."

"It's gone, along with my derringer. I stuck them in my pocket before I left the hotel, but someone swiped them."

Jack muttered under his breath as he removed the meat from the fire. "So far there is nothing to prove you didn't seek out Dex and dispose of him because he roughed you up a couple of weeks ago. Plus, Stony mentioned the bloody knife, which makes you look guilty as hell."

"You think I killed him, don't you?" Her voice was flat.

"In self-defense, maybe." He could tell that he'd hurt her feelings because she shrank into herself and refused to meet his gaze. But damn it, she did look guilty.

"You think I'm so dense as to be wandering around in the alley beside a dead body that had a knife sticking out of it? Give me a little credit," she muttered resentfully. "I told you, it wasn't self-defense because Dex didn't attack me. He was dead when I arrived. The note said to meet him behind the saloon. It was signed by Dexter Hanes..." She frowned pensively. "Not that I can identify his signature, damn it."

"So you put on your urchin disguise and tramped off," Jack said, angered. "Hell, Pru. Wondering if the note really was from Dex should've been your *first* thought."

She blew out her breath. "I know that now. But I was tired and I obviously wasn't thinking clearly."

"Sorry, I didn't mean to jump down your throat." After all, he hadn't been thinking clearly last night after their initial kiss. So who was he to criticize? "Let's put this in chronological order. There was a knock at the door, followed by a note on the floor that was supposedly signed by Dex. You changed into your concealing disguise.... Then what happened?"

"I used the fire escape and walked to the alley behind the saloon," she replied.

"And?" he prompted when she paused to nibble on her meal.

"And I thought I'd be the first to arrive in the alley, but I found Dex lying facedown in the dirt with a knife in his back. When I crouched down to see if he was still alive, someone hammered my skull."

Jack reached over to check to see if there was a new knot on the back of her head. Sure enough, there was.

"That's the last thing I remember until I awakened and staggered to my feet. I was wobbling down the alley, trying to get my bearings, when Stony and several men showed up unexpectedly."

"Where was the knife?" Jack asked grimly. "In your hand?"

She shook her head, thankful the mysterious killer hadn't planted the murder weapon in her hand to make her look guiltier than she did already. "Still buried in his back.

There was also a puncture wound in his chest. The speculation was that I confronted him and stabbed him. When he collapsed I supposedly stabbed him in the back to make sure I accomplished the dastardly deed."

Jack inwardly winced. "Someone went to considerable effort to build a strong case against you. Someone who objects to your social reform could be using your conflict with Dex to set you up and make you look bad."

"I know," she said deflatedly. "The suspects are too numerous to mention. It could be Dex's accomplice or a vengeful husband repaying me for inspiring his wife to become involved in the women's movement."

She looked him straight in the eye and he nearly drowned in those hypnotic blue pools. "I swear I didn't kill him, Jack. I was foolish and careless, but I did not kill him."

"I believe you," he murmured. "We'll get to the bottom of this, but it might take time."

"I don't have time. I have two jobs and a debt to pay to you. I also have important causes to promote."

Jack smiled dryly. "You better put them on a back burner until you're exonerated. I don't need to tell you how Joan of Arc ended up."

"If I turn my back on my kindred spirits, I'll let them down."

Jack surged to his feet then pulled her up beside him. "Nevertheless, you need to lie low until things cool down."

When he pivoted toward his horse, she clutched his hand. "I want you to go home, back to the life you've built for yourself. This isn't your problem to fix."

"The hell it isn't—"

She pressed her index finger to his lips to shush him.

"You should marry one of the women I sent to you. Each one has her special qualities."

Too bad he was attracted to trouble—trouble who went by the name of Prudence Perkins. "How is that going to help?"

"When word gets around town that you're courting someone else, your involvement with me will be forgotten."

"You're right, that'd do it," he mumbled as he walked away. "I'll consider it in a couple of weeks."

"Do it now, Jack," she insisted. "You were prepared to marry *me*, sight unseen. You already know these other respectable women will make good wives."

"That was different."

"How is it different?"

"Because you were supposed to be so grateful for a new lease on life that you didn't care if your new husband was an extra person in the world who has no family history or connections. Jack McCavett isn't even my name," he burst out. "One of the hired help at the orphanage named me when she found me in the middle of the night on the front step. I was two years old and I could have been the son of a prostitute, an outlaw or both. I have no idea."

Jack slammed his mouth shut so fast that he bit his tongue. "Hell!"

Pru circled around to block his path and stared at him intently. "That's what the mail-order bride business is all about? You were prepared to marry a complete stranger who might've been down on her luck and so grateful for protection and security that she didn't care who you are or where you came from? Give yourself some credit, Jack."

"Credit for what? I don't know who the hell I am! How would you like to go through life without an identity?" he flung at her. "I don't belong anywhere. There are no family mementos, no family reunions, no birthday celebrations and no holiday get-togethers."

"If I'd known you craved them so much we could have exchanged places years ago," she insisted. "One meal with Gram telling you to sit up straight, mind your manners and don't speak unless spoken to and you would have lost your appetite. It would have cured your craving to belong to a clan."

Jack chuckled at her dour expression. "I wanted a family desperately. You couldn't get rid of yours fast enough. A fine pair we make."

"Right. The former lawman and the ex-bride-to-be outlaw," she added caustically. "Aren't we the envy of Paradise?"

Jack scooped her up and set her atop the bareback horse. "We'll swing by the ranch to gather a few supplies. Then I'm going to take you somewhere that you won't be easily found."

"And leave me there until the furor dies down," she predicted dispiritedly.

"Something like that." Jack mounted his horse. "Stony and I will test the waters in Paradise and decide when it's safe for you to return. Maybe we'll get lucky and find some leads as to who set you up for Dex's murder."

Thirty minutes later Jack drew his horse to a halt on the hill overlooking his cabin. A raft of foul curses flooded from his lips.

"Dear God! They destroyed the progress you made on your new barn!" Pru railed in dismay.

Jack stared at the scattered and broken lumber that had once been stacked neatly beside the corrals. The framework he had sweated and toiled over to erect for the barn was in a twisted pile on the ground.

"Damn it all." He scowled furiously.

"That's it, Jack. We are parting company here and now," she declared as she rode off. "I will not have you suffering because of my crusades."

She raced away with her blond hair flying out behind her like a banner. She made it a hundred yards before the horse leaped a small creek and Pru had nothing to anchor herself to. Her shrill shriek filled the air when she and the horse parted company.

She landed with a splat in the mud then glanced skyward. "Lord, I'd ask what else could possibly go wrong but I'm not sure I want to know."

# Chapter Ten

Jack trotted downhill then leaned away from his horse to offer Pru a hand so she could crawl up behind him. "You okay?"

"No," she muttered as Jack trotted off to retrieve her horse. "My life is hell and it's spilling over into yours."

"At least your grandmother isn't here to harass you about it," he reminded her.

"You're right, things could be worse for me, but I hate that I'm the cause of your loss and extra expenses."

Pru felt terrible. She was responsible for the broken lumber that would have to be replaced for the framework of Jack's new barn.

Jack surveyed the extensive damage. "At least they didn't torch my house."

"I couldn't live with myself if those spiteful marauders had done that, too."

Jack set her to her feet. "Let's grab some supplies and leave, in case we're being watched."

Pru glanced every which way, wondering if Dexter's

killer or a vengeful protester was waiting to strike. The uneasy thought prompted her to quicken her pace. She bumped into Jack who'd halted abruptly when he stepped inside the door. Pru peered around his shoulder and her temper exploded again.

A note had been propped up on the table. It said, Get rid of the imported troublemaking rabble-rouser or your house will be the next to fall.

"Son of a bitch," Jack muttered as he snatched up the note. "Recognize the handwriting, Pru?"

"No, it doesn't match the note slipped under my door, if that's what you're asking."

"But that doesn't mean your mysterious friend didn't incite this attack or participate in it," he reminded her.

Hurriedly they gathered makeshift sleeping pallets and food to tide Pru over. Despite the thought of facing Gram's wrath, she seriously considered returning home, if only to take the pressure off Jack. He didn't deserve this cruel retaliation. She'd wanted her freedom, despite the consequences, but not at *Jack's* expense. Now she'd have to reimburse him for every scrap of lumber damaged in the attack.

Provided that she survived and was acquitted of the charges against her, she told herself glumly.

Jack ushered her across the main room. He halted by the door to stuff a spare pistol into the waistband of her breeches. "If we're ambushed going out, drop and roll. Come up shooting while you scramble for cover."

Pru swallowed hard, knowing this was the kind of deadly reception Jack had encountered in years past. No wonder he wanted to leave that dangerous life behind. This kind of excitement and adventure wasn't exactly what she'd hoped for. Naturally, she'd wanted to pick and choose whichever exciting adventure that appealed to her.

This wasn't it.

"Ready? I'll go first, just in case…. Damn it, Pru!" he yelled when she bolted past him to draw whatever gunfire might be awaiting them.

Sure enough, shots rang out from the clump of cedar trees to the east. Pru did as instructed and managed to get off two wild shots while she rolled across the planked porch. She fired off two more shots while Jack bounded over to grab the horses' reins.

*"Ooofff!"* Pru grunted when Jack swooped down to jerk her roughly to her feet and thrust her toward the horses.

"Keep your head down," he growled as he heaved her onto her horse then bounded onto his mount.

Pru clutched the steed's neck and held on for dear life while Jack controlled the reins. They thundered off, accompanied by the sound of flying bullets. She glanced over her shoulder when she and Jack were out of range, but no one appeared from the trees and bushes to be easily identified.

As they plunged into the underbrush to follow the creek, another round of guilt pelted Pru. This was so unfair to Jack. She had become the curse of his life and there was no way to adequately repay him.

"Stay in the creek," he instructed as he tossed her the reins. "It will be more difficult to track us through water."

"Where are we going?"

"To the dugout where I lived when I first staked my claim," he informed her. "It's nothing more than a hollowed cavern in the creek bank, but you can't see it unless you accidentally stumble onto it."

Ten minutes later Jack directed her attention to a spot surrounded by willow trees and tangled vines. He pulled her from the horse then clutched her hand to lead her up the steep embankment to the dugout.

He tossed the pallets and sack of supplies aside. "It's crude and isolated, but it's the best place for you right now. I'll ride into town and confer with Stony. He needs to hear your side of the story."

"I tried to tell him, but the group of men accompanying him kept interrupting and spouting that I was trying to get away with murder because I was a woman," Pru remarked sourly.

"I'll make sure Stony knows about the setup," Jack promised. "I'll have to take your horse to avoid any suspicion about your presence in the dugout, you know."

Pru nodded. And then she impulsively flung her arms around his neck and kissed him—hard. She decided to hug the stuffing out of him while she was at it. Being afoot in the middle of nowhere, isolated with nothing but the mud-splattered clothes on her back, was unnerving. If the lynch mob found her, she'd never see Jack again. She intended to make the most of their last few moments together.

To her relief, he kissed her back, devouring her mouth with the same hungry impatience. She considered telling him that she was a little bit in love with him, but she just kept kissing him instead of wasting time with words he didn't want to hear. Besides, it would hurt her feelings to have him say that he didn't feel the same way about his cast-off mail-order bride-to-be.

Eventually, Jack set her to her feet and smiled wryly. "If you're thinking that was our fare-thee-well kiss, it wasn't. You're going to live through this, if I have anything to say about it."

"You might not," she murmured deflatedly.

"Stony and I will figure this out," he reassured her.

He was trying to make her feel better, but there was no guarantee her life would improve. It might get even worse.

"I'll be back after dark. In the meantime, you'll have to stay inside as much as possible to avoid notice."

Then he strode off, leaving her stranded, not knowing what to do with herself. She had the sinking feeling that she'd have to make a new start in another fledgling town in Oklahoma Territory and learn from the mistakes she'd blundered through in Paradise. Dispiritedly, she plunked down on her pallet and stared out at the sun-dappled creek and overhanging trees.

She sighed heavily, realizing that she was a lot more than a little bit in love with Jack McCavett. Last night wouldn't have happened if that weren't true. Unfortunately, she and Jack had conflicting goals in life. Not to mention her run-in with the law and his legendary career as a marshal. Her name was an infamous household word and he wanted out of the public eye.

Plus, if her father tracked her down and dragged her home, she had no excuse to stay, no leverage to counter his wishes.

"You should have married Jack when you had the chance so Papa couldn't uproot you," she muttered at herself. But then, that would've made Jack's life more miserable than it was. He wouldn't want her now, even if she got down on her knees and *begged* him to marry her.

"This is not what you need right now," Pru told herself as she flopped back on her pallet. "A tangled-up life is more than enough. Ill-fated love will only break your heart. If you have any sense at all you won't let yourself forget that."

Jack couldn't believe his eyes when he rode into Paradise. Women and children strode down one side of the street and the men used the other boardwalk. Plus, he hadn't received a single nod of greeting from his male counterparts. They stared at him as if he were a traitor of the worst sort.

Jack sighed in frustration as he dismounted in front of the marshal's office. Stony stood with one shoulder propped against the supporting beam, surveying the town divided.

"This is one hell of a mess." He gestured toward the broken brooms and shovels in the street. "Battle lines were drawn last night. All because of a few newspaper articles and the mysterious death of a man who commanded little respect to begin with. No need to make a martyr of that ruffian."

Jack ambled into the office and closed the door to ensure their privacy. "You don't honestly think Pru is responsible, do you?"

Stony dropped down in his chair and propped his boot heels on the corner of his desk. "I don't know what to believe. No one had seen Dex anywhere near Wild Horse Saloon for the past two weeks. Yet, there he was with two fatal stab wounds. We found Pru wobbling around, as if she'd been in a fight that left her dazed and bloody. In addition, it's public knowledge that those two came to blows recently."

"She insists that someone slipped a note under her hotel-room door, luring her to the saloon," Jack reported. "She had the note and a derringer in her pocket, but someone knocked her unconscious and took the incriminating note and her weapon. Which, by the way, she probably would have used instead of a knife if she wanted to ensure Dex's demise."

Stony threw up his hands in frustration. "No note and no way of proving she's telling the truth. Men are calling for her head, if only to stop the rabble-rousing newspaper articles that stir up women." He sent Jack a withering glance. "Next time you send off for a mail-order bride, do me a favor and try to pick one without spunk and spirit. Someone who isn't on a personal mission to free women from male oppression and human bondage would be nice, too."

Jack's lips twitched. "I'll try to keep that in mind. Homely, dull and dutiful. Right?"

A reluctant smile formed beneath Stony's mustache. "That's what you thought you wanted, as I recall."

"Yeah, but things change. The world around us is changing…and the women in it, too."

Stony sighed as he linked his fingers behind his head and stared up at Jack. "This fiasco makes me wish for the good old days in Kansas where trail hands rode into town to get liquored up, camped out at brothels and shot a few windows."

"Ah, yes, just think of the fun we had." Jack smirked.

"We broke up a few fights, crammed offenders in jail to sleep off their hangovers then escorted them to the city limits. A few shoot-outs here and there. A few murder cases to solve. But this?" Stony hitched his thumb toward the street. "I don't know how to handle social unrest and the makings of a gender war. What do I have to do to return things to normal?"

"First we examine Pru's hotel room and the alley behind Wild Horse Saloon for clues," Jack suggested. "I have the unmistakable feeling that someone probably left incriminating evidence for us to find. We might as well get to it."

On the way to the hotel, Jack briefed his friend on the morning's incidents and the necessity of tucking Pru away at the dugout. Stony muttered and scowled as he followed Jack into the lobby to request a spare key to Pru's room.

"No need," the desk clerk said. "Someone kicked in the door and ransacked the place. Miz Perkins' belongings are scattered everywhere."

Jack swore under his breath when he surveyed Pru's room a few moments later. "Someone is very displeased with Pru."

"To the extreme," Stony noted.

Not only were Pru's garments strewn about, but many of them had been ripped into pieces.

"All she has left are the clothes on her back and they're muddy," Jack murmured.

"So where is the incriminating evidence?" Stony asked.

"Maybe the assailant never had the chance to plant more evidence against her because the place was swarming with other disgruntled men," he suggested as he gathered up the shredded clothes and stuffed them into the satchels. He paused abruptly when he noticed the pile of jewelry in the bottom of the bag. "What the hell—?"

Stony peered over Jack's shoulder at the items and then they stared bemusedly at each other. "I'll have to recheck the list, but that might be the stolen valuables from the stagecoach robbery. Do you think Pru might've been involved and tried to double-cross her cohorts?"

Jack made a slashing gesture with his hand. "Don't be absurd. Pru came from Saint Louis."

"Or so she said. We haven't verified that."

"I don't think she was mixed up with the outlaws and suddenly decided to dispose of Dex."

"Then you explain her clash with Dex, his dead body in the alley and all these stolen items," Stony challenged.

"My guess is that they were planted before or after the ransacking brigade showed up last night. I think there might be *two* vindictive parties or individuals tormenting Pru. One might be the surviving outlaw and the other could be a group of angry husbands or boyfriends who oppose Pru's cause."

While Stony made a thorough search of the room, Jack tucked away the torn garments. As much as he would have liked to replace her wardrobe, he didn't dare. That would attract too much attention and he was too visible already. He would contact Rozalie discreetly and ask her to select a few garments from the boutique to tide Pru over.

Jack wrote a quick note to Rozalie and paid a young lad to deliver it. Then he and Stony walked across town to inspect the area behind Wild Horse Saloon. He frowned curiously when he noticed a set of smeared tracks in the loose dirt beside the building. He called Stony over to take a look.

"These tracks were purposely distorted," he contended. "Why do that unless you planned premeditated murder and didn't want to risk being discovered at the scene? I'd bet the ranch that Dexter Hanes was dead before Pru received the note."

Stony murmured in agreement then stood over the trampled prints near the back door. "This is where I found Dex. The men who followed me over here stamped all over everything."

"Could have been on purpose," Jack remarked. "Who first reported finding the body and seeing Pru in the alley?"

"The new janitor, who replaced Dex at the saloon. He went outside to discard trash," said Stony. "He didn't know it was Pru that he saw in the distance. He thought it was a boy in an oversized cap, vest and cloddish boots."

"Pru's disguise threw the new janitor off track, but it also suggests that she used the disguise to conceal her identity while she committed the murder," Jack remarked.

"Who would've thought that her protective disguise would work to her disadvantage," Stony mused aloud.

Jack glanced curiously at his friend. "Who was on hand when you arrived to investigate the murder?"

"The same five men who overheard the janitor tell me about the dead body. They were a step behind me when I went to investigate."

Stony rattled off Earl Thorton and Henry Palmer's names. Jack had met those two no-accounts. The other three were unfamiliar to him.

Jack panned the area impatiently. He was frustrated and no closer to figuring out who'd lured in Pru than he was when he arrived in town. But at least he knew of two abusive husbands who might have motives for getting rid of Pru.

"I'm buying lunch," Stony announced as he turned on his heels. "I'll interview the five men after we eat."

When they entered the hotel restaurant, Terrence Miller appeared at their table. "In case you see Pru—" he stared deliberately at Jack, "—tell her that she's fired. I don't want someone working for me who will give the place a bad name." He stared curiously at Stony. "Did she do it or not?"

"No," Stony declared. "But someone is trying hard to make us think she did. She's been collecting enemies since she began writing those newspaper editorials. You don't have a rebellious wife at home, do you? Are you feeling spiteful toward Pru for putting ideas in her head?"

Terrence grinned. "Yeah, but I'm a cook not a killer."

Jack caught Myrna Bates staring at him from a distance and he shifted uncomfortably in his chair. He'd practically dumped her on the floor in his haste to rescue Pru last night. If Myrna was annoyed with him, she had a right to be.

"What's with you and Myrna?" Stony asked when he intercepted the glance. "You've turned into a regular Romeo."

"No, it's just that Pru sent Myrna over last night, in case I might be interested in her as a potential wife."

"So you think Myrna tore down your barn because you bounded off to answer my call for help?"

Jack chuckled. "Not likely."

"You've never heard the adage about the wrath of a woman scorned? Anyone, man or woman, could have tied ropes to the framework, secured them to horses and pulled it down. Maybe Myrna knew she didn't stand a chance with you unless Pru was shamed and jailed and your property was destroyed to the point that you blamed Pru for it."

"You're leaping to wild conclusions like a mountain goat," Jack said. "Myrna is one of Pru's staunch converts. I don't think she's involved in a murder setup and the destruction of my property."

"If Thorton and Palmer had nothing to do with this, then I'm stumped," Stony mumbled.

So was Jack, but he wrote off Myrna immediately. She was smiling at him in far too provocative a manner to be spiteful.

Too bad he couldn't return the interested glance. As luck would have it, he'd developed a dangerous attraction to the holy terror of Paradise.

\* \* \*

It was just past dark when Jack reached the newspaper office to speak with Oscar. Shortly thereafter, Jack arrived at the designated spot where he'd asked Rozalie to meet him with a change of clothes for Pru. He waited fifteen minutes before he saw the silhouette of a woman scurrying toward the edge of town on foot. He frowned curiously when he realized it wasn't Rozalie but rather the seamstress, Samantha Graham.

"Is she all right?" Samantha asked anxiously as she handed the package of clothing to Jack.

"Exhausted but okay," he reported. "I'm keeping her safe until the charges are dropped."

"I offered to bring her clothing tonight because I'm very fond of Pru," Sam murmured. "She's been an inspiration to me."

*Unfortunately, I'm fond of her, too*, thought Jack.

"Pru has helped so many of us gain self-esteem with her inspiring articles. She's been particularly nice to me, Amelia and Molly." She glanced solemnly at Jack. "You rejected Pru as a bride. Was it because you don't believe women should have the right to vote, hold public office and share the same protection under the laws that men receive?"

Jack was pleased with Samantha's newfound confidence. When he'd seen her in the dry-goods store two weeks earlier she'd been too timid to look him or Tom Jenkins squarely in the eye. Now she held herself with pride and confidence.

"I never gave it much thought before, but I think Pru makes valid points," Jack replied belatedly. "I don't see why women shouldn't chase their own dreams. They should enjoy the same privileges as men. They work right alongside them, especially here on the frontier."

"I wish more men saw things the way you do," Sam said, studying him for a pensive moment. "If it's not because Pru is a champion for women's rights, why did you reject her?"

"She came here to campaign for women's rights. She wanted me to call off the wedding to save face and ensure I wasn't blamed for her crusade," he said honestly.

Samantha pulled the hood of her jacket over her head before turning to leave. "That sounds like her, kind and considerate of others."

"But I'm catching heat nonetheless. It seems the flames of social reform have back drafts," Jack remarked wryly. "You can't stand on the fringes of barnstorming without getting burned."

Samantha chortled in amusement. "That is a good way to put it. Tell Pru that we are thinking of her and that we're keeping the cause alive while she awaits exoneration."

"She'll be pleased to hear it." Jack mounted up and rode off to see if Pru had gone stir-crazy after spending the whole day stuck out in the middle of nowhere.

Pru paced the confines of the dugout—which didn't take long because the area was slightly larger than her bedroom closet in Saint Louis. It was getting late and Jack hadn't returned. What if he'd been ambushed again? He could be lying out there somewhere, fighting for his life. Or dead...

Her fretful thoughts trailed off when she heard the thud of hooves. She poked her head around the corner to see a moon-dappled silhouette on horseback. She was out of the dugout in two seconds flat, dashing anxiously toward Jack.

"You're okay?" she asked as he dismounted.

"I'm fine, but you're supposed to be tucked out of sight," he said accusingly.

"Dugout fever," she said dismissively.

Then she flung herself at him and kissed him hungrily. Hours ago, Pru had decided that she was going to make the most of her seclusion with Jack. She craved the pleasure of his touch and, after facing the prospect of murder charges, she vowed to make the most of every moment. Life held no guarantees and the frontier was fraught with unexpected danger.

"Glad you're home, dear," she teased as she dropped back on her heels. "I missed you terribly."

He tapped the tip of her nose then chuckled as he grasped her hand and led the way to the dugout. "Isolation makes you behave strangely."

That was a good enough excuse. She decided to go with it. "Stranger than usual?"

He hooked his arm around her waist and hauled her against his muscular form. "Not that I'm complaining, you understand."

His warm lips skimmed the column of her neck and she shivered in anticipation. Pru was all in favor of letting passion take its scintillating course. She sighed in disappointment when Jack stepped back a pace.

"Something wrong?" she asked.

He handed her a package. "I brought you new clothes."

"What happened to the old ones?"

"Samantha Graham said to tell you that all the women in town think of you as their inspiration."

"Sam has come a long way since I first met her," Pru

agreed then stared pointedly at Jack. "Now where are my other clothes?"

Jack wheeled around and strode outside. He returned a moment later with her satchels. Then he felt his way along the dirt wall to light the lantern. Golden light flickered over the shredded garments. Pru muttered a curse to whoever had destroyed her belongings to display his anger with her.

"Your room was ransacked," Jack reported. "The stolen jewelry from the stagecoach robbery was inside your satchel."

She blinked, stunned. "Now I'm being set up as the inside person for the robbery?"

"Apparently," Jack replied. "Someone is trying to blame you for every crime and misfortune that plagues Paradise. Lucky for you that Stony is skilled enough to recognize planted evidence and a setup when he sees one. He's dismissing the charges, but you need to lie low for a few days until this blows over."

"Oh, goody. I get to run and hide like a frightened rabbit," she grumbled resentfully.

"More bad news," he said. "Terrence Miller fired you. He says you're bad for the restaurant's reputation. Personally, I think business would be brisk if a murder suspect waited tables." He grinned wryly. "The good news is that Oscar Epperson has no qualms about keeping you on staff. He wants you to write articles while you're hiding out. He thinks it will be a sensational idea that'll sell more papers."

Pru was so touched by Jack's consideration in replacing her clothes and his efforts to exonerate her that she tossed aside the satchels and walked deliberately toward him. She had made a serious mistake when she didn't marry Jack the night of the town-wide celebration. Then he would have been hers permanently rather than temporarily. It wouldn't have been in his best interest, of course, but she would have loved her husband. Unlike her feelings for Edwin Donald and the dull life he had to offer in Saint Louis.

"Thank you for everything you've done, Jack."

He bent to kiss her then he grinned wickedly. "You're welcome, but you should know that the new clothes are gonna cost you."

"I know. I'll pay you back eventually. Until then..."

She leaned suggestively against him, leaving no doubt as to what she wanted. It seemed so natural, so easy to be with Jack. She supposed that's the way it was when you found yourself in love for the very first time. Ironically, she had come looking for independence on the frontier and discovered that she wanted Jack more than her precious freedom.

"Are you trying to seduce me?" he teased as she spread a row of kisses along his jaw.

"Yes, is it working?" She splayed her hand over the hard wall of his chest then let her fingertips drift lower.

"Like a charm..." he assured her hoarsely.

# Chapter Eleven

Jack groaned in helpless pleasure when Pru's supple body glided familiarly against his. The frustration of the day melted away when her left arm slid over his chest and her right hand skimmed over the bulge in his breeches.

*Why this woman?* he asked himself while his body throbbed heavily with desire. Why did he crave *her* scent, *her* touch, *her* taste? There were other women better suited to his new lifestyle. Why did he look into her enchanting face and forget every argument about getting so deeply involved with her?

"Come with me. I've been thinking about this all day," she murmured after she broke the breathless kiss.

Dazed and aroused to the extreme, Jack followed when she exited the dugout. "Considering that you seem to know where you're going, I'd say you didn't spend the entire day tucked from sight as I requested."

She glanced over her shoulder and grinned mischievously. Another jolt of need pelted him. He wasn't sure what she had in mind or where she was leading him, but he went eagerly. Which indicated that his life was spinning out of his control. He'd lost focus when Pru blew into his life.

When she halted on the creek bank and gestured toward moonlit water sparkling like diamonds over the gentle rapids and rippling across the pool beyond, Jack smiled. "Turns out this was my favorite place during the first six months at my new homestead."

"I've been longing for a bath and a swim." She peeked up at him and smiled provocatively. "I had erotic visions of sharing both with you."

Jack stood mesmerized while Pru disrobed and walked into the water. Then he shed his clothes in record time and joined her in the creek. She swam toward him then reached out to trace his aroused flesh with her forefinger. Her experimental touch had him burning from inside out and he swore there wasn't enough water in the pool to cool him off.

"You drive me crazy, you know that, don't you?" he wheezed as he snaked his arm around her waist and pulled her against him.

"Nice to know," she replied as she caressed him. "I want to make it my mission to learn to pleasure you as thoroughly as you pleasure me."

"You already do," he admitted huskily.

Her hand glided over his chest and down his abdomen while they stood in the shallows. Jack arched a dark brow when she glanced up at him and smiled seductively. And then he forgot to breathe—couldn't remember why that was necessary—when she knelt before him to cup him in her hand. Then she stroked him gently and need blazed through him. His knees nearly buckled when she lowered her head to flick at him with her tongue.

"Pru—" His voice gave out when she took him into her mouth and suckled him gently.

Pleasure burgeoned inside him and he groaned in unholy torment. He had never granted a woman the freedom to touch him as intimately as Pru. She alone had the power to turn him into her willing slave. Whatever she wanted, however she wanted it, had suddenly become his motto.

His thoughts swirled into a dizzying haze as she trailed her hands from his knees to his hips and inner thighs. All the while, she measured him with her lips and tongue. Fire blazed across every nerve and muscle in his body. Incredible pleasure burned in its wake, turning his flesh to pinpoints of fire and his mind to ashes.

"I love the feel of you," she whispered as her warm lips drifted over his thigh. "I love the taste of you. Everything about you fascinates me."

Jack knew it was only the newness of passion talking. Plus, Pru's world had tumbled down around her and she was searching desperately for distraction. But it still pleased him to hear her whispered words and feel her hands and lips moving provocatively over his sensitized body.

When her teeth closed playfully over his throbbing manhood and she took him deeply into her mouth, Jack groaned. His pulse hammered so hard against his ribs that he swore they would crack. Need clenched deep inside him, squeezing like a vise.

"Enough," he hissed between his teeth. "My turn."

"Equal rights?" she asked impishly.

"I'm all for 'em. Where do I sign up?"

He swooped to lift her into his arms. He walked into

deeper water, his aroused body shuddering as he battled for hard-won control.

"I know I'm being unfair to want to be with you when I'm trying to find you the perfect bride—"

Jack kissed her into silence. His desire for her amazed and tormented him. He had spent years ensuring that no woman got close enough to him that her absence from his life could torture him. It was easier on the heart not to care, not to form emotional attachments. Children from the orphanage had come and gone and he had to regroup emotionally with the loss of each friend. Then he had lost Davy Freeman, who'd been like a little brother. The pain had taken years to fade. Since then, Jack had allowed only his longtime attachment to Stony to be a part of his life.

But somehow this blue-eyed, spirited beauty had slipped past his defenses and took up residence in his heart. She had become too important, too necessary. That was dangerous because Pru would leave, too, and it would hurt like hell.

But until then he was going to enjoy her, savor her, delight in the intimacy between them. He was going to let his guard down...because he didn't seem capable of fighting his feelings for her.

"Ah, Jack..." she whispered as he bent his head to skim his lips over the peaks of her breasts. "Why can't I resist what you make me feel?"

"Same reason I can't resist the pleasure you give me," he replied. "We're addicted."

He left her adrift in the water while he mapped her feminine body one languid caress at a time.

"We're shameless...mmm..." She arched upward, her body shimmering with sparkling water droplets.

"Completely shameless," he agreed before he trailed his lips over her rib cage. "And I'm enjoying every moment of it."

Pru's breath broke when his warm lips skimmed her belly and his roaming hands drifted over her inner thighs. It still amazed her that she felt so uninhibited and eager for Jack's seductive touch. He knew how to make her burn, how to make her beg for his caresses. She yielded to him without protest, wanting all he had to offer.

When he shifted her in his arms to spread heated kisses from knee to hip, she quivered helplessly. She cried out in pleasure when he kissed her intimately and stroked her with his fingertip. She watched him watch her succumb to his skillful seduction and she knew beyond all doubt that she could never share this intimate bond with another man. She had bared body and soul to Jack McCavett and nothing would change these overwhelming feelings for him—

Her thoughts scattered like leaves in a windstorm when fiery pleasure burst over her. Desperate to have him deep inside her, she twisted in his arms.

"I need you." She curled her hand around his thick shaft, drawing him to her. "I want you inside me. Now."

She guided him to her and he surged forward. She moved urgently against him as she clamped her hands on his shoulders then kissed him for all she was worth. His hands cradled her hips, holding her as he plunged and re-treated, setting a frantic cadence that matched the hungry need pulsating through her.

Pru struggled to draw a breath as wild, mindless ecstasy swamped and buffeted her. She couldn't look away from the expression on Jack's face, from the glow in his amber eyes. She wondered if he could see all the way to her soul and knew the depth of her feelings for him, wondered if he realized how much pleasure and satisfaction he gave her.

With a sense of wonder, she watched passion overtake him. She saw his jaw clench, his eyes flare, felt him hard and deep inside her. He groaned as he clutched her to him and shuddered. With a cry of completion, she laid her cheek on his laboring chest and locked her arms tightly around his neck. The emotions she longed to express rose in her mind and flocked to the tip of her tongue but she bit them back.

Jack chuckled softly as he sank into the water with Pru's legs still locked around his hips. "I wondered what it would be like to return to the dugout and have someone here waiting for me…like this…after a hard day of building the cabin. Where were you a year ago?"

"I was listening to my grandmother plan my life and hoping my father would come to my defense rather than kowtowing to Gram." She pressed a light kiss to his collarbone. "Believe me, I'd have been here if I could."

Pru understood now why Jack had decided to find himself a bride. He'd wanted companionship while he was out here alone in the wilds. He'd wanted passion and conversation and—

Her thoughts broke off abruptly when Jack pulled her protectively behind him and glanced south. She didn't hear or see anything, but then her survival instincts weren't as acute as Jack's. She didn't object when he towed her through the water to reach shore.

Despite the potential danger waiting in the darkness, she

found herself gawking at his incredible male body as he crouched down to gather his weapons and clothes.

When he pointed the Colt in the direction of whatever sound had alerted him, she came ashore to grab her garments. Using his body as a shield, he led her to the dugout.

"Stay here and don't come out unless I call you," he instructed as he pulled on his breeches.

Pru nodded as she donned her clothes then combed her fingers through her damp hair. The moment Jack exited she scooped up the spare pistol and tucked herself in a shadowed corner. Then she pointed the weapon at the exit and waited.

Jack sank onto his haunches and listened attentively. He tried to figure out what had niggled his well-honed senses a few minutes earlier. A predator, no doubt. Unfortunately, he didn't know if it was the two- or four-legged variety. He wasn't taking any chances with Pru's safety.

The rustle of underbrush brought him to high alert. He watched a coyote and two pups trot to the creek to drink. The instant they caught his scent they turned tail and darted off.

Jack waited another five minutes to make sure the coast was clear. If there was one thing he had learned in law enforcement, it was caution. You had to outwait trouble so it wouldn't pounce the minute you turned your back.

Jack rose to his feet and move silently toward the dugout. A wry smile twitched lips, remembering the steamy tryst in the stream. Pru had no idea that she had fulfilled a couple of erotic fantasies this evening—fantasies that remained with him since he claimed this property. Their lovemaking, however, was even more fantastic than he could have imagined and he swore he'd carry the memory until the day he died.

"If you grow too accustomed to having her around you'll drive yourself insane later," he muttered at himself.

He knew he was Pru's first experiment with passion. Plus, dealing with danger prompted you to live for the moment— until you grew accustomed to dealing with it on a daily basis. Pru wasn't used to it. The unusual circumstances and close proximity had gotten to her. Not *him* specifically. He better not let himself forget that or he'd be sunk.

"It's me, Pru. I'm coming inside," he called out.

He watched her materialize from the dark corner like an angel absorbing into the light. Emotion thumped him in the chest and made him swallow hard. *You're getting too attached to this free-spirited woman*, came that lecturing voice in his head. *When her troubles are resolved, she'll be off crusading and you'll be here, tormented by your empty fantasies.*

"See anything?" she asked anxiously.

"Coyotes. But that doesn't mean something or someone else wasn't there. To be on the safe side we'll move the pallet to the corner behind the table."

"And sleep with one eye open," she presumed.

"Probably a good idea."

A few minutes later Jack and Pru cuddled up on the pallet behind the small table he had overturned as a blockade for protection. His pistol was within arm's reach. Pru brushed her hand leisurely down his arm and her breath caused gooseflesh to pop up on his neck.

"How much is this extra bodyguard duty going to cost me?" she asked playfully.

The smile in her voice and the touch of her hand sent need pulsing through his body again. "It's costing you plenty," he said before he kissed her passionately.

He wondered if he'd ever grow tired of her taste, tired of the feel of her exquisite body molded intimately to his. As urgent desire flared like a match set to dry kindling, Jack heard the taunting voice in his head whisper, *You're going to fall for this unique woman if you don't watch out, Jack McCavett. And that spells disaster.*

The next morning, Jack brushed his lips over the curve of Pru's neck and said, "I don't want to leave, but I need to go back to the cabin to check on my livestock."

Pru sighed contentedly—until she remembered the isolated world of pleasure always gave way to reality and unforeseen dangers. "I'm coming with you."

"Not a good idea." He levered himself upright and worked the kinks from his back. "It will take at least another day for Stony to spread word that you aren't a murder suspect and that he is looking for someone else. Plus, there are still plenty of disgruntled men in town who blame you for the female rebellion."

Pru stared into his ruggedly handsome face for a pensive moment. "Do you think I'm a troublemaker because I want women to have the same rights as men?" she asked somberly.

Jack toyed with a silver-blond ringlet coiled beside her ear. "Samantha Graham asked me the same thing when she brought clothes for you last night."

"I'm surprised her husband permitted her out of the house after dark. He tries to rule her with an iron hand, the same way Molly and Amelia's husbands do. I've seen evidence that when their wives take a stand, those men abuse them. If ever three women needed to be liberated, it's them."

She arched a curious brow. "What did you tell Sam when she asked about your opinion of women's rights?"

"I told her that I've seen women toil and work right alongside men on the frontier and I see no reason why they shouldn't enjoy the same rights and privileges." He shrugged a broad shoulder. "It's just that no one brought it to my attention before. I didn't give it much thought, but you have legitimate grievances that should be addressed."

Pru sat up to kiss him soundly. Smiling, she dropped back to the pallet. "I can't tell you what a relief it is to hear you say that. I feel horrible that you've suffered because of my crusades. I would feel a hundred times worse if you fiercely opposed my views."

"I doubt I agree with *all* your theories, but I respect your right to speak out for change." Jack tapped the tip of her nose and grinned. "But dragging me back into the public eye? Now that's something different entirely."

She shrugged nonchalantly. "Ah well, I don't think you would have made a good recluse anyway."

"No?"

"No. Much too dynamic a man to be isolated," she insisted. "That's why I'm doing my best to find you a wife...." Her voice trailed off when guilt stabbed at her conscience.

"I don't want you matchmaking for me," he insisted. "You have too much on your plate already."

A moment later, he cocked his head and breathed deeply. "Do you smell smoke?"

Pru bounded to her feet when Jack headed to the exit. An uneasy feeling settled over her when she saw the curl of smoke in the distance. When it seemed to double in size in the blink of an eye Jack swore foully. Pru knew from the direction of the plume of smoke that it was near his cabin. If his homestead had been attacked again she was never going to forgive herself.

Hurriedly they burst outside to fetch his horse.

"Stay here," he demanded.

"No, this is my fight, Jack."

He wheeled on her and shook his finger in her face. "Damn it, Pru, for once—"

She took advantage of the moment and ducked under his arm to retrieve his horse. She struggled to climb aboard then glanced down to see Jack standing with his feet askance. His arms were crossed over his broad chest and he wore a pensive frown.

"Now what?" she demanded hurriedly.

"Are all martyrs this headstrong and defiant?"

"I'm not a martyr. I'm just a woman who's been held back and held down too long," she said. "I'm not that much different than you."

"How's that?" he asked as he bounded up behind her.

"You grew up in an orphanage, ended up on a train headed west and went from one cow town to the next until this territory was opened for settlement."

"What's your point?" he asked as he nudged the horse toward his cabin.

"Given your past, all you wanted was a place to call your own. The chance to lead the life you envisioned for yourself. It took hard work and sweat to establish this homestead, but it was *your* dream. Freedom is *my* dream. Freedom of choice. Is it so hard to understand that I want to come and go as I please without needing someone's permission constantly?"

He sighed audibly as he veered in and around the willow trees. "If someone shoots you on my watch I still won't be happy about it."

"I won't be happy if someone harms you, either," she insisted as she stared at the puff of black smoke.

They rode uphill at a fast clip and Pru mentally crossed her fingers, hoping the rising smoke wasn't consuming Jack's property. A few minutes later, her hopes died beneath the flames leaping skyward.

The cabin Jack had built with his own hands was a mass of smoke and flames. His belongings and possessions were gone because of his association with her. His herd of cattle and horses were nowhere to be seen and the corrals had suffered serious damage. She didn't know how she could possibly feel worse about herself and more outraged on Jack's behalf.

"I'm so terribly sorry," she said through the wash of tears and frustration that overwhelmed her. It nearly killed her that his dreams had gone up in smoke—literally. She didn't even want to consider the financial setback he faced.

"This is the last straw," she muttered as Jack urged the horse downhill toward another clump of trees, rather than exposing them to a potential ambush. "I'm going back to Saint Louis to marry the man Gram picked out for me. Then I can use my stipend to reimburse you for your losses."

She started when he grabbed her shoulder and twisted her around so he could get right in her face while they were on horseback. He glared at her and he said, "You're giving up your freedom because of a burning house? I thought you were made of sturdier stuff."

"It's *your* house," she blurted in exasperation.

"I still have the dugout. You think I won't be aggravated as hell at you if you turn tail and run when things get difficult? If I'm going to sacrifice my hard work and money, only to have you run home then you're going to hear about it!"

Pru didn't know why he was so irritated. Probably because they were watching his house and his dreams go up in smoke. He was taking his outrage out on her, even if he didn't realize it. But catching the brunt of his frustration was the least she could do for him.

"I'm sorry." Jack blew out his breath and settled himself behind her. "I appreciate your sympathy and concern, but I won't let you tramp off to marry a man you don't love, just so you can repay me to pacify your guilty conscience."

"I *owe* you," she insisted firmly. "You've spared me from getting shot, from going hungry and from a lynching. All I've given you is a breach of contract and a wagonload of trouble. I'm surprised you don't hate me as much as whoever it is who's trying to bring false charges against me. If I go home to marry Edwin Donald I can solve all your financial problems."

"You think I could live with the fact that you sacrificed your dreams so you could repay me?" He snorted derisively. "No thanks, Pru. I'd rather live in the dugout for another six months while I rebuild."

The thought of Jack's numerous setbacks tormented her to no end. Furthermore, she'd give anything to get her hands on the person or persons responsible for the vindictive destruction. Her enemies were transferring their vengeance for her to Jack and she hated the unfairness.

Her bitter thoughts trailed off when she saw the Dawson brothers thundering across the pasture like a two-man rescue brigade. As they approached, Jack searched the shadows of the trees carefully for bushwhackers before riding into the clearing to reach the bonfire that had once been his home.

"Did you see who did this?" Chester asked as he skidded his horse to a halt.

Jack shook his tousled head. "I kept Pru tucked out of sight last night and we saw the smoke this morning from a distance."

"Damn shame," Leroy muttered. "All that hard work gone up in flames. I'd like to strangle whoever did this."

"So would I," Pru put in.

She clamped her mouth shut when the brothers Dawson glanced at her. She could tell by the looks on their faces that they thought she was to blame.

But then, so did she. So who was she to complain?

Horatio glanced up from the paperwork on his desk to see his pesky business rival grinning wickedly at him. Theodore Porter occasionally showed up to harass him. His upstart trading company had gained a foothold in Missouri five years earlier. Horatio didn't mind the competition but he disliked Theodore's smug attitude. And here Theo was again, bound to spoil Horatio's mood.

"One of my acquaintances brought me something interesting from his travels across the new Oklahoma Territory." Theo dropped the frontier newspaper on Horatio's desk.

Horatio's eyes bulged from their sockets and he choked on his breath when he read the article naming Pru Perkins as the head of the women's rights movement and the prime suspect in a murder investigation.

"I thought you said your daughter was visiting family in the East," Theodore goaded him.

Good God, Pru was in Paradise—wherever the hell that was—working on a crusade that led to a man's death. His wide-eyed gaze drifted down the page to notice that Pru had penned an article about relocating gaming halls and brothels to the outskirts of town. Muttering at the exasperating turn of events, Horatio bolted to his feet.

"Where are you off to in such a rush? As if I don't know," Theo mocked. "Apparently your daughter found a forum to express her radical opinions. Makes me wonder about how she was raised. Not with a firm hand, obviously—"

Theo slammed his mouth shut when Horatio rounded on him, his blue eyes shooting hot sparks. "One word about this around town, Theo, and I will ruin you. Do you understand me?" He smiled tightly as he loomed over the annoying little man. "You have a few skeletons in your closet, like your penchant for young men. I will appoint my mother to expose you in our social circle if you start any rumors before I have a chance to check on this situation."

Theo's face turned the color of raw liver. He swallowed hard, stepped back a pace then scurried off when Horatio thrust out his arm to show him the door.

Scowling, Horatio tucked the newspaper under his arm and walked off. He needed to catch a train, call off this ridiculous bet and bring Pru home. Immediately.

Horatio was out the door and in his carriage in two

shakes. He hurried home to pack a bag so he could race off to purchase a ticket on the next train heading west.

He winced, anticipating that his mother would give him the third degree about this unexpected trip. Well, he'd dream up some excuse, he assured himself as he careened around the corner. The less his mother knew about Pru's present predicament and where she was, the better off he would be. If she knew, she'd pitch a full-fledged fit. Horatio preferred to avoid her tirade. There had been far too many of them the past month.

# Chapter Twelve

Jack surveyed the smoldering pile of ashes that had taken most of the day to burn out. He reminded himself that he'd begun life with little of nothing—and was right back where he'd started. Well, not precisely, he mused. He still had one-hundred-sixty acres of prime farmland, pasture and a spring-fed creek. Plus, he had machinery to work the land and a herd of cattle and horses—most of which were scattered to kingdom come at the moment. Only two horses had wandered back to the broken corral.

He also had a very miserable female on his hands. He wanted to shake the stuffing out of Chester and Leroy for treating Pru as if she were the curse of his life. Clearly, she felt terrible about his losses without the Dawsons heaping more guilt and resentment on her.

Pru had busied herself by stacking what was left of the lumber for the barn in an orderly fashion while he plowed more space for the garden. Fifteen minutes later he saw Pru walk toward him, a determined look on her flushed face.

"I'm going into town," she announced. "I'll ask Oscar

for an advance on my wages to replace the lumber needed to rebuild your home."

Jack halted the plow horse then took a long swig from the canteen. Then he said, "No, someone might take potshots at you."

Pru tilted her smudged chin at him. "You are fired as my bodyguard. I'm finding that I like to be shot at. It keeps my heart pumping and my senses on full alert."

The woman was so full of sass and spunk that he couldn't help but grin at her comment. "I don't need your money, Pru. I have a nest egg in savings from salary and bounties."

"I'm relieved to hear that, but that doesn't change the fact that your house and the framework of your barn would still be standing if not for your connection to me."

He frowned darkly at her. "We have been through this already. I do not blame you for what happened."

"*I* blame me and you can't talk me out of it." Pru lurched around. "I'm borrowing one of your horses."

"No, I'll have you arrested for horse thieving," he threatened the exasperating woman. "That charge carries the same sentence as murder. *A hanging.* Trust me, Pru. You would not look good with a noose around your neck."

"Well, at least I'd be out of your hair for good and people wouldn't treat you like a social outcast because you had the misfortune of getting mixed up with me," she countered.

When she bounded onto the horse and trotted off, Jack muttered under his breath. He planned to give chase, of course, but he had to unhook the machinery and feed the plow horse. He couldn't leave the exhausted animal standing in the field half the night.

Pru had been gone thirty minutes before Jack rode off

after her. He glanced over his shoulder at the two remaining buildings—the henhouse and small shed—and wondered if they would still be standing when he got back.

His troubles would be over if he disassociated himself from Pru, as she demanded. He had every reason to write her off as too much trouble. So why hadn't he? he asked himself as he trotted his black gelding toward town.

Pru followed Jack's cautious practice of clinging to the security of the tree-lined creek to avoid becoming a target. When she rode into town, she was greeted with scowls from men. Only the women nodded cordially. Pru made a beeline for Stony's office, hoping he had scared up a few facts about who had stabbed Dexter Hanes.

When she passed the boutique, Rozalie and Samantha burst outside to greet her. Molly Palmer from the bakery rushed out to check on her, too.

"Thank goodness you're all right," Samantha said with a relieved smile. "We heard that Jack's home burned down. I sincerely hope you weren't in it and had to battle smoke!"

Pru smiled reassuringly and made a point to survey Molly and Samantha's arms and faces. The unsightly bruise Sam had sustained earlier had faded away. Pru hoped Sam's bully of a husband had backed off after Pru began writing articles advocating courteous treatment for all women and calling for social reform. There was a noticeable change in Sam's demeanor and Molly's, as well. Amelia had made great strides, too. They possessed a new confidence that radiated from the inside out. If Pru accomplished nothing else in Paradise, she was proud these women had taken her words to heart and improved their situations.

"Jack and I weren't at the ranch when the fire broke out," she reported belatedly. "He found a place for me to hide out in the wilderness, so we're both fine."

Rozalie fisted her hands on her ample hips and sniffed distastefully. "Well, I'd like to get hold of the scoundrels who destroyed Jack's house and threatened you. At least you have been exonerated of that ridiculous murder charge."

"That's good to hear," she said with a gusty sigh. "Any new suspects?"

Rozalie shrugged. "I don't know. Stony didn't say. He just sent word around town that you were set up for the crime and that someone ransacked your room while you were lying unconscious in the alley beside Dex. If Stony has any leads he didn't make them public."

"We have more clothes for you," Samantha said as she whirled toward the shop.

"That isn't necessary—"

"Nonsense," Roz interrupted. "Maybe Lady Godiva could ride around naked in the streets to protest injustice, but you better not try it so soon after the Petticoat Rebellion, as our sisters are calling it. Besides, you need something to wear for tomorrow's rally at town square. You are the guest speaker."

Dumbfounded, Pru accepted the garments that Samantha handed to her. "Guest speaker?" she chirped.

"Who else? You are the voice of oppressed sisters who want the same rights those women in Wyoming and Colorado have enjoyed for years," Molly commented. "We need to elect delegates to send to the new territorial capitol in Guthrie to pressure our representatives and to unite other women for the cause."

"Oscar has been by twice today, asking after you," Sam reported. "He says he's expecting the exclusive story of your ordeal for the paper, as soon as possible."

After a heartfelt thank-you for the clothes and unfaltering support, Pru detoured to the newspaper office.

"Well, here is our local rabble-rouser," Oscar greeted cheerfully. "The newspaper sold out again today. I guess everyone wanted to hear what you had to say before you were jailed and what I added to support your innocence." He beamed in delight. "You are a walking gold mine, Pru. My lucky charm."

She might be making money for Oscar hand over fist, but she was a bad omen to Jack McCavett.

"Now that you're here you can issue a statement for tomorrow's paper. We'll put it on the press."

"I'll be happy to." She grinned wryly then borrowed one of Jack's favorite comments. "But it's gonna cost you. Sensationalism has its price and I need a raise."

Oscar didn't so much as blink. "I'll double your salary," he said generously. "I've billed you as the next feminine activist who ranks up there with Oregon's Abigail Scott Duniway, Wyoming's Esther Morris, Utah's Emmeline Wells and Clarina Nichols from Kansas. I've received a half-dozen wires from eastern and western newspapers wanting information about the Petticoat Rebellion and about you."

Pru inwardly grimaced. She needed to stop at the telegraph office to wire her father before he received word of her notoriety from someone else. Then she'd have to disappoint her kindred spirits in Oklahoma Territory in order to acquire sufficient funds to reimburse Jack for the destruction of his property. Hopefully, women like Rozalie, Samantha, Amelia and Molly would take up the cause, even if Pru had to conform to social restrictions back home in order to reimburse Jack.

She shuddered at the thought of tolerating Edwin Donald's companionship after reveling in the passion she'd discovered in Jack's arms, the pleasure of simply being *with* him. Her future would be dull indeed, she mused dispiritedly.

"Here," Oscar said, jostling her from her thoughts. "Jot down some comments to appease your devoted followers and mention the rally scheduled for tomorrow at town square."

Hurriedly, Pru wrote out her comments about being relieved that she'd been found innocent and that she hoped Dexter's killer would be brought to justice quickly. As requested, she mentioned the need for women's rights in Oklahoma Territory and the upcoming rally.

"This should tide you over a few days," Oscar said as he dropped a heavy pouch of coins into her palm.

Pru nodded gratefully then exited to see a small crowd of men glaring at her as if she were public enemy number one.

"Radical," one of the men muttered as she walked away. "Now you've taken to wearing men's breeches in public."

"Are those Jack's?" Someone smirked sarcastically. "You wearing *his* breeches these days? Wouldn't be surprised since he's turned into a sissified plow boy."

"I still have my own breeches and plan to keep them."

Startled, Pru whipped around to see Jack seated on horseback, staring down the hecklers who followed her.

"I always thought a self-assured man had no trouble dealing with a strong-willed woman." He smiled wryly.

"You know what I think? I think you boys are afraid of Pru and intimidated by her progressive ideas."

"Afraid? Ha!" one of the other men said and snorted.

"Yes, afraid," Jack confirmed. "She's better educated than most of us. She's certainly more eloquent because we've seen evidence of it in her newspaper articles. She also possesses the polished manners that we've never learned. And, as you recall, Pru never asked you to give up a single one of *your* rights and privileges, just to give your wives, girlfriends or daughters the same consideration and respect that you expect from others."

"Hell, she wants to shut down gaming halls and brothels!" someone erupted from the center of the crowd. "We don't want that to happen."

"I only suggested limiting hours of operation," Pru reminded them. "And has it occurred to you that the ladies of the evening name their own price, while the rest of us receive less pay for doing the same jobs as men? Double standards of any type will not be tolerated, gentlemen. Fair is fair."

"Should've tarred and feathered you when we had the chance," someone muttered spitefully. "Jack, too. He turned out to be a traitor!"

Jack didn't respond verbally, but he did ride his horse through the crowd so Pru could climb up behind him, just in case the situation turned sour, as it had in front of Stony's office.

Pru rode off with Jack, listening to the hecklers grumble about the audacity of a woman riding astride and in breeches, to boot. It was disappointing that these men were the same well-wishers who'd greeted her with open arms the first night she arrived in Paradise. She seemed to have a knack of offending people and turning them against her.

"Did you come to press charges for horse stealing?" she asked Jack as they rode to the marshal's office.

"Nope. Changed my mind." He glanced at the package she'd tied to the saddle of his borrowed horse that she'd tethered by the boutique. "More gifts from your kindred spirits?"

"Roz and Samantha were very generous. Plus, Oscar gave me a raise so I can pay for your room at the hotel, since you don't have a home."

"Not necessary. I can cover that, plus new clothes."

Jack set her to her feet, then dismounted. He gestured toward the dry-goods store. "I'll pick up a few things then meet you at the marshal's office."

The moment Jack disappeared into the store Pru headed for the telegraph office. She was determined to make things right for Jack, even if it meant giving up her dream of independence and freedom. It was the least she could do to compensate for all the trouble Jack suffered because of her.

Stony glanced up from filling out forms when Jack and Pru entered the office. He grinned wickedly. "What do you two have in store for the good citizens of Paradise tonight? A near lynching? Another rebellion?" His smile faded as he focused on Jack. "I'm damn sorry about that bonfire at your place. You're welcome to stay with me at the boardinghouse."

"Thanks for the offer, friend. As for the wild goings-on from two days' past, Pru and I were hoping for a quiet evening." He raised a thick black brow. "Any leads on the murder investigation?"

Stony shook his dark head. "No, afraid not. I questioned Palmer and Thorton, but they provided alibis for each other. Dexter's replacement at Wild Horse Saloon tells the same story about what he saw the night of the murder. Went out to discard trash. Saw Dex in the dirt and spotted the young boy who turned out to be Pru. Then he sent for me."

"He saw no one else?" Jack asked. "Heard nothing else?"

Stony shrugged. "Three other men rushed outside when the janitor dashed into the saloon with the news. None of them saw anything, either. Except Dex dead and Pru in the distance."

"What if the killer hid in the alley?" Pru suggested. "Maybe he slipped in the rear exit of the saloon, mingled with the crowd and waited for Dex's body to be discovered."

"Then we have suspects galore to interrogate," Stony said. "Plus, only motive we're aware of is your conflict with Dexter. I don't know what problem anyone else had with him."

"Except maybe his cohort in the robbery," Jack added.

"Dex did admit to robbing me. And I know for a fact that Dex had an accomplice," Pru commented. "The thieves could have had a falling out and Dex's partner might have set me up."

"I agree with Pru," Jack chimed in. "The accomplice could have disposed of Dex, knocked Pru over the head, then slipped into the saloon to blend in with the crowd."

"Yes, and if not for the fact that Pru has stirred up a hornet's nest with her talk of women's rights that have menfolk fussing at her, I'd agree that the mysterious accomplice is our prime suspect. But anyone could have set up Pru for spite, hoping to have her jailed instead of inciting women to join her cause."

Stony leaned back in his chair and frowned pensively. "It has even occurred to me that whoever sent that note to Pru had planned to intercept her and to retaliate. But since she used a disguise and left by the fire escape, her nemesis missed his chance. In which case there are two mysterious assailants running around loose instead of one."

"That's a definite possibility," Jack agreed. "Dex could have had his own set of enemies and one of them could have taken advantage of Pru being at the wrong place at the wrong time. Dex could've sent for Pru and someone else interceded to make her the prime suspect of murder."

"Were Dex's pockets picked clean?" Pru asked.

Stony nodded. "I didn't give it much thought, what with all the turmoil surrounding you that night. But Dex didn't have a weapon or a single coin on him. He could've been robbed before you had the misfortune of showing up."

Pru pivoted toward the door. This fiasco had too many complications and possibilities. It would take time to sort it all out. She might not be here to assist with the investigation. It all depended on how quickly her father reacted to the message she'd sent off to him today. But one thing was clear to Pru. She'd made several enemies who could have set her up. In addition, Dex could've had his own set of enemies working against him that fateful night.

"Where are you going?" Jack questioned her.

"To rent a room at the hotel."

"Watch your back," he cautioned.

She glanced over her shoulder at him. "Why? Is there a bull's-eye drawn on it?"

"That's not funny," Jack muttered before she closed the door behind her.

* * *

"Mrs. Perkins?"

Gram glanced up to see Elva Foster, the housekeeper, standing in the doorway to the parlor. She frowned at the concerned expression on the woman's face. "Yes, what is it? Have you received word from Horatio?"

The housekeeper shook her frizzy head then sailed in to stand beside the sofa where Gram was taking tea. "A messenger from the telegraph office delivered this. It's for Mr. Perkins. But since he left town I thought I should deliver it to you." She extended the missive. "It's from your granddaughter."

*"What!"* Gram snatched the note from the house-keeper's hand. "It's bad enough that Horatio took off for parts unknown and tried to convince me that he was on a business trip. Ha! How dense does he think I am?"

She gasped and then muttered several unladylike curses under her breath when she read the note from Pru. *You win the bet. I'm in trouble. Send money soon.*

Send money? Not likely. She would deliver it in person.

Gram made note of the name of the town at the bottom of the missive. "Paradise, Oklahoma Territory? What in God's name is she doing there? That's the middle of nowhere!"

"I'm sure I don't know, ma'am," the housekeeper murmured.

Gram gave her the evil eye as she heaved herself to her feet. "Not one word to anyone about this, Elva, or you'll be dismissed from your position. I'll make certain you're blacklisted from working for anyone in high society." She flicked her wrist. "Now fetch the butler and have him purchase me a ticket on the next train. Then come to my room and help me pack for my trip. I intend to bring my granddaughter home where she belongs.

"What is the reckless hoyden thinking?" Gram said to herself as she pelted down the hall, pounding her cane at irregular intervals. "Oklahoma Territory? With her background and breeding? She isn't supposed to mix and mingle with common homesteaders. She's ruining her upstanding reputation!"

It was dark by the time Pru retrieved her horse from the hitching post in front of the boutique and tethered it near the hotel. She glanced toward the lobby then changed her mind about renting a room immediately. She had another errand to tend to before she bathed and changed clothes.

Glancing over her shoulder to ensure a crowd of hecklers wasn't gathering behind her, Pru ducked into the alley and scurried off. She wanted to question the new janitor at the saloon herself. Not that she expected better results than Stony, but she had a vested interest in this case. She wanted to solve it before she left for Missouri.

Pru peered around the corner of a brick building to make sure she was alone, then scurried toward the gaming-hall and bordello district. There was no telling who was lurking behind the overturned crates and trash bins, waiting to pounce. She cautioned herself to pay close attention to her surroundings.

Clinging to the shadows, Pru inched toward Wild Horse Saloon. She heard the tinkling sound of piano music, guffaws of laughter and the murmur of voices inside the saloon. She marshaled her resolve and vowed not to let her guard down for even a second. She didn't want another dead body to turn up at her feet.

She nearly jumped out of her skin when a scrawny alley cat leaped from a stack of garbage and tore off into the darkness. Pru clutched her chest, drew a steadying breath and approached the back door of Wild Horse Saloon.

She had just plastered herself against the clapboard wall when the door leading to the storeroom of the saloon swung open unexpectedly. Unfortunately, the man opening the door spotted her.

"What the hell are you doin' here?"

Despite the thick Southern drawl in the man's voice, there was something faintly familiar about it. Pru wracked her brain, trying to make a connection but coming up empty.

"Are you the new janitor?" she asked as she emerged from the shadows.

"That's right. And you're that rabble-rouser in breeches that I saw in the alley the night Dexter Hanes was stabbed. Am I your next victim?"

"I didn't kill Dex, but I would like to ask you a few questions about what happened that night," Pru requested of the sturdily built janitor who was wore a dingy white apron over his shirt and breeches. She studied his square jaw, rimmed with bristly stubble and tried to recall if she'd seen him before. His ruddy features were puckered in a scowl, indicating his dislike for her.

There seemed to be a lot of that going around town.

"I already told Marshal Mason everything I remember," he drawled. "If you're tryin' to get me to back up your story of innocence then you're knockin' on the wrong door. Personally, I think you did it. You're just tryin' to get off because you're a woman and you're friends with the marshal. I didn't see anyone else in the alley that night so don't expect me to make up somethin' to get you off the hook."

"Phil, get in here. There's a spill you need to clean up!" Charley Rutherford, the proprietor, yelled over the sound of music and conversation.

"I'll be there in a minute!" he called back.

Pru froze like a block of ice when Phil, the janitor, spoke to his boss without his exaggerated Southern drawl—which he'd obviously used for *her* benefit. This, she suddenly realized, was the voice she'd heard during the robbery and each time she'd been accosted and threatened into silence.

Recognition hit her like a landslide. This was Dex's cohort. He had likely killed his partner and laid the blame at her feet. He had also taken Dex's job when he skipped town after the altercation, she noted.

Pru yelped when Phil leaped on her, slamming her against the outer wall so hard that she smacked her head and shoulders—hard—forcing the air from her lungs in a whoosh. She couldn't scream for help because she couldn't breathe, especially when he wedged her between his bulky body and the wall and stuck his face in hers.

"You make one peep, bitch, and you're dead where you stand," he snarled.

Yes, definitely this man had issued hateful threats during and after the robbery. He'd also been on hand for the confrontations at the hotel.

"Or maybe I'll just cut out your sassy tongue so you can't start another riot for women's rights. Bad enough that I left an eyewitness from a robbery. An eyewitness who decided to squat in the same town where I live. That complication never happened before. Then your barnstorming for women's rights made things even worse. When you got Samantha all fired up and talked her into standing up to me that was the last straw. You've made my life hell in every direction and you're gonna pay dearly."

Pru's eyes popped when she finally made the connection. "Phil? As in Samantha Graham's husband?" she croaked when she finally got her breath back. "Give back my bracelet!"

He sneered at her demand. "I'll have it buried with you."

"That's not exactly what I had in mind," she said.

"Didn't think so." He yanked off his apron and used it as a hood and a gag to restrain Pru.

She struggled against him but to no avail. She was no match for his strength and he was careful to keep her arms pinned against her sides so she couldn't fight back. She tried to kick when he slung her over his shoulder and stalked up the steps into the storeroom.

"Damn it, Phil!" the proprietor yelled again. "Get your ass in here right now!"

"I'm on my way, boss!" Phil called back as he dumped Pru in the corner. "I'm just cleaning out the dirty mop!"

When Pru tried to roll to her feet, Phil clamped a hand on her shoulder and shoved her down. "Settle down, bitch. You're too much damn trouble. You need someone who knows how to keep a woman in her place to straighten you out."

He grabbed rope to tie her hands and feet then anchored her to whatever heavy object sat beside her—she didn't know since she couldn't see past the blindfold.

"Jack McCavett couldn't teach you a few important lessons, but I sure as hell can. Of course, you probably used sex to control him. The two of you had yourselves quite a time down at the creek, didn't you?"

Pru winced, disgusted by the thought of this brute spying on them. Phil must have been hiding in the underbrush and it was his presence that had caught Jack's attention. This was the two-legged predator that had been lurking about.

Frantic to escape, Pru kicked out with her feet, hoping to knock Phil off balance with enough force that he'd slam into the storage shelves and cause enough racket to prompt the proprietor to investigate. She heard Phil grunt and swear when her feet connected with his shin, but being shackled didn't allow her enough force or momentum to do major damage to her captor. It only made him mad.

"Pesky bitch," he snarled as he thumped her on the head with what she presumed to be the butt of his pistol. And damn the luck, he managed to connect with the tender spot that he'd hammered the night Dex died.

"Phil, where are you? If you don't get in here right this minute then you're fired!"

"On my way!"

The voices seemed to come from a long winding tunnel. Pru tried to keep her wits about her, but she slumped on the floor and passed out.

# Chapter Thirteen

Jack frowned, bemused, when he looked at the hotel register and noticed Pru hadn't checked in. Now where the hell had she gotten off to? The horse she'd borrowed was hitched outside and the package of clothes was still strapped behind the saddle.

He sighed. It was late, it had been a long frustrating day and he wanted to sprawl out and relax. But he couldn't when he didn't know where Pru was.

"Damn," he grumbled after he checked the newspaper office and found it closed up for the night.

Then he remembered what Pru had said about the possibility of the killer entering the back door of the saloon to lose himself in the crowd. Surely she hadn't taken it upon herself to investigate.

An unsettling sensation slithered down his spine. Pru? Assertive enough to pursue the investigation, the same way she took on a crusade or squared off against a couple of stagecoach thieves? Hell yes, she'd take matters into her own hands!

Jack whipped around and jogged down the boardwalk. He headed straight toward West Side, the unruly part of town where the streets were lined with gaming halls, dance halls and brothels. Five minutes later, he strode through the alley where Pru had been found near a dead body. He inwardly winced, hoping her daring nature hadn't left her standing over another corpse—or ended up as one herself.

"Pru?" he called quietly. "Are you here?"

He heard nothing. Saw no one.

His concern escalated with every step he took. He approached Wild Horse Saloon and pounded on the back door.

"Yeah? Who is it and wha'd ya want?"

Jack studied the stocky man who appeared at the door. "Are you the new janitor?"

"What's it to you?" he asked sarcastically.

Jack glanced into the dark storeroom. "I want to ask you a few questions."

"I'm working. Come back later," he said rudely.

"Have you seen the woman accused of killing Dex?"

The janitor shook his head. "Nope, not since the night she was wandering around in the alley."

"Mind if I have a look around?"

"The marshal already did."

"He deputized me to take a second look," Jack hedged as he shouldered past the uncooperative janitor.

"She did it, you know," the janitor insisted. "She's been trouble since she showed up in town. Don't know why you're taking up for her."

Jack glanced back at the janitor who was a head shorter but just as broad. "Don't know why it's any business of yours, friend," he replied.

"It ain't." The janitor veered around him. "I'm telling the boss that you're back here snooping around. Better come out through the saloon when you're done."

Jack focused his attention on the cluttered storeroom. He didn't see anything out of the ordinary, just stacks of supplies. If Pru had been here, Jack didn't see any sign of her.

If she hadn't come here, where could she have gone? He ambled through the saloon to see several men gathered around the card tables and a half-dozen scantily dressed women hanging over their shoulders.

He suspected that if Pru had ventured in here there would have been a riot. The clientele was outraged by her suggestion of shortening the hours of operation. If she'd dared to make one remark, a fight would have broken out.

Jack nodded to Charley Rutherford, the proprietor, then exited the front door. *You're not her keeper, you know,* he thought to himself. Still, he had the twitchy feeling that something was amiss. He wasn't going to rest easy until he located Pru and tucked her in for the night.

"Boss, I need to take off for an hour to see to some business," Phil Graham requested the moment Jack left.

Charley Rutherford shook his gray head then hitched his thumb toward the crowd. "We're busy tonight."

"I'll work an extra hour to make up," Phil negotiated.

"You haven't worked here long enough to get special privileges," Charley replied as he puffed on his cigar.

"It's important or I wouldn't ask," Phil insisted, wishing he could walk out on the hidebound old bastard without drawing the kind of suspicion he didn't need right now.

"I'll make up the time and work *two* extra hours for free. I'll even tidy up the storeroom tomorrow."

Charley regarded him through the curl of smoke rising from his cigar. Finally, he nodded. "Okay. But you had damn well better be back here in exactly one hour. If you aren't, I'll withhold your salary for the week, you hear?"

"Yes, sir." Phil wheeled toward the storeroom. "I'm mighty grateful."

Phil scurried out the back exit, relieved that he'd found time to move Pru to a secluded hiding place before Jack McCavett showed up. He had stuffed her in a trash bin and covered her with crates and garbage. When he fished her out, she was a wriggling bundle of nuisance. He stole the first horse he came across so he could toss Pru on its back and secure her before she had the chance to escape.

A wry smile pursed his lips as he led the horse into the darkness. His captive would become a hostage held for ransom, he decided. If Jack McCavett couldn't afford to pay, then all those female drumbeaters could take up a collection to get their mouthpiece back.

With mounting enthusiasm for his latest scheme, Phil hurried off to retrieve his mount. A few minutes later, he trotted from town, leading the stolen horse and his hostage behind him.

Pru struggled for all she was worth, trying to throw herself off the cantering horse. Unfortunately, Phil had taken the precaution of strapping her down. She'd heard Jack calling to her earlier but she'd been unable to gain his attention. She'd felt helpless and completely at Phil's mercy and that frustrated her to no end.

Now there was no telling what this low-down, conniving murderer had in mind for her. Whatever his latest scheme she knew it wouldn't bode well for her. And that made her furious. And scared. Her future looked grim. Nonexistent even.

"You're going to be my meal ticket out of this town, bitch," Phil said twenty minutes later.

Since Phil had gagged her, she silently consigned him to hell and hoped he suffered all the torments of the eternally damned when he got there.

"How much do you think I should ask for ransom?" he taunted. "What's McCavett's personal *whore* worth to him, do you think? And your female cohorts? What's the going rate for recovering a troublesome rabble-rouser?"

Pru silently cursed Phil Graham, hoping that he'd break out in hives and scabs before a lightning bolt zapped him and fried him to a crisp.

"You brought all this on yourself and Jack, you know," he goaded. "Because of Jack's ties to you, it didn't take much to convince and encourage Palmer and Thorton to ransack his homestead. I was trying to get Jack to back away from you so I could grab you but the fool never did it."

He was trying to intimidate Pru, but she refused to react to his taunts.

"I think your stupid cause is a waste of time. Women don't deserve the same rights and wages because they aren't smart enough or strong enough to do more than they're born to do. Which is appease men's desires and tend household chores."

Pru swore into her gag. She was getting a taste of the harangue Samantha endured during her marriage to this bastard. No wonder Samantha had possessed so little confidence in herself—until recently. Phil intentionally made her feel subservient so he could keep her under his thumb.

"You're going to pay dearly for forcing me to dispose of Dex after he flapped his jaws about our robberies. You'll also pay for putting radical ideas in Samantha's head. My wife didn't give me an ounce of trouble until you showed up and told her that she deserved a better life. She was one of eight kids and I traded her pa some stolen cash for her three years ago. Now, because of *you*, she thinks she isn't beholden to me," Phil muttered resentfully. "I'd like to whip the son of a bitch who let you grow up thinking you were a man's equal."

A lot he knew, Pru mused. Her father hadn't instilled independence and freethinking in her. She'd come to crave it after years of being restrained and held back by Gram. It was the lack of freedom that inspired Pru to crusade for herself and her kindred spirits—

Her thoughts dried up abruptly when Phil brought the horses to a halt. He jerked her into his arms then tossed her roughly on the ground. Pru landed with a thud and a groan.

"This is the dugout that Dex and me used to stash our loot," he said as he dragged her across the ground by her heels. "Don't think somebody will accidentally happen onto you here. This stretch of rocky ravines and dense blackjack trees is known as Rattlesnake Gulch. It ain't fit for homesteads. Nobody comes around here, so don't expect company."

Pru swore silently when she felt Phil pulling on the rope that bound her ankles. He anchored her to some object—she had no idea what—so that it was impossible for her to roll outside the dugout and attempt to flee. Although *how* she might escape when he'd made movement practically impossible, she didn't know. This latest ordeal nearly depleted her unfaltering optimism. She wondered if she'd see the light of day again.

"Damn, look at the time," Phil noted as he exited the dugout. "Gotta get back before that crotchety old bastard who owns the saloon chews on my ass or fires me."

Then he was gone and all Pru heard was eerie silence, broken only by the chirp of crickets and frogs. She was sporting a hellish headache and she was shaky from missing two meals. Plus, she predicted she'd never see Jack again and she'd never have the chance to tell him that she was in love with him and that she'd marry him, if only he'd ask again.

In addition, she'd sent a telegram to her father who would likely hop a train rather than send money as she'd requested. He would wonder what had become of her.

Pru winced when her thoughts turned to Gram. Her grandmother would never forgive her for getting herself killed before she married Edwin Donald and produced an heir. Gram had the next twenty years of Pru's life mapped out. Without Pru to catch the brunt of Gram's criticism, she expected her father would become Gram's new project. Pru stopped feeling sorry for herself long enough to sympathize with her father.

Jack paced back and forth across the hotel lobby then checked the grandfather clock in the corner for the umpteenth time. It was two in the morning and no one had seen anything of Pru. He'd looked up every heckler who'd pestered her outside the newspaper office and he'd reverted to his hard-nosed methods of interrogation to get answers. But every story ended the same. No one had seen Pru after pestering her outside the newspaper office.

"Still no word?" Stony asked as he trudged tiredly into the hotel lobby.

Jack shook his head. "She vanished into thin air."

"Did you ride back to your ranch to see if she's there? Considering the jeers and threats she received, she might have opted for a quiet night at your place."

"Leave without her horse?" Jack countered. "Doubt it. She's in trouble, Stony. I can feel it."

"I've never doubted your instincts," Stony murmured. "But hell, Jack, I don't know where else to look. We'll have trouble raising a search party now that Pru has become so unpopular with the menfolk."

*And so have I*, Jack mused. He predicted that if either he or Pru were drowning, no one would lift a hand to save them. They'd sink like a couple of rocks and no one would care.

When the sound of shattering glass exploded behind him, Jack wheeled and grabbed his pistol in one swift motion. Old habits died hard, he thought as he watched a rock bounce across the floor. A piece of paper was tied to it.

Jack refused to be distracted by the note. He crouched down and scurried toward the broken window, hoping to catch sight of whoever had pitched the rock. To his annoyance, he didn't see anyone and heard nothing but the nicker of horses that were startled by shattering glass.

"Well, son of a bitch," Stony growled as he stormed up behind Jack.

Jack lurched around to take the note his friend thrust at

him. "Five thousand dollars ransom to return the rabble-rouser," he read aloud, then swore a blue streak.

"Damn it, the menfolk who dreamed up this ransom scheme have gone too far," Stony rumbled. "We're going to make national headlines if we don't watch out. That isn't the kind of publicity a new territory needs."

"To hell with unwanted publicity," Jack muttered. "Pru's in danger and this note didn't mention a drop site for the ransom money. Which means we have to wait it out." The thought had him cursing foully again. He was already going crazy wondering what torment she was enduring and the waiting game would only grow worse.

"We'll put together a ransom when the bank opens in the morning…. Oh, hell. Tomorrow is Sunday so we won't hear back from the kidnappers until Monday," Jack scowled.

The prospect of Pru being held captive for two days was guaranteed to drive Jack loco. He felt helpless and frustrated. He'd been a man of action for years. Sitting and waiting felt unnatural. He wasn't sure he could do it.

Sure enough, he couldn't. When he bedded down for the night, he tossed, turned and cursed Pru's mysterious abductor.

Looking as haggard as he felt, Jack propped himself against the outer wall of the marshal's office. It was Sunday evening and the rally for women's rights was gearing up at the town square. Although the whereabouts of the guest speaker were unknown, the women paraded down Main Street, demanding the release of their ringleader and banging on pots and pans.

"I hope this doesn't turn into another riot," Stony grumbled when he saw the congregation of men surging down the street like an incoming tide. "No offense, Jack, but you have to admit life around here was less eventful before Pru showed up. You should have picked a local for your wife."

Jack gnashed his teeth. "When your best friend starts placing the blame at your feet you can guess how the rest of the men in town feel."

"I don't have to guess," Stony remarked. "They've been giving me an earful for weeks."

"So you think we should stand aside and let whoever kidnapped Pru have her and refuse to pay the ransom?" he challenged.

"I didn't say that."

"No, but I expect that's what a lot of men around here are thinking. Good riddance to the rabble-rouser…. Well, hell!" No sooner were the words out of Jack's mouth than the same chant rose up around him.

"Good riddance to the rabble-rouser. We say don't pay!" the mob of men shouted in unison.

Stony glanced helplessly at Jack when the irate women, pots and pans upraised, charged at the men. The fight was on again. Husbands badmouthed wives. Daughters railed disrespectfully at fathers. Mothers chided sons.

The pot-and-pan brigade showed no mercy. The men pushed and shoved to prevent being walloped upside the head. Tempers flared and foul oaths erupted. Then the train pulled into town and Jack could barely hear the shrill whistle and whoosh of steam over the irate shouts in the street.

He noticed Oscar Epperson, the newspaper editor, standing aside. He jotted notes as fast as he could write. He wondered if Oscar might have absconded with Pru, just to keep things astir so he could sell more papers. Better not have or Jack was going to wring the man's skinny neck!

Five minutes later the desk clerk from the hotel scurried down the boardwalk with a rock in his hand. Jack muttered several pithy epithets. With all this commotion, the kidnapper had no trouble coming and going without being noticed.

"This came flying through the broken window," the clerk panted as he extended the stone and the note to Jack.

"Did you see who threw it?" Jack asked anxiously.

The clerk shook his head then shoved his glasses up to the bridge of his nose. "No. It came flying while the men marched down the street toward the marshal's office. I couldn't tell precisely where it came from."

Jack unfolded the note. "The money is to be delivered to Three Mile Corner tomorrow night after dark." He glanced at Stony. "With no guarantee of Pru's release. Damn it!"

His frustration mounted while he watched the men and women battle each other. This town was misnamed, he decided. Paradise had gone to *hell*.

"How long do you think I should let this battle go on?" Stony asked.

"Give it five minutes," Jack suggested. "If they don't give up and go home then we'll break it up."

Jack stared over the crowd to see the passengers step down from the train. His attention settled on a well-dressed gentleman in wire-rimmed spectacles. He lingered on the platform of the train, watching the goings-on. Was he a reporter from back east, come to poke fun at the trouble in Paradise? He wouldn't be the first, Jack reminded himself. According to Stony, two reporters—one from Boston and the other from Philadelphia—had arrived the previous day.

Jack frowned as he watched the newcomer grab his expensive-looking luggage and descend the steps. There was something oddly familiar about the man, but Jack couldn't imagine where they had met. In Kansas a few years ago? In Texas during his heydays as a trail driver?

Pausing at irregular intervals to scan the crowd, the new arrival approached. He zeroed in on the badge pinned on Stony's chest.

"Do you have these brouhahas often?" he asked.

"Not until recently," Stony replied. "Are you another reporter?"

"No, I was hoping you could point me toward adequate accommodations for the evening." He panned the group of women.

"Are you looking for someone in particular?" Jack asked as he offered his hand. "I'm Jack McCavett. And you are?"

"Horatio Perkins. I'm looking for my daughter, Pru."

Jack appraised Horatio and decided the man was far more than the wagon driver Pru claimed he was.

"One of your town's newspapers turned up in Saint Louis with Pru's name as a murder suspect," Horatio continued. "Is she in jail or in the middle of this crazed battle?"

Jack inwardly groaned as Stony cast him an uncomfortable glance. Clearly, Stony wanted Jack to field the questions.

"Her name is Pru. Blond hair. Eyes the same color of blue as mine," he described when Jack said nothing. "She advocates women's rights—yow!"

All three men ducked when a copper pot sailed through the air—missing them by inches—and banged into the wall behind them with a *clang* and a *clunk* before dropping on the boardwalk.

"Your daughter is no longer a murder suspect," Stony hurriedly informed him. "And she isn't in the riot."

"Well, that's a relief," Horatio said with a gusty sigh.

"Excuse us for a minute, Horatio. These good folks have aired their differences of opinion long enough. It's time to put a stop to it." Jack stalked into the street.

It took ten minutes to restore order in Paradise. Jack caught an inadvertent elbow in the chin and one in the hip. Stony fared about the same. However, they managed to clear a path that left the men on one side of the street and the women on the other.

"Stony plans to arrest every man who antagonizes the women during their protest marches," Jack called out loudly. "And I'm going to be here to enforce his orders."

While the men grumbled, the women looked smug and triumphant. Stony returned to Jack's side. "What are you going to tell Pru's father?" he questioned.

"The truth."

"He won't like it."

"Can't say that I do, either," Jack murmured as he mentally prepared himself to break the disturbing news of the kidnapping to Pru's father.

A full day had passed since Pru had been dumped in the dugout in Rattlesnake Gulch. She had concluded that Phil Graham—thief, murderer, wife beater and kidnapper—planned to let her rot away. She only hoped Jack and her sisters-in-suffrage would see that the ruthless bastard paid for his dastardly deeds. She also pitied Samantha who would be shamed and embarrassed—but finally emancipated—if Phil was arrested.

Pru had wormed and squired for hours, trying to get loose. Then she'd collapsed in exhaustion and regenerated her strength before beginning again. She scraped the grimy apron from her face so she could see. Although she'd skinned the hide off both cheeks, she finally managed to force the gag downward. She could see and speak but it wasn't doing her a damn bit of good since she was stuck in the middle of nowhere.

Pru glanced around the dark dugout, unable to see much of anything. The only light source was the moon and it didn't reach into the recesses of the dugout, which was smaller in size than Jack's. She inched across the dirt floor to note that Phil had tied her to a stake driven into the ground. She had no idea what purpose it served originally. To tie horses nearby for a fast getaway after robberies? Most likely.

Hope rose inside Pru when her eyes finally adjusted to the darkness well enough to identify a small wooden cupboard with two glass doors. She scooted across the floor then used her shoulder to nudge the cabinet. Nothing happened. She slumped on the floor to rest then tried again. Still nothing.

Gritting her teeth, Pru forced herself to lie still and rejuvenate her strength. She was hungry and thirsty and she tired easily. *Give yourself time to rest*, she thought while she tried to ignore her growling stomach. It wasn't easy because the gnawing sound echoed in the darkness and came at her from all directions.

*By damned, I refuse to let my life end like this*, she vowed defiantly. *I'll escape…or die trying….*

# Chapter Fourteen

Horatio studied Jack as Jack stepped onto the boardwalk in front of the jail. "My guess is that you've quelled riots before, young man."

"A time or two." Jack gestured toward the hotel. "This way, sir. I'll show you to the best accommodations Paradise has to offer, but I'm sure they are below your standards."

"Were you a policeman somewhere before you came to the territory?" Horatio persisted as he fell into step.

"No, a town marshal in a few rowdy cow towns in Kansas during the height of the cattle drives to railheads. Paradise is tame in comparison," Jack remarked. "Well, except for these recent riots."

"How long do you intend to stall before you tell me where I can find my daughter?" Horatio asked.

Jack glanced sideways to meet Horatio's intense stare. Damn, he really hated to have this conversation. He had hoped to delay it until Horatio had the chance to sit—in case the unsettling news knocked him off his feet.

He gestured toward the bench outside the barbershop,

silently suggesting that Horatio take a seat. But the older man clenched his jaw and refused.

"Your daughter has been kidnapped," Jack told him straight-out. "Either by disgruntled men who resent her leadership in the women's movement or because she was a victim who witnessed a stagecoach robbery. We aren't sure which."

"Kidnapped?" Horatio croaked, his eyes bulging behind his spectacles. "Good God!" His legs wobbled so he plunked down on the bench. "She was robbed on the stagecoach? At gunpoint?"

The horrified look on Horatio's peaked face assured Jack that this man didn't know the real Pru Perkins, the daredevil who was assertive and bold to a fault. No doubt, Horatio's perception of his daughter sharply contrasted the woman Jack had come to know.

"Two men held up the stagecoach Pru arrived in. They stole her bracelet. She…uh…didn't take it well. Seems it was an important keepsake from her mother."

Horatio raked his hands through his thinning hair. "Dear God," he breathed shakily.

"Then someone tried to pin a murder on Pru. She landed in jail. But she's been cleared of the charges," Jack reported.

"That's a relief," Horatio murmured. "I feared I would have to send for my lawyer to defend her."

"She was released into my protective custody because the men opposing the women's movement were stirred up and demanding a lynching."

Horatio slumped back on the bench and swore under his breath. Jack didn't ask him to repeat the mumbled curses. They sounded as foul as the ones Jack had uttered a time—or three.

Jack retrieved the two notes from his pocket and presented them to Horatio. The poor man looked stunned to the bone and equally exhausted.

"I have enough money set aside to pay her ransom," Jack said hurriedly.

Of course, it would take every cent he had and he was afraid his efforts would be in vain. Jack had dealt with several ransom cases in his time. Most of them had turned out badly. The very thought made his skin crawl. Helpless frustration ate him alive.

"I'll pay it," Horatio insisted. "It's not like I don't have the money." He shook his head, bemused. "Pru has access to all the money she wants and all the social connections she needs. She can live like a queen her entire life. She wants for nothing. I've made sure of it. Yet, she chose to go out west to battle the entrenched traditions against women." Baffled, Horatio looked up at Jack. "Where did I go wrong?"

Jack knew Pru hadn't been completely honest with him. From the cut of Horatio's clothes, his polished manners and his comments, he was wealthy to the extreme. He was *not* a common wagon driver, as Pru had him believe.

Pru had turned her back on the wealth and social connections that most women dreamed of having. Pru had wanted freedom to follow her own dreams and to make a difference in the world. Problem was, her life might be the sacrifice she would have to make to have enjoyed a few weeks of independence.

She'd penned newspaper articles and organized rallies to call attention to the unfair conditions women encountered. Unfortunately, she wasn't around to enjoy the fruits of her labor. She was at the mercy of her captor and her life was in jeopardy.

Horatio surged to his feet and stared Jack squarely in the eye. "Her chances of survival aren't good, are they?"

"Depends on who kidnapped her," Jack hedged.

"Right, the disgruntled men or the murderer who set her up. Or perhaps the thief from the stagecoach robbery." He raised a curious brow. "By the way, how did you get mixed up with my daughter?"

Jack shifted self-consciously from one scuffed boot to the other. "I sent off for a mail-order bride and she answered the ad. I chose her from the list of applicants."

Horatio's brows nearly shot off his forehead. "The two of you are married?" he asked in amazement.

"No, she wasn't interested in marriage," Jack explained. "I was the means to an end. Her ticket to freedom."

"So she won the bet," Horatio muttered.

Jack's gaze sharpened. "The bet?"

Horatio bobbed his head as he pivoted around to stride down the boardwalk. "Like a fool, her grandmother and I bet her that she couldn't survive without Perkins money. She took the dare. Two weeks later, she disappeared from town without a trace. I even hired a private detective to track her down, but he turned up nothing.

"I suspect she used a disguise and traveled under an assumed name to leave town. By stage, obviously. My annoying business competitor somehow got his hands on a recent issue of *Paradise Times Star* that named Pru as a murder suspect. If not for Theo Porter waving it in my face, I wouldn't have known where to look for Pru."

Jack was torn between his concern for Pru and his frustration over the news Horatio had imparted. Pru had turned his life completely upside down and destroyed all of his lifelong dreams because of a damn *bet?* Hell's bells! If she survived this latest disaster, Jack wasn't sure what he wanted to do first. Hug the stuffing out of her in relief or strangle her.

Pru struggled to come to her knees. She gritted her teeth and told herself that she wouldn't rest until she managed to tip the cupboard off balance. After several attempts, the cabinet teetered. With a determined heave-ho, she rammed her shoulder into the cabinet and pushed with all her might.

To her relief it crashed to the dirt floor and the brittle glass shattered. Several dishes and cups spilled out. Pru couldn't believe her luck when she noticed a paring knife among the broken glass and cups. Unfortunately, she couldn't reach the knife since her hands were lashed to her sides.

Determined, she stretched forward to dislodge the knife from the other three pieces of silverware with her shoulder. Then she rolled onto her side, hoping to grasp the knife. She stabbed herself with shards of glass but she kept contorting her body until she clenched the knife in her left hand.

Pru blew out her breath, paused a moment to rest, then rolled over. She was so lightheaded from lack of nourishment and overexertion that she almost passed out.

She jerked up her head when she saw a flash of lightning then heard the rumble of thunder. But she didn't care if she had to trudge through a thunderstorm after she cut herself loose. As long as she was gone when Phil Graham returned she would be well satisfied. She wanted to survive this ordeal so she could point an accusing finger at the ruthless bastard.

She maneuvered herself so she could use the knife to saw through the rope on her wrist. She sliced herself a time or two, cursed the pain and kept hacking away at the restraints. Eventually, she severed the rope and freed her hands. Sitting upright, she untied the strands of rope that bound her ankles.

Pru surged to her feet then braced herself against the wall. The room spun furiously around her as she dragged in several panting breaths of stale air. Right there and then she vowed to extract a few more ounces of Phil's flesh for every hardship he'd caused her. And that went double for the torment Samantha had tolerated.

She hoped Sam would be as relieved to see her abusive husband behind bars as Pru would be. The man was a menace to society and to women everywhere. The mere thought of being married to that brute made Pru shudder in disgust.

When another flash of lightning speared into the dugout, Pru noticed a lantern in the corner. She found matches nearby then lit the lantern. Since Phil claimed that he and Dex used this as a hideout she suspected the loot was around somewhere. Sure enough, she found a pouch of watches, rings, necklaces and her heirloom bracelet stashed beneath a stack of firewood.

A devilish smile pursed her lips as she tucked the bracelet in her pocket then walked outside to hide the pouch of jewelry where Phil couldn't find it. If he overtook her, he still wouldn't get his loot back. Served that bastard right, she thought spitefully as she walked off.

An hour later, Pru dropped to her knees beside the stream she encountered during her exodus from the dugout.

She gulped water then splashed some on her face to revive herself. She had no idea where she was and it didn't help that it was the middle of the night. Her travels were limited to Paradise and the two-mile stretch of road leading to Jack's homestead. Or rather to the pile of ashes where his house once stood.

Resolving to find her way back to town before Phil showed up to recapture her, Pru tramped off. Five minutes later, she heard an eerie rattle off to the left. Rattlesnake, she thought as she backed up a step. She didn't need a snakebite right now. She had endured plenty of adversity these past two days, thank you very much.

To her relief the snake, wherever it was, didn't strike. She descended the rocky hillside with more caution than before. In the moonlight, she could see a rutted path that she hoped would lead her to Paradise. She also noted the bank of gray clouds and flicker of lightning that indicated she would be soaked to the bone before she reached town.

The whistle of an approaching train caught her attention and she noticed moonlight glinting off the steel rails before the rolling clouds plunged the countryside into darkness. She remembered the evening train came south to reach Paradise, which meant the town was north of her present location. Which meant Phil's hideout was west of town—and she'd wasted time walking in circles trying to figure out where she was. If she traveled as the crow flew, she'd save valuable time.

Hungry though she was, Pru trudged off, hoping the gulps of water would sustain her. With rain pelting her, she felt as if she'd walked for hours before she spotted the distant street-lights. The prospect of returning to town, unpopular though she was in the county, raised her flagging spirits.

A half hour later, Pru staggered down the abandoned street, headed for the hotel. When she noticed Jack's black gelding tethered at the hitching post she sent a prayer of thanks winging heavenward. She stepped into the hotel lobby and noticed the broken window.

"You're alive!" the sleepy-eyed clerk said when he saw her standing there, dripping all over herself. "How did you—?"

"Wasn't easy," she interrupted. "Where's Jack McCavett?"

"Room number seven."

Pru stared at the mountain of steps and wondered if she had enough strength left to make the climb. She was weak, starved, wobbly and exhausted. She was so close to passing out that it didn't bear thinking about.

She clamped her hand on the banister and pulled herself upward one step at a time. She braced her hand on the wall for support as she moved down the hall. When she tapped lightly on door number seven it opened only wide enough for a pistol barrel to greet her.

"Jack?" she whispered.

"Pru? Thank God!"

And suddenly Jack's arms snaked around her waist and she slumped against his solid strength. "I need to borrow a bed for a few hours—"

Her voice fizzled out when darkness crowded in on her. The sheer will and determination that had brought her to town gave out when she finally reached her destination. Her knees folded up on their own accord and her head rolled against Jack's shoulder as she collapsed in his arms.

"Pru?" Jack uplifted her limp body and wheeled toward the bed. Even though she was covered with mud and smelled like a musty root cellar, she had somehow survived and returned to him. He wanted to shout to high heaven.

Holding her in one arm, he tugged off her filthy clothes before putting her in bed. He made note of the ever-present bump on her head. It seemed she'd had one—or was recovering from one—since the day the thieves tossed her off the horse, causing her to smack her skull against a tree. Although she was scuffed up, she looked beautiful to him. Whoever was responsible for the patches of raw skin on her cheeks and wrists was going to pay dearly, he vowed as he cleaned her injuries with a damp cloth. There were only a few minor wounds from shards of glass, he noticed. He was grateful for that.

For several moments, Jack sat watching her bare chest rise and fall methodically in sleep. He was mightily relieved that she'd managed to escape captivity by her own ingenuity and resourcefulness. He still wanted to choke her for putting him through such emotional turmoil, of course, but at least she was alive and in one piece—more or less.

Jack glanced pensively at the door, wondering if he should stuff Pru into one of the new garments Sam and Roz had given her then alert her father to her arrival. The man couldn't be getting much more sleep than Jack had—which was close to none. *He* had lain in bed, worrying himself crazy for hours. No doubt, Horatio was also suffering from insomnia.

Rising, he found a nightgown among the garments then gently fastened Pru into it. He padded barefoot down the hall to summon Horatio.

"She made it back," Jack murmured when Horatio answered the quiet rap at the door.

"Thank goodness!"

Horatio followed Jack down the hall to see Pru tucked in bed. He muttered in outrage when he got his first close look at Pru's battered face and arms.

"Whoever did this to her will pay dearly," Horatio growled in a vindictive voice.

"You can count on it. I'll personally see to it."

"Did she say who it was? Did she know her kidnapper?"

Jack shrugged a bare shoulder. "She showed up at my door, asked to borrow my bed then collapsed. I checked her for life-threatening injuries but didn't find any. I figured she needed rest more than I needed to interrogate her."

Horatio nodded as he looked Pru up and down. "You're right, of course. First things first." His gaze swung to Jack. "So where are you sleeping now that you've lent her your bed?"

"On the floor right beside her," Jack insisted. "I'm not letting her out of my sight, in case her abductor thinks he can reclaim her." He gestured toward the door. "Go back to bed, Horatio. You've had a long journey and a harrowing evening."

"Thank you." Horatio cast Pru one last glance then turned toward the door. "You will be generously reimbursed for your time and efforts," he assured Jack.

"No need." Jack grabbed the spare quilt and spread it out on the floor.

"Nonetheless, you will be compensated," Horatio declared.

Jack didn't argue. He wanted Horatio gone so he could close the door. Then he gave up the pretentious offer to sleep on the floor. Jack stretched out in bed beside Pru and cuddled her close.

For the first time since he'd discovered Pru missing, Jack breathed easily. Even though his life had been turned upside down and his homestead had been ransacked and burned to the ground, all that mattered was that he had Pru back in his arms and she was safe. He chose not to delve too deeply into why that was so essential to him. Pru was here and he was mightily relieved that she was okay.

He predicted the ordeals Pru had faced would increase her father's determination to take her home. Considering that she was the most controversial personality in town, it was probably for the best.

Of course, Jack was going to miss her like nobody's business, but she still wasn't what he wanted and needed to complement the new life he'd made for himself. Not that it mattered, he mused as he tucked Pru's cheek against his chest and rested his chin on the crown of her silver-blond head. She hadn't wanted to marry him in the first place. But for tonight she was in his arms and his world felt right again.

Pru came slowly awake. Her stomach growled something fierce, objecting to the fact that it had been days rather than hours since she'd eaten. She smiled when she felt the warm protective strength beside her. Being with Jack made everything right.

She accepted the drink of water pressed to her lips then pried open one eye when Jack insisted that she bite into a fluffy biscuit.

"Ah, that tastes wonderful," she said appreciatively.

"Who did this to you?" Jack asked without preamble.

Pru appraised the fierce expression etched on Jack's stubbled face. He clenched his jaw. His thick brows were bunched over his narrowed golden eyes. He looked every bit the predator, the avenging angel of injustice—

Her thoughts broke off when the door opened unexpectedly. Pru nearly choked on the biscuit when she saw her father. His alarmed gaze leaped back and forth between her and Jack.

"Well, hell," Jack muttered as he swung his long legs over the edge of the bed to sit up.

Clearly, her father disapproved of the casual intimacy they shared while Jack fed her breakfast. And how did her father get here so quickly anyway? He must have dropped what he was doing the instant he received her telegram to board a train bound for Oklahoma Territory.

"I thought Jack said you two didn't get married," Horatio muttered suspiciously.

"We didn't." Pru propped herself up on her elbow to rake her tangled hair away from her skinned face. "I decided I wasn't good enough for him."

"Not good enough?" Horatio harrumphed. "You have a blue-blood pedigree as long as your leg and you know it!"

Pru darted Jack a discreet glance and noted that he was staring accusingly at her. Apparently, he and her father had shared enough information for Jack to know that Horatio wasn't your everyday, average wagon driver.

"Out here on the frontier, pedigrees aren't worth much," she said dismissively. "Hard work and know-how count most."

Jack braced his hands on either side of her hips, even though Horatio had made it clear that he disliked the familiarity between them. "Who did this to you?" he persisted.

"If you think I'm going to tell you so you can ride off

alone to avenge me then you better think again. *I'm* the one who got hurt and scared spitless and *I* demand vindication."

Horatio waved both arms in expansive gestures to gain attention. "You aren't going anywhere but home, Pru. Apprehending criminals is a job for the marshal and this former marshal. Now what happened? Start at the beginning and don't leave out the details."

"Yeah, let's hear it." Jack sank down on the edge of the bed and stared intently at her. "You walked out of the marshal's office Saturday evening. Your horse was tied in front of the hotel and you never showed up."

Pru took a sip of the coffee Jack had brought up from the restaurant with the plate of biscuits and jelly. "I decided to swing by Wild Horse Saloon to question the new janitor."

"Saloon?" Her father bleated. "For God's sake, Pru!"

She waved him off. "I went to the back exit where the murder took place. I suppose Jack told you that I was a suspect because Dexter Hanes and I clashed a few weeks ago."

"I wasn't thoroughly briefed, but you can skip over that and get to the part about this kidnapping," he said with an impatient flick of his wrist.

"I met Phil Graham, who is the new employee."

"Samantha's husband?" Jack's brows shot up in surprise.

"One and the same. He's burly, abusive and rude," Pru muttered. "He wasn't the least bit cooperative about answering my questions. His voice and physical appearance kept niggling me. I didn't think I had met him before, although something about him seemed familiar." She stared grimly at Jack. "It suddenly struck me that his voice was the same as one of the stagecoach robbers. The one who backhanded me and knocked me into the tree."

Jack swore foully. He was going to take great pleasure in dishing out the same physical abuse that had become Phil Graham's forte. But he also wanted to hear the details before he went looking for that devious bastard.

"When I realized who he was, I tried to run, but Phil pounced." She took another sip of coffee then continued. "He bound and gagged me and knocked me unconscious. When I woke up I was in the alley, buried under the garbage." Her attention shifted to Jack. "I heard you calling to me that night, but I couldn't move or speak or alert you to my whereabouts."

Jack swallowed several pithy oaths. If he'd gone looking for Pru sooner he might have spared her the pain and suffering. He stared into her battered face and blamed himself for every cut, bruise and scrape.

"Later, Phil dragged me from the trash and tossed me over the back of a horse. He stashed me in a dugout in a rocky ravine that he referred to as Rattlesnake Gulch."

Jack nodded in recognition. "According to the Indian tribe that owned this land, evil spirits inhabit that area."

"Phil Graham, for one," she added bitterly.

"The legends say that bad omens—owls, snakes and haunting spirits—congregate there. Not a good place to be."

"Sure enough, it wasn't," Pru confirmed. "I'm thankful I escaped the rope restraints before Phil returned from his shift at work last night. He planned to hold me for ransom."

"I received a note demanding five thousand dollars," Jack informed her. "Since the bank was closed Sunday I was instructed to make the drop this evening."

Her eyes widened. "You were going to pay to get me back? You know I probably wouldn't have survived, don't you? Haven't I caused enough trouble and cost you enough money without wasting any more of it—?"

"*Wasting* it?" Horatio interrupted, outraged. "We are talking about your *life*, Pru."

"Didn't Jack tell you how much it has already cost him, just to associate with me?" she asked. "No? I didn't think so. For starters, I dragged him into one riot after another and unintentionally ruined his upstanding reputation in town. As retaliation against *me*, a mob of disgruntled men tore down the framework to the barn Jack is building."

Horatio studied Jack consideringly. Jack had no idea what the man was thinking.

"After I was jailed on murder charges, Jack came to my rescue. Shortly thereafter, his home and his worldly possessions went up in flames. Again, thanks to Graham's prompts."

Horatio's eyes widened as he fixed his undivided attention on Jack again. "I'm sorry for your losses."

"I traveled light for years," Jack said with a lackadaisical shrug. "I don't have many worldly possessions. Besides, it was just a house, a roof over my head."

"Just a house?" Pru sniffed in contradiction as she sat up a little straighter then shook her tangled blond head. "It was your first real home on your very own homestead after being raised in an orphanage. It was your life's dream so don't minimize its importance to you. I've unintentionally taken everything from you and left you with nothing. That includes your honorable reputation, your home, your livestock and barn. And I'm indebted to you because you loaned me money so I could survive."

"Good gad, Pru. You make it sound as if you've become the curse of the man's life," said Horatio.

"I have," she didn't hesitate to say.

"That isn't true," Jack tried to deny but she waved him off.

"It is true and you know it," she insisted. "You were doing fine until I showed up in Paradise."

Jack shrugged dismissively. "Never mind about all that. Go on. What happened next?"

"Phil dumped me in the dugout that he and Dex used to stash their loot. He left me without food and water for two days. I expect he planned to leave me to die after he collected the ransom." She paused to take another bite of the biscuit she'd smeared with an extra spoonful of jelly. "I was so weak from hunger that I had difficulty getting free from the stake where he tied me."

"He tied you up like a dog?" Horatio howled, horrified.

Jack made a mental note to give that bastard a taste of his own medicine when he caught him.

Pru nodded then gestured to her scraped face. "Once I rubbed off the blindfold and gag I noticed a small cupboard. I managed to contort my body so I could overturn it. I planned to sever the ropes with the broken glass from the doors—"

"My God!" Horatio cried in dismay.

"But I found a paring knife in the rubble and cut myself loose," she continued. "I found the loot from the robberies and I hid it outside so Phil couldn't retrieve it."

She gestured for Jack to hand her the pair of soiled breeches that he'd draped over the chair. Smiling triumphantly, she fished out her valuable bracelet, which was embedded with enough diamonds to choke a horse. When she held it up for his inspection, he calculated the damn thing was worth a fortune. No wonder she'd been so determined not to let the bandits steal her bracelet.

"Then I walked to town during the storm," she finished.

While Horatio muttered in outrage, Jack stared at Pru with renewed respect and admiration. He predicted most women would have accepted their bleak fate and succumbed to tears rather than taking the initiative and battling for freedom. Pru might look like a dainty angel, but she was tough and determined and absolutely amazing.

"Graham underestimated you when he didn't return to the dugout to make sure you were still in captivity," Jack commented. "He'll pay for that mistake and for the pain he caused you."

"I want revenge," Pru insisted, "but I know his wife, Samantha, will suffer humiliation and regret." She shot Jack another apologetic glance. "Like you did when you caught flak because of your association with me. I don't want Sam to be ostracized because she's married to Phil."

"You said Phil abused Sam," Jack reminded her. "She might jump for joy if she has the brute out of the house and out of her life."

"Or she might hold me responsible for turning her life upside down," she speculated. "I don't want to lose her friendship or cause an emotional setback. She's gained self-confidence and I don't want her to feel ashamed."

"Whatever else happens, Phil Graham will be prosecuted," Jack insisted. "He murdered his own partner and would have disposed of you if you hadn't escaped. So don't turn into a bleeding heart, Pru. The man owes a debt to society and his wife will be much better off without the abusive bastard, even if she has to suffer some embarrassment and regret."

When Jack wheeled toward the door, Pru sat up abruptly on the edge of the bed. "I'm coming with you—"

Her voice wobbled—and so did her legs—when she stood too quickly. Jack grabbed her arm before she crashlanded at her father's feet. Clearly, she wasn't ready for vigorous activity.

"There's the answer to whether you're fit to join a posse," he said as he stuffed her back in bed. "And stay there." He glanced over at Horatio. "I'm placing you in charge to make sure she doesn't get up until she's recovered."

Jack handed a pistol to Horatio, who gaped at him in astonishment. "I'm going to fetch Stony so he can take Pru's statement and bring charges against Graham. If she tries to follow me, shoot her."

Horatio's blue eyes popped then he chuckled when he noticed Jack's teasing grin. "After she finishes her breakfast I'll blast her for scaring ten years off my life."

"You're not the only one who's aged a decade in a couple of days," Jack said as he headed for the door.

"By the way," Horatio called, "you and I are going to have a private chat after we get this matter squared away."

"About what?" Pru wanted to know.

"Just hush up and eat," Horatio ordered. "That's between Jack and me."

Jack inwardly cringed as he exited the room. A private chat? That sounded ominous. He suspected Horatio planned to rake him over live coals for being so familiar with Pru while she was sprawled in his bed.

Ah well, if he had to listen to Horatio's livid tirade then

so be it. Horatio hadn't threatened to make him the guest of honor at a private *shooting*. A private *chat* had to be better than a shooting, he thought as he hurried to Stony's office. Besides, Jack knew he had it coming. Just like the lecture Jack planned to give Pru for misinforming him about her background.

# Chapter Fifteen

Phil Graham ducked into the dugout then swore furiously when he saw the overturned cupboard and the severed ropes. "How the hell did she get loose?" he asked himself.

When broken glass crunched beneath his boots, he figured she'd used it to cut herself loose. "Damn it to hell!" he muttered as he dashed outside. He hoped she didn't have much of a head start. But the rabble-rouser was nowhere to be seen.

"She's screwed up everything," Phil growled bitterly.

The ransom wouldn't be delivered until the following night and that bitch would likely alert Jack McCavett and Stony Mason. The thought made Phil cringe. He didn't need a marshal and ex-lawman breathing down his neck.

Lurching around, Phil scurried back inside the dugout to retrieve the loot he'd collected from the last three robberies. With all the goings-on lately, he hadn't taken time to ride to neighboring towns to pawn the jewels for cash.

He roared in outrage when he realized the leather pouch he'd tucked beneath the firewood was gone. Damn that woman! She had ruined his life and corrupted his wife's thinking. Now she'd stolen his loot and was pointing an accusing finger at him. He had to get out of here—fast. And Samantha was going to pack up and go with him, he vowed as he stormed outside to retrieve his horse. Samantha had provided the perfect front while he worked at the livery stable and organized the robberies. He'd need her to provide him with a respectable reputation in a new town.

Phil bounded onto his horse just as dawn filtered across the sky. He didn't have much time to pack up, repay that Perkins bitch for the trouble she'd caused, then clear out.

Pru focused her attention on her plate rather than on her father. Now that Jack had left the room she expected him to launch into a scathing lecture. Thankfully, he watched her eat for ten minutes without scolding her. Then he set aside the pistol Jack gave him and she thought *here it comes*.

"Pru, I'd like to shake you until your teeth fall out," he said for starters. "But Jack seems very protective of you so he'd probably pummel me if I dared."

She smiled wryly. "I doubt it. He put a pistol in your hand, didn't he?"

"To protect you, I suspect, despite what he said to the contrary," her father replied.

"If you're girding up to scold me then save your breath." Pru set aside the empty tray. "I wanted an adventure and I got more than I bargained for."

"I'll say you did," her father snorted.

She looked her father straight in the eye. "I will agree to go home with you and live the life you and Gram expect of me…on one condition."

Horatio steepled his fingers and regarded her for a pensive moment. "What's the one condition?"

"I want to see Jack McCavett fully compensated for the calamity I brought down around him. I was so determined to have my independence and freedom, and to escape your and Gram's expectations, that I took advantage of a good, honest, hardworking man. Jack has sacrificed years of his life and faced constant peril to keep law and order. Now he wants to lead a quiet, unassuming life. I've brought him havoc and ridicule because of my crusade."

*Plus, I'm so in love with him that I will do anything, even sacrifice my own independence, to restore his life*, she added silently.

"I want his home rebuilt to three times its original size. The same for the barn and outbuildings. His livestock scattered to kingdom come and I want it replaced…and the size of the herds increased," she negotiated. "I want to ensure that Jack receives the grand prize for tolerating all the misery he had to endure because of me."

Horatio nodded thoughtfully. "Essentially, you want to make his life three times better than it was before you arrived. Why, Pru?"

She stared somberly at her father. "Because he *deserves* it. Because I *owe* him for his trouble and for assistance."

"And if I fulfill Jack's dreams then you will agree to marry Edwin and provide an heir for the Perkins family?"

Pru inwardly grimaced as her father's probing gaze zeroed in on her. The prospect of joining Edwin in bed was not a pleasant thought. Sure as the world, she'd close her eyes and see Jack in her mind's eye. She would lie there wishing it were Jack who shared her life. She figured she'd have to fantasize about Jack to tolerate the touch of another man. But that was the price she had to pay to ensure Jack's reversal of fortune.

"I will do whatever it takes to make Jack's life satisfying and prosperous," she vowed determinedly. "Plus I want you to forget having a *private chat* with Jack. Most especially if it is to lecture him about this fiasco. None of this was his fault so don't blame him. Do I make myself clear?"

"Perfectly clear. I'll make the necessary arrangements to restore Jack's homestead before I leave town." Horatio rose to his feet. "I'll order a bath for you while I have my breakfast downstairs. I assume you have more suitable clothing than those ripped trousers and shirt to wear?"

In other words, dress like the lady you are supposed to be, she interpreted. "Yes, Papa. I'll meet you later for lunch. I'll bathe and rest and—"

He flung up his hand and frowned in disapproval. "You will not track down your kidnapper after you rest, if that's what you're planning. I don't care what you told Jack. You are not going anywhere near that dreadful scoundrel. You can poke a stick at him once Jack has him behind bars. But you will not be in on the chase and capture. That is one of *my* stipulations, if Jack is to be rewarded for his trouble."

Pru pulled a face, knowing that she'd given her father bargaining power by pleading with him to leave Jack better off than he'd been before she showed up.

"Well? Do we have a deal?" he prodded.

"Yes," she said begrudgingly. "But I want a stick with a very sharp point on it for prodding and gouging Phil Graham."

Horatio grinned before he turned to leave. "I'll see what I can do about that, too."

* * *

Jack burst into Stony's office, only to find him gone. With a growing sense of urgency, he lurched around and headed over to Harper's Café where his friend routinely ate breakfast. He found Stony in the middle of a stack of pancakes as tall as his fist. As Jack recalled, Stony had loved them since childhood. But today he would have to forgo them because they had a killer to catch.

Stony glanced up when Jack approached. "Any news?"

"Plenty." Jack hitched his thumb toward the door. "We need to go now."

Stony took one last bite of pancakes, grabbed his hat and surged to his feet.

The instant they were out of earshot Jack said, "Pru managed to escape and walked to town during last night's downpour."

"Thank God," Stony murmured. "Is she okay?"

"More or less," Jack reported. "Phil Graham kidnapped her and he's the one who killed his partner, Dex. He admitted to Pru that he instigated the raids on my home-stead, hoping to get me to distance myself from her so he could get hold of her."

In between Stony's scowls and muttered profanity, Jack related the incident leading up to Pru's captivity and her escape.

"I presume you want to be on hand when I arrest Phil," Stony said as he strode past his office.

"Damn right I do. Since he works the evening shift at Wild Horse Saloon, I figure he's at home, pretending he isn't involved in this fiasco."

"You're deputized," Stony said with a flick of his wrist.

Then he chuckled. "It seems strange to be saying that to you after I was your deputy for so many years."

Jack wasn't in the mood to revisit old times. He was focused intently on arresting Phil Graham and seeing that he was charged for his various and sundry crimes.

Five minutes later Jack and Stony walked through the residential area and reached the Grahams' modest-size home. There was no white picket fence like the neighboring houses, but the place was neat and tidy. Due to Samantha's industrious efforts, no doubt.

Jack knocked on the door and waited impatiently. Then he knocked again. When the door finally opened, Jack and Stony cursed in unison. It was evident that Samantha Graham had endured a recent beating. Her face was swollen and discolored and her lip was split. Tears streamed down her puffy cheeks.

"Are you all right?" Jack and Stony asked simultaneously.

Samantha drew a shuddering breath and nodded as she pulled her robe tightly around her.

Jack noticed the fresh circular burn on her forearm and he swore mightily. Phil had burned his wife's arm with the hot tip of a cigar. That brutal bastard!

"Where is he?" Jack demanded with a hiss.

"He told me this morning that we were moving away and I should get packed," she said shakily. "I told him he could go without me because I had no intention of leaving Paradise."

"So he hit you a few times to convince you to go," Stony presumed. His voice was so cold and harsh that Jack glanced sharply at him.

"It made him furious when I stood up to him and told him that I was making half the salary in our household and that I had a say." She stared solemnly at Jack and Stony. "Pru gave me the courage to make my wishes known instead of bowing to him. It was worth the abuse not to let him frighten and intimidate me the way he's always done."

"Phil kidnapped Pru," Jack reported grimly.

Samantha sagged against the doorjamb. "Oh God, no!"

"Afraid so," Stony murmured. "You should also know that your husband set up Pru to take the blame for killing his accomplice who helped him rob the stage line."

"Sweet mercy!" Samantha bleated as she grabbed the edge of the door for support. "It's bad enough that Phil vented his anger on me, but not Pru, too!"

"You didn't deserve it, either," Stony told her quickly. "No woman does. I want you to stay with Rozalie until we locate Phil. He might double back here and I don't want to see you hurt again."

Jack lurched around. His sixth sense was jumping alive, not knowing where Phil was. "You can bring Samantha while I check on Pru."

"I'll meet you at the hotel in a few minutes," Stony called after him. But Jack was jogging down the street, tormented by the unshakable feeling that something bad was about to happen—if it hadn't happened already.

Pru rose from the tub, feeling rested and refreshed. One glance in the mirror assured her that she still looked the worse for wear. Thankfully, a good night's sleep, a hearty meal and a bath had put her on the road to recovery. Unfortunately, selling her freedom in exchange for Jack's soon-to-be prosperity depressed her.

"At least you enjoyed a month of independence," she

consoled herself as she fastened the calico dress Roz and Sam had given her.

She smiled ruefully as she brushed her hand over the soft fabric, noticing the excellent needlework. Samantha was a fine seamstress. Would she remain in Paradise once Phil was arrested? Or, like Pru, would she end up somewhere else to begin the next phase of her life?

"At least Sam has a choice for the first time in her life," Pru murmured as she slipped on her shoes. "I'm glad one of us does."

Her thoughts trailed off when she heard the faint tap on the door. Expecting her father or Jack, she unbolted the lock. Pru yelped in surprise when the door shot open so forcefully that it smacked her in the forehead and knocked her off balance. Before she could upright herself and lunge toward the pistol lying on the nightstand, Phil Graham grabbed her by the hair, jammed his pistol into her throat and shut the door.

"Thought you could outsmart me, did you?" he snarled.

Pru wanted to tell him that it didn't take a genius to outsmart an imbecile like him, but he'd clamped his fingers so deeply into her windpipe that she couldn't speak.

"Now where'd you stash my loot?" he demanded, giving her a hard shake.

Pru moved her lips, showing him that she couldn't reply.

"Doesn't matter. You're gonna show me in person anyway. Now where's Lover Boy McCavett? I need him to fetch the ransom money he owes me—"

His voice dried up and he tensed when another knock sounded at the door. "Tell whoever it is to come in," Phil breathed down her neck and loosened the grasp on her throat.

When she defied his command, he yanked on her hair and jerked her head back so roughly that she yelped in pain.

"Pru, I'm coming in."

Pru inwardly cursed her father's poor timing. He obviously hadn't trusted her to stay put and had come to check on her. Her father stopped in his tracks when he saw the pistol barrel rammed in her throat and her head tilted at an awkward angle.

"Who the hell are you?" Phil demanded.

"An old friend of Jack's," Pru squeaked before her father could give himself away. "His name is Horatio."

"A friend of Jack's, are you?" Phil grinned devilishly. "Good. Find Jack. Tell him that this bitch is gonna drown in a pool of her own blood if he doesn't hand over the ransom money in fifteen minutes. No, make it ten," he decided abruptly. "I'm not giving that bastard time to double-cross me."

Pru could see the fear and concern in her father's expression and she inwardly cringed when he said, "Take me as your hostage instead of her."

The fact that her father was prepared to risk his life to save her tugged at her heartstrings. For years, she'd wondered if he even cared about her happiness since he'd left most of her raising to Gram. But when things became difficult, Horatio Perkins had come through for her.

"You think I'm crazy?" Phil snorted sarcastically. "She's a lot easier to manhandle than you'd be. Besides, she ruined my life and turned my wife against me. She deserves to suffer for it." He canted his head toward the door. "Now skedaddle, Horatio. Leave the door open behind you—I want to see who's coming and going. Don't come back without the money…or else."

"Then you will release her," Horatio said. It wasn't a statement; it was a demand.

"Don't get pushy with me, old man," Phil snapped. "I'm making the rules around here. I want the money placed in the open doorway. *By you.* Then I want the hall and lobby cleared. I also want a covered buggy so I'm not exposed to an ambush. I want a spare horse tied behind it. If anyone even looks like he's gonna try something, I'll shoot her. If anyone follows us while we're riding out of town, I'll shoot her. You understand me? No matter what, she'll get shot if you disobey."

Her father nodded, then glared murderously at Phil. He wheeled around and scurried away, leaving the door slightly ajar.

"You wanna be a martyr for your stupid cause?" Phil backed across the room. "Here's your big chance. Rah, rah for women's rights," he mocked caustically. "Hell, women aren't smart enough to have any rights. They count for nothing. Especially you. Too bad you didn't have anyone around to remind you of that daily. And if you don't think you're gonna pay for turning Samantha against me, then think again."

"I hardly think it's fair to blame me because you're a liar, thief and murderer," she muttered as he positioned the chair in the corner to provide himself with a clear view of the door and the window.

"Shut up," Phil growled as he plopped down on the chair and yanked her onto his lap so she'd be his shield of armor. "I can still drag you out of here with me, shot and bleeding. So keep your trap shut unless you're asked to speak."

Pru silently fumed. She hated that she didn't have the

strength to counter Phil's domineering physical force. He kept such a fierce hold on her hair that she couldn't move her head. The pistol practically dug a tunnel into her neck, making it difficult to swallow. She had to bide her time and hope Phil would let his guard down for a split second, giving her a sporting chance.

Jack knew something was dreadfully wrong when he saw Horatio Perkins scuttling toward him with a bulging pouch clutched in his fist.

"Thank God!" Horatio huffed and puffed. "Our ten minutes is almost up. I couldn't find you and—"

Jack clamped his hand on Horatio's shoulder, giving it a reassuring squeeze. "Calm down and tell me what's wrong."

"That beast showed up in Pru's room and he's holding her hostage again," Horatio erupted like a geyser.

Jack's heart skipped a beat and hung in his chest like a rock. He dragged in a strained breath as he glanced up at the hotel window, calculating his chances of bursting in from an alternate route.

"Phil demanded the ransom money in ten minutes so you wouldn't have time to come up with a counterattack," Horatio said as he pivoted toward the hotel. "I tried to exchange places with Pru but he refused. He wants a covered buggy and spare horse waiting for him. If we try to follow he'll shoot her."

Jack spewed several crude curses to Phil's name. "I'll take care of everything. How much time do we have left?"

Horatio swallowed hard as he looked at his timepiece. "Four minutes."

"Hell!" Jack took off for the livery stable at a dead run.

When he saw the proprietor, he explained the dire circumstances while he grabbed the first horse he could get his hands on then hitched up a buggy.

"Phil Graham is responsible?" the proprietor croaked as he helped to hitch the horse to the buggy. "I knew he was lazy when he used to work for me before he took the job at the saloon, but I never dreamed he was using our contract to furnish horses for the stage company to learn the schedule. He robbed my client? Damn him!"

Jack remembered the night he'd escorted Pru from jail then rented horses. He'd had the uneasy feeling someone was watching them. Obviously, Phil had been lurking in the shadows. "He also incited the other men in town to join forces against Pru," Jack said hurriedly. "He burned down my house and committed murder to protect his secret identity."

Jack raced the buggy from the stable and skidded to a halt beside Horatio, who was wearing a rut in the boardwalk. The livery-stable owner barked orders to clear the street in case gunfire broke out. People scattered like a covey of quail.

Stony, looking baffled, arrived on the scene with only a minute to spare. "What the hell's going on now?"

"You tell him, Jack. I'm supposed to deliver the money and clear the lobby and hall." Horatio dashed off to beat the ticking clock.

"Phil Graham went directly from battering his wife to recapturing Pru for ransom," Jack explained.

"Well, damn it," Stony grumbled then gestured toward the spare horse and buggy. "He's demanding free passage out of town with Pru as insurance against getting shot, right?"

Jack nodded sharply, feeling his anger and frustration

mounting with each passing second. He hated feeling helpless. Hated that Pru had escaped one horrifying ordeal, only to be plunged headlong into another.

He jerked up his head abruptly when a thought occurred to him. "I'll wager Phil is furious because Pru hid the stash of stolen jewelry. I don't know exactly where she hid it, but she described Rattlesnake Gulch as the place he held her captive. I plan to be there when he arrives."

"You better still be here when he leaves. Otherwise he'll get suspicious," Stony predicted.

"I need a rifle with a scope," Jack said to no one in particular.

"I'll see that you have it," said the mayor—and owner of the dry-goods store—who poked his head from the doorway. "It's my way of apologizing for thinking the worst about Pru."

Tom Jenkins darted down the boardwalk, lickety-split, then veered into the gunsmith's shop. A few moments later, he returned with a rifle in hand. Jack retrieved his horse from in front of the hotel and tied the rifle in place.

Then he waited for Phil to appear—and cursed the son of a bitch to hell and back with each bated breath.


Pru tensed when she saw her father place the pouch inside the partially opened door.

"Now go away," Phil ordered rudely. "Get everyone out of here. If I see anyone, I'll shoot her. Make sure Jack knows that no matter what else happens, this rabble-rouser will be the first to die. You got that, Horatio?"

Her father nodded bleakly as he backed away.

"Now get up nice and easy," Phil hissed in Pru's ear.

"You put up a fuss and I'll shoot you in the foot. And then in the other foot if you fail to cooperate."

Pru hated being intimidated, hated this bully for having an advantage over her and for controlling everyone else in town so he could escape. She figured Jack was going to hold himself personally accountable if things turned out badly for her. She suspected that he already blamed himself for allowing her to be recaptured. No doubt, he blamed himself for every case-gone-bad during his years in law enforcement. He was too responsible and conscientious not to feel that way.

Her thoughts trailed off when Phil gave her hair another hard yank to get her moving. He had twisted the long strands around his wrist—a technique she suspected that he'd used on his wife too many times.

"Now crouch down and pick up the money pouch," he demanded. "Open it so I can see that the money is there."

Begrudgingly Pru did as she was told. For a half second she considered bolting to her feet, in hopes of ramming the top of her head into his chin. But he kept such a fierce grip on her hair that she was powerless to attack him. God, how she hated him. Given half a chance, she'd scratch the man's eyes out for the humiliation and pain he'd caused her and Samantha.

"Hanging will be too quick and easy for you," she sneered at him. "I want to see you tortured within an inch of your life before you're boiled in oil then strung up to dry."

"You ain't seeing nothing, bitch," he jeered as he looked over her shoulder to double-check for the money crammed in the leather pouch. "I'll be long gone, headed for parts unknown. You'll be a buzzard's meal. You can't win against me. You're a useless, helpless female. You're not supposed to be doing any thinking or speaking, either. Remember?"

Pru gritted her teeth, knowing Phil was resorting to the demeaning tactics that he'd perfected on Samantha. He tried to humiliate and belittle her, but all it did was make Pru furious. She couldn't recall despising anyone as much as she despised this ruffian.

Although Pru set her feet Phil uprooted her and frog-marched her down the hall to the staircase. Sure enough, Horatio had evacuated the lobby. The place was deathly quiet.

The uncomfortable angle of her head, thanks to Phil's painful grasp, made it difficult to see where to step. Pru tripped on the hem of her gown and listened to Phil spew foul curses at her while he jerked her upright.

"Clumsy bitch," he ridiculed. "Can't you do anything right?"

Pru wondered how many times Samantha had been subjected to hurtful comments. Probably more than she cared to count.

He paused three steps from the bottom of the staircase. He craned his neck around the corner to make sure no one was lying in wait beside the interior entrance to Miller Restaurant. The door had been shut tightly.

"Hurry up," Phil demanded as he bustled Pru across the lobby to reach the exit.

Pru noticed Jack's squinty-eyed stare the instant Phil stepped onto the boardwalk. His stubbled jaw was clenched and there was murder in his eyes. When his attention shifted to her, she could read the apology in his glance. She'd known he was the kind of man who would hold himself accountable for this unexpected abduction.

"It's not your fault," she felt compelled to tell him.

His expression became grimmer, if that were possible.

"Sure it's your fault," Phil taunted as he inched carefully toward the waiting buggy. "It's your fault she's here and your fault she got the women in town all riled up. You should've stood guard at her hotel room door so I'd have had the pleasure of burying a knife in your back before kidnapping her."

Pru noticed the shocked expressions on the faces of the men and women who were peering through the windows of the businesses across the street. She knew she looked awful with her black eye, bruised chin and skinned cheeks. Plus, Phil was about to pull out her hair by the roots with one hand and he kept a pistol crammed against her neck with the other.

Despite the bitterness and animosity she'd acquired because of her crusade, the locals were now offering a smidgen of sympathy. Clearly, no one expected her to survive this ordeal.

Optimistic though she usually tried to be, she had serious doubts about surviving. She glanced at Jack, memorizing his powerful physique, the sensuous shape of his lips, the golden glow in his eyes and each bronzed, angular feature of his face.

Just in case this was the last time she saw him….

## Chapter Sixteen

The train whistle pierced the morning air as Jack watched Phil clench his elbow around Pru's throat and drag her to the buggy. The sound of the approaching train barely registered—all of Jack's thoughts and emotions centered on Pru and her ruthless captor. Murderous rage boiled inside him as he stood helplessly watching the bastard drag her upward by the hair of her head, making her yelp in pain.

Despite what Pru had said, it *was* his fault that Phil had managed to sneak into the hotel. Jack was supposed to protect her and he had failed. Again.

When Phil clamped his arm diagonally across Pru's chest, using her as his shield and forcing her to take the reins to drive off, everything inside Jack rebelled. Icy dread twisted in his gut. The pessimistic voice in his head kept whispering that he'd never see her alive again. He battled that bleak thought, but he couldn't defeat it completely.

His attention shifted momentarily to Horatio, whose face was the color of salt. Jack sympathized with the man. No doubt, it was killing him, inch by inch, to see his daughter riding off to an unknown fate. This was certainly Jack's worst nightmare.

The clatter of the departing horses and buggy filled the silence like a death knell. Then the train whistle split the air again and steam billowed upward as the locomotive ground to a halt at the depot. As the buggy careened around the corner, a shrill voice erupted from out of nowhere.

"Prudence Elizabeth Perkins, come back here this instant!"

"Holy hell!" Horatio chirped in astonishment.

Jack glanced back at Horatio. The whites of his blue eyes were like boiled eggs. Jack focused on the train platform where an elderly woman, dressed from head to toe in black, carrying a lacquered cane, stepped up beside the conductor. She shook her cane in the air and spat threats as the buggy rolled out of sight.

"Gram?" Jack presumed. "What the devil is she doing here?"

Horatio shrugged, bewildered. "Damn if I know. I didn't tell her where I was going or what I was doing when I left Saint Louis."

Jack bounded into the saddle and reined his black gelding in the opposite direction of the buggy. "I'm taking the shortcut to reach Rattlesnake Gulch." He glanced down at Stony. "Block the west side of the gulch in case Phil gets past me."

Stony nodded then sprinted off to fetch his horse.

Horatio grabbed Jack's leg before he could gallop away. "If you bring Pru back to me I'll give you a generous reward."

Jack didn't hang around to reject the offer. He nudged his horse in the flanks and thundered off. Frantic urgency pounded through him. He wanted to be lying in wait when

Phil showed up. If not, that murdering bastard might have the advantage again.

Don't let that happen, Jack chanted as he raced off, demanding all the horse had to give.

Gram was in Paradise? Pru thought bewilderedly as she drove the buggy down the path. Why had her father told Gram where she was? That's all Pru needed on top of everything else. Gram would give Pru an earful when she returned....

*Rather presumptuous, aren't you?* Pru asked herself. There was a very real possibility that she wouldn't survive the day. It would upset Gram if she weren't allowed to spout the lecture she was probably rehearsing at this very moment.

"Speed up." Phil craned his neck around the leather hood to check for the appearance of a posse behind him. "So far so good. Now veer off the road."

When Pru didn't do as he demanded immediately, he gave another hard yank on her hair. Pru gritted her teeth and vowed to defy him, even if he pulled out every hair on her head.

"Damn you, you contrary bitch!" Phil snarled then let go of her hair long enough to backhand her.

Pain exploded through Pru's injured cheek and jaw. Her eyes watered to such extremes that she could barely see. But she took advantage of the fact that he'd let go momentarily. She launched herself from the buggy but he leaped on her. Before she could buck him off and scramble to her feet, he shoved her face in the grass and wrenched her arm up her back. She shrieked in agony then cursed him soundly.

"You're the most troublesome she-male I ever met," he growled in her ear.

"Thank you," she mumbled into the grass.

To her dismay, Phil had thought far enough ahead to bring a few more strands of rope. He tied her hands behind her back then jerked her to her feet to cram the pistol into her neck again. Then he tossed her onto the horse and secured her hands and feet so she couldn't leap off.

Frustrated, she strained against the ropes while he bounded into the buggy to lead the way to Rattlesnake Gulch. When they reached the rocky terrain, he left the buggy and climbed on behind her to guide the horse around the perpendicular slabs of stone that led toward the dugout.

When Phil rounded the corner to the dugout and spewed foul oaths, Pru glanced up to see what had upset him. To her astonishment, Jack was leaning casually against a tree. He trained his pistol on Phil's shoulder. Naturally, he shifted and hunkered down in his attempt to hide behind her skirts—literally.

How Jack had managed to beat them to the dugout— and figured out where to look in the first place—baffled her. She hadn't provided many details during the telling of her harrowing ideal. Yet here he was and she was so relieved to see him that she slumped in the saddle.

"Don't bother asking Pru where she hid your loot, Phil." Jack smiled craftily. "I'm playing hide-and-seek with it. You'll have to be especially nice to me if you want me to tell you where it is."

"You go to hell, McCavett," Phil roared furiously.

"You go first," Jack insisted. "But release Pru before you leave."

"Not a chance. I'll shoot her before I let you get the best of me."

"No, you won't," Jack contradicted. "You'll be dead before she breathes her last breath. The ransom money and stolen jewelry won't do you a damn bit of good where you're going, you son of a bitch."

Pru's attention settled on Jack's uncompromising expression—one that he'd probably relied on hundreds of times during his stint as a lawman. He looked tough, fearless and hell-bent on justice. And as cold-blooded and deadly as a rattlesnake.

Phil, on the other hand, was shifting restlessly in the saddle and desperately trying to figure out how to gain the advantage. As far as Pru could tell, this stalemate could go on for several minutes, even hours. She was impatient and eager to have it over and done. The consequences be damned.

While Phil was holding onto her, she flung her head back, catching him in the face, causing his teeth to snap together. She also heard the crunch of bone that indicated she had broken his nose. He yelped and cursed and she could feel the pistol barrel bearing down on her throat, making it impossible to breathe or speak.

She dug her heels into the horse's flanks, causing it to bolt sideways. But Phil refused to let go of her as he fought for control of the alarmed steed. Pru silently cursed when Jack bolted forward, shouting Phil's name to gain his attention.

Pru had heard fantastic tales about gunfighters who were lightning fast on the draw, but she had never seen one in action. She had never stared into a gunfighter's eyes during a deadly showdown, either.

When Jack aimed and fired in one blur of motion, she saw the look on his face that promised and delivered hell.

She knew she was seeing a snippet of what Jack McCavett was like in his previous profession. And he was incredible!

His pistol spit lead. Phil Graham was too slow on the draw to match Jack. Which was fine with Pru because the murdering scoundrel deserved a good shooting. Plus, he hadn't planned to give her or Jack a sporting chance.

Jack's well-aimed shot hit Phil in the chest, causing him to slump against Pru for support. She tried to worm away, but he had enough strength left to cock the trigger of the weapon that he crammed in her throat.

"Tell him good bye, bitch," Phil panted shallowly. "I'm taking you with me."

Gunfire split the silence. Pru awaited the inevitable. Since her face was pulsating from the pain rendered by Phil's backhanded blow and her head was tender from being yanked on so fiercely, it was difficult to tell precisely where she had been hit. But she figured it had to be in the neck because Phil had rammed the pistol barrel into her throat more times than not.

A moment later, when Phil pitched off the side of the horse and landed with a thud, Pru realized that he hadn't had the chance to shoot her. Jack had fired a second deadly shot that stopped him cold.

Jack stalked over to kick the weapon from Phil's hand.

"Bastard," Phil snarled on a seesaw breath.

"Maybe so. Don't really know for sure," Jack commented as he watched the bloodstains spread across Phil's laboring chest. "But I damn sure know a heartless son of a bitch when I see one. I buried several of your kind in boot hill cemeteries outside Kansas cow towns. I'll do the same for you in Paradise. Go to hell, Graham, and give my regards to the devil."

When Phil's jaw went slack and he stared sightlessly at the sky, dozens of emotions bombarded Pru simultaneously. Relief was at the forefront. *It's over. At last*, she realized. This cruel, devious cutthroat was on his way to Hades. He wouldn't have the chance to lay another hand on Pru or Samantha again.

"It's okay, sweetheart," Jack cooed. "You're safe now."

He reached up to brush his thumb lightly over her stinging cheek to reroute the salty tears that were about to scald her injured face. She didn't even realize she was crying until he wiped away her tears.

"You were amazing," he praised her. "You have more courage than most men I know."

"I do?" she said with a sniffle.

"Definitely." He reached down to untie her hands and feet from the pommel and stirrups. "You gave that bastard all he wanted…and then some."

The moment she was free Pru flung herself sideways and clamped her arms around Jack's neck. She held onto him so tightly she wondered if he could breathe. As for her, she savored Jack's scent, the feel of his sinewy arms encircling her, keeping her safe. She shook all over and her tears came in great huge sobs that she couldn't control.

"So much for defiant courage," she blubbered.

"This is just aftershock," he assured her. "It will pass and you'll be fine. The point is that you were tough when you needed to be."

Jack didn't add that, on the inside, *he* was a mass of frazzled nerves. Earlier, when Phil pointed his pistol at Pru, determined to blow her out of the saddle, Jack had nearly suffered apoplexy. He'd never been so terrified in his life, not even when William Carter, the gruff-talking rancher from Texas, had grabbed him by the scruff of his shirt, hauled him off the train and he feared he'd never see Stony and Davy again.

And then, when Pru reared back to smash Phil's face, breaking the stalemate and bringing his furious wrath on her, Jack had been so frightened that he couldn't think straight. Fortunately, well-honed skills and instincts had kicked in and he'd reacted quickly.

Now, he held Pru close to his heart, relieved that she was alive and the nightmare was over. His lingering annoyance with her misleading comments about her background and her bet with her family fizzled out. Nothing mattered except that she was safe. He hugged her and rocked her while she bawled her head off. He wanted to wail right along with her to release his pent-up tension so he'd feel better.

He glanced over the top of Pru's disheveled blond head to see Stony trotting toward them. He halted to stare at Graham unsympathetically. "This will make Samantha's life easier."

"Graham was still going to kill Pru after I shot him the first time." Jack lifted Pru into his arms and held her while she continued to cry. "I was forced to shoot twice."

"Phil should have asked me about his chances going up against you," Stony remarked, his attention fixed on Pru's fierce grasp on Jack. "I would have told him he didn't have an icicle's chance in hell…. You okay, Pru?"

"Fine. Wonderful. Couldn't be better," she mumbled against Jack's neck. "Is Gram still in town?" *Sob. Shuddering gasp.* "Could I be so lucky that she got right back on the train and left?"

Stony grinned when she lifted her bruised, tearstained face. "Nope. Sorry. Last time I saw her, she was letting your father have it with both barrels blazing. I hear that you're named after her."

She wrinkled her nose and sniffled. "Yes, lucky me."

"Stony, I'll help you drag Phil over the horse," Jack offered as he propped Pru against a thick tree trunk. "I'd appreciate it if you rode on ahead so Pru has time to compose herself before she's reunited with her family in town."

"Sure thing," Stony said as he dismounted.

When Stony rode away five minutes later, Jack clasped Pru's hand in his and led her to the stream. He used his kerchief to blot her face with cool water. By that time, she was down to muffled sobs and hiccups.

Every time Jack glanced at Pru's swollen and battered face, he wanted to shoot the bastard a few more times for good measure. Before Phil got hold of her, Pru'd had a flawless complexion. Now one eye was partially swollen shut and her puffy lip was split like Samantha's. There was raw skin on her cheeks, her chin and both elbows. Plus, scrapes and cuts on her arms and shoulders.

Jack longed to trace her elegant features with his finger, but he figured it would bring her pain rather than provide comfort.

"This wasn't your fault. None of it was, Jack," she insisted as she took the kerchief and bent to dip it in the stream.

"I feel guilty as hell," he said stubbornly. "No one is going to talk me out of it."

"May I try?" she murmured.

When she leaned forward to brush her lips against his, he stopped beating himself black and blue and savored the

tantalizing taste of her. Lord, he had come perilously close
to losing her today. The prospect had terrified him to no end.

He knew she wouldn't be staying in Paradise. He told
himself that he could deal with that, as long as Pru was out
there *somewhere* in the world. No doubt, Horatio had taken
one look at this fledgling frontier town, watched the
horrible drama unfold around his daughter and decided to
take her back to Missouri on the first train leaving town.

Naturally, Pru's grandmother would agree wholeheartedly.

Jack smiled wryly. Now there was a formidable obstacle
wrapped in black satin and petticoats. No wonder Pru had
accepted the challenge and left home. *The bet* was simply
her excuse to test her independent wings and make her
own choices for the first time in her life. He couldn't blame
her for that.

"Thank you for saving my life. Again," she whispered.

"Sure, but it's gonna cost you," he teased before he
helped himself to another tantalizing kiss.

To his everlasting relief his comment coaxed a smile
from her. Emotions robbed him of breath. Words flocked
to his tongue but Jack bit them back. Damn if he was going
to let Pru's departure be more difficult than it already was.
Hell, he missed her like crazy and she hadn't even set foot
on the train, bookended by that hidebound curmudgeon in
black and her overprotective father.

"C'mon, might as well face the music then order up
another relaxing bath to ease the next round of aches and pains
you're destined to feel," he said as he drew her to her feet.

Pru opened her mouth to voice a comment then must
have thought better of it. She compressed her lips and

squeezed his hand. An overload of emotion bombarded him. It tied him in knots and demanded release. Valiantly he held it all inside and didn't give his feelings away.

"I'll say one thing," he remarked, striving for a light tone.

"What's that, Jack?"

"There's never a dull moment when you're underfoot."

"Sorry about that," she murmured as he set her atop his horse then swung up behind her. "All you wanted was to be left in peace and live the life you've dreamed about."

He made a neutral sound as he guided his steed down the rocky slopes to reach the abandoned buggy. He smiled, remembering that it had been his greatest desire to live a simple life after he'd turned in his badge and walked away from law enforcement.

Now he looked at Pru and decided that it was going to be entirely too dull and quiet in Paradise when her family bustled her back to Saint Louis.

Why was it, he wondered, that what you *thought* you wanted and needed wasn't what you wanted and needed at all? Usually Jack appreciated irony, but today it didn't make him feel better because he knew that the precious few hours he had to spend with Pru were dwindling by the minute.

Pru felt her apprehension coil tightly when she and Jack reached town. Gram and her father were ensconced on the bench outside the hotel. Gram was tapping her cane impatiently—a clear indication that she was in a foul mood.

Dozens of curious citizens milled about. Several women she passed wished her a speedy recovery. Even some of the men commented that they were sorry about her unnerving ordeal.

The moment Jack set her to her feet, Gram rose from her perch to survey her battered condition. "Dear God, child, if this is the abominable treatment a proper lady must tolerate in this god-awful frontier society, then we shall endeavor to avoid it like the plague."

"I don't think it's fair to blame a town of decent people for the ruthless actions of only a few," Pru replied as she stepped onto the boardwalk to place a dutiful kiss on Gram's wrinkled cheek. She pivoted toward Jack. "Gram, this is the man who has saved my life more than once and has suffered personal consequences to see that I'm safe and sound—"

*"Sound?"* Gram harrumphed. "You cannot be of sound mind if you came to this godforsaken wasteland in the first place." In what appeared to be an afterthought—when it was actually a good snubbing—she nodded a stiff greeting in Jack's general direction.

Pru gritted her teeth at her grandmother's slight then added, "Jack McCavett, this is Prudence Meriwether Perkins."

Jack tipped his hat politely. "Nice to meet you, ma'am. Now if you'll excuse us, Pru needs a soaking bath and medical attention. Sturdy and tough though she is, the past few days have been a trying ordeal."

"Well, I never!" Gram gasped as Jack more or less brushed her off as an unwanted obstacle in his path, then escorted Pru inside the hotel.

"Young man," Gram snapped, as only Gram could, "do you have the slightest idea who you are speaking to?"

"No, ma'am. Do *you*?"

Pru swallowed a giggle while Gram puffed up like a toad and sputtered in offended dignity. "Beware, Jack," she whispered confidentially. "An immediate fall from Gram's good graces usually results in a fiery landing. If you were on her stomping ground she would blackball you from every social event and see to it that you were not welcome in the uppity circles."

"I didn't figure she planned to like me much anyway," he said, unconcerned. "Besides, I've faced down worse than crotchety widows carrying dragonhead canes."

Indeed he had, thought Pru. He'd recently engaged in a deadly showdown. She would have to inform Gram that Jack McCavett was lethal with a weapon and as tough as nails. *She* had fallen to pieces in the aftermath of the frightening incident. Jack seemed rock-steady, as usual.

By the time they reached Jack's room, two youngsters were scurrying to fill water buckets. Jack positioned the dressing screen in front of the brass tub.

"This will provide privacy, in case you're plagued with unwanted company," he said then placed a gentle kiss to the only spot on her cheek that wasn't raw and bruised. "I'll check with Doc Quinn to see if he has a salve to ease the pain."

Pru threw her arms around his neck and kissed him as if there were no tomorrow. Which, of course, there wouldn't be because she'd struck a deal with her father. She was bound for Missouri. She'd traded dutiful compliance for Jack's prosperity.

With that in mind, she put everything she was, all that she felt for Jack, into that parting kiss. She tried to convey her affection for him without burdening him with the words of a confession. Jack wanted no more than an arranged, symbiotic marriage to suit his simple life. She had complicated his life enough without telling him that she was in love with him.

"Ahem!" Gram's gravely voice intruded into the moment like shattering glass.

To Pru's amusement Jack took his own sweet time about breaking their kiss, rather than leaping back guiltily. If Gram thought she could make Jack McCavett kowtow, she had seriously miscalculated.

Gram's stern gaze swept over the room, noting Jack's set of clothes on the dresser. "Tell me this is not what I think it is," she huffed in outrage.

"I returned from captivity in the middle of the night," Pru explained. "I came to Jack because I had no idea that Papa had arrived earlier that evening. When I passed out from starvation and exhaustion Jack gave up his bed for me, just as he risked his life to save me two hours ago."

Gram flicked her hand, dismissing Jack as if he were a lowly servant. "All well and good. But remove your belongings immediately, young man. Pru's fiancé will not be pleased if he discovers she shared a room with another man. I doubt anyone in this backwoods has heard of propriety and etiquette, but I assure it thrives in Saint Louis. Now grab your things and go away, McCavett."

Jack scooped up his belongings on his way to the door. He paused to loom over Gram—who looked like a midget beside his tall, masculine frame. "If Pru has a fiancé then it's a good thing I turned her down before we were to marry."

Gram's eyes rounded and bulged like walnuts. She opened her mouth but no words came out. She had been struck speechless—a rare occurrence indeed. She was still gaping at Jack as he sauntered down the hall.

"You were considering marrying that…backward bumpkin?" Gram snorted derisively. "You have gone mad!"

Pru sorely wished again that she had married Jack when she had the chance. It was the biggest mistake of her life. Although Jack would have been stuck with her, for better or worse, Gram couldn't have dragged her back to Saint Louis to serve a lifelong sentence as Edwin Donald's wife.

Suddenly all the physical exertion and high-flying emotion caught up with Pru. She felt bone weary and wrung out. She wanted to plunk in the tub and soak to her heart's content.

"Papa, please find a room for Gram," she requested when her father arrived. "I'm exhausted and I need to rest."

"A room in this fleabag hotel?" Gram sniffed distastefully.

"This is the best available," Pru assured her.

"Gad, I was afraid you were going to say that."

"Come along, Mother," her father requested as he took Gram's arm. "Pru needs time to recuperate before our trip home."

Gram glanced around warily. "Who will stand guard to make sure that disrespectful McCavett character doesn't come barging in here again?"

"He's not all that bad," her father defended on the way down the hall.

"As a servant or bodyguard, probably not. As a chaperone or companion for Pru? Hardly! I will not permit it."

Pru closed and locked the door then sagged in relief. The past that she'd tried desperately to outrun had caught up with her in Paradise. She still couldn't imagine why her father had told Gram where she was, because then Gram had taken it upon herself to track Pru down, too.

Gram was an added complication that she didn't need right now. But what did it matter now? Pru asked herself as she peeled off the soiled gown. She had made a deal with her father for Jack's benefit and she was sticking with it. She was determined to repay him for his trouble and his financial setbacks.

Tired, Pru sank into the tub of warm water and told herself that she'd had her day in the sun, her month of limitless freedom and wild adventure. Also, she had discovered what it was like to fall in love, all the way to the bottom of her heart.

A sob burst from her throat. She remembered the adage that what didn't kill you was supposed to make you stronger. Well, it wasn't true, she mused while she cried her eyes out. Losing Jack was killing her, bit by excruciating bit.

# Chapter Seventeen

Jack shot upright in bed when he heard the light tap at the hotel-room door. He pulled on his breeches and, with pistol in hand, he inched open the door. To his bewildered surprise, Pru was standing in the dimly lit hall in the middle of the night.

Because of his taunting remarks, Gram had forbidden him from seeing Pru before she went to bed. To be honest though, those comments had been a self-defense tactic to ensure he had help keeping his distance from a woman who was far above his social and economic class. Not to mention her fire-breathing dragon of a grandmother saw him as a thorn in the side.

His thoughts swirled off when Pru stepped into the room and closed the door quietly behind her. Then she kissed him with the same sense of urgent desperation as she had that afternoon. She had set him on fire then, as now. He eagerly accepted the feel of her supple body meshed familiarly to his. He knew he would never be this close to Pru again and he vowed to make the most of the moment.

Self-defense tactics be damned for the night.

"Make love to me once more before I have to go away," she whispered against his lips.

"You don't have to go," Jack heard himself say, knowing it was wishful thinking even as he said it.

"Yes, I do," she murmured as her fingers glided through his hair. "For a dozen important reasons, some you don't understand. Yet."

Then she kissed him again and the cryptic comment swirled into the fog of desire. Jack lost the ability to think. His male body urged him to live in the moment, to share the passion Pru offered and make the most of their private tryst. He scooped her into his arms and carried her to bed then followed her down, refusing to break their heated kiss.

His hand drifted from her ankle to her knee, drawing her chemise upward, baring a few more inches of her satiny flesh. When his fingertips glided over her inner thigh, she moaned his name and moved restlessly toward him.

Jack told himself to be gentle with Pru. She was scuffed up and bruised and his impatience would deprive her of pleasure. He vowed to prolong their time together, to savor the magic he had discovered with her and her alone.

He heard her sigh raggedly as he spread a row of kisses over her bruised throat then skimmed his lips over the filmy fabric covering her breasts. He unbuttoned the bodice to flick his tongue at the taut peaks. He was rewarded with her shuddering gasp of pleasure. Jack took his time in pulling the chemise over her head. He feasted his hungry eyes on her shapely body, marveling at how the moonlight spearing through the window made her skin glow. She was like a magical creature from beyond the realm of reality and she mystified him completely. She was breathtaking. She was so wildly responsive, so passionate, so lovely, so…everything.

She was every man's dream come true and he regretted making those comments about how this blue-eyed beauty was more trouble than she was worth. Turned out that she was priceless to him.

"You have entirely too many clothes on," she murmured as her fingers brushed over the waistband of his breeches. "Help me get these off of you."

When her hand dipped lower to brush his rigid length, Jack lost the ability to breathe momentarily. He noted that Pru wasn't helping remove his breeches at all. She left the task to him while her caresses drove him just short of crazy.

"You don't play fair," he chirped, when he finally dragged enough air into his lungs to speak.

"Where's the fun in that?" she teased as she twisted away from him to kiss her way down his shoulder. "No rules tonight, Jack. Only boundless pleasure, okay?"

Her lips skimmed the dark furring of hair on his chest and his belly. His breath fizzled out again as he tried to reach for her. She positioned his hand on his thigh then traced his throbbing length with the tip of her tongue. Pleasure burned in the wake of her caress. Flames leaped through his blood when she took him into her mouth and suckled him. Jack groaned in unholy torment as she stroked him with tongue and teeth, caressed him with her fingertips. Need pelted him so fiercely that he panted to drag in more air to prevent passing out from the intense sensations assailing him.

In that tantalizing moment, when one fantastic pleasure

coiled atop of another, the intolerable thought of Pru in bed with the fiancé Gram had picked out for her nearly drove him out of his mind. If he was ruined for life with other women then it seemed only fitting that his memory should color her trysts with another man.

Maybe he couldn't or shouldn't have Pru as his own, but he vowed she would remember him in the years to come.

Jack shifted sideways then uplifted Pru until she was propped against the pillows and headboard. Then he went down her body one kiss and caress at a time, sensitizing every inch of her flesh with erotic pleasure, branding her with his tender touch.

She gasped as immeasurable pleasure burgeoned inside her, fearing she would burst with it. "Jack?"

"Yes, and don't ever forget it," he whispered against her quivering flesh. "I want to be more to you than a bet you made with your father and grandmother."

"The bet was never about you or *us*," she murmured. "You simply got caught in the middle of a family conflict. I never meant to hurt you. Never that, I swear. You mean too much to me…"

Her thoughts whirled away. He was weaving a silky web of ecstasy around her and nothing else fazed her, nothing else mattered except making love with him this one last time.

Her breath broke as his lips brushed her inner thigh and he traced her secret flesh with his thumb and fingertips. Need bombarded her when he dipped his finger inside her then kissed her intimately. Pru's senses reeled as one fiery sensation after another riveted her. She arched instinctively toward him, feeling her body tense in hungry need, burning with indescribable pleasure.

When the first wave of ecstasy crested over her, she clutched desperately at Jack's shoulder, urging him to take her there and then.

"Not yet," he murmured as he stroked her intimately again.

"I'll be dead in another minute," she assured him frantically. "Jack…ah…"

Another incredible spasm of rapture rippled through her. She dug her nails into his shoulder in frantic desperation. "Come here, damn you," she panted. "Now, Jack!"

His quiet laugher drifted around her as he grabbed her ankles and tugged her downward. She glanced up to see his powerfully built body poised over her, saw the endearing smile that would live in her memory always and forevermore. She fell in love with him all over again.

"Demanding little thing, aren't—?"

She didn't allow him to finish the playful taunt. She curled her hand around his erection and guided him to her. She wanted to be as close to him as she could possibly get. Now. She wanted to share the same breath, the same skin, the same wild pleasure for as long as the moment lasted.

A sigh escaped her lips as he drove into her then retreated. She grabbed his tousled hair, pulled his head to hers and kissed him as he plunged deeply inside her again. And again. The wild cadence of their lovemaking brought them together, apart, and sent pleasure searing through them like a shooting star arcing across the midnight sky. She could taste her hungry need for him on his lips and the intimacy of it sent a shudder rippling straight to the very core of her being.

This was the man her heart desired. This man could fulfill all her wants, needs and dreams. It was killing her that she didn't have forever to spend with him.

She only had tonight.

"Jack, I lo—"

Pru had just enough presence of mind left to shut her mouth before she verbally expressed her love for him. She clamped her lips shut and arched into his driving thrusts, wanting all he had to give, giving all that she was to the man who had come to mean more to her than the freedom and independence she craved.

Her thoughts exploded like a meteor bursting into flames. Soul-shattering passion consumed her, burning her from the inside out. She held on to Jack as if she never meant to let go—knowing she would have to in a few short hours. She savored every indescribable sensation that throbbed through her body. Tears misted her eyes as he shuddered above her then pulled her tightly against him, as if she were as important to his existence as he was to hers.

She knew better, but she let herself think that he loved her in his own way, if only for the night.

Pru tucked her cheek against his chest and cherished the moment. This was her last night in Jack's arms. Her last night of inexpressible pleasure and unparalleled contentment. Gram had already purchased tickets at the railroad depot and her father had made the arrangements with the owner of the lumberyard to begin construction at Jack's homestead immediately. A large deposit had been made into Jack's bank account, though Jack didn't know it yet.

It was part of the bargain she had negotiated with her father. She would leave Jack better off than he'd been before he made the critical mistake of selecting her from the applications of mail-order brides.

She pressed an adoring kiss to his chest before he

eased down beside her. Then she cuddled up against him, feeling content and protected…and loving him to the depths of her soul. She had gone in search of long-awaited freedom and she had discovered how it felt to love wholeheartedly.

She wondered if her father or Gram understood how it felt to love so fiercely. Had Gram forsaken her soul mate to wed Grandpapa? Was that what left Gram bitter and tormented all these years? Had she also placed family duty for her arranged marriage above love? And what of Pru's father? Had he loved her mother as devotedly as Pru loved Jack?

Pru fell asleep, wondering if anyone else in the world understood or experienced these same intense feelings. If they did, she hoped to high heaven that they didn't have to turn their backs on love, as she had been forced to do with Jack. It was going to be sheer torture to leave him behind and return to Saint Louis to live a lie.

The dismal thought prompted her to snuggle even closer to Jack in sleep and make the most of the few hours she had left.

Jack awoke to the vacant space beside him. It looked as empty and rumpled as he felt.

He and Pru had said their intimate farewells the previous night and Pru had tiptoed back to her room before dawn. There was nothing left to say, only dozens of tormenting feelings to bury deep inside and pretend didn't exist.

Jack had expected Horatio to come calling to reprimand him for behaving all too familiarly with his daughter. To his surprise, Horatio hadn't dropped by before he bustled his mother and his daughter off to catch the early morning train. He supposed that since he had saved Pru's life Horatio decided not to press the issue.

Rising from bed, Jack splattered water on his face, considered shaving and rejected the idea. He tramped downstairs and headed for Harper's Café to meet Stony for breakfast. Sure enough, Stony was hovering over a stack of pancakes and chasing it with coffee.

"Morning," Jack mumbled as he plunked down at the table.

"It *is* a good morning because this town is back to normal," Stony said cheerily.

"Yeah, I suppose it is." So why did normal suddenly feel so dull and uninspiring?

"I'm going over to Samantha Graham's place to help her with the arrangements," Stony informed him between bites. "She feels terrible about what happened to Pru." Stony shook his head. "Every time I think about how that bastard mistreated and ridiculed Samantha the past three years I want to—"

"I know," Jack cut in bitterly.

"Yeah, but you got to shoot him—twice—to appease your need for revenge," Stony complained. "I only got to haul him to the undertaker."

Jack studied his friend's scowl. He had been so immersed in his own misery that he hadn't realized what was going on. Obviously, Stony had formed an instant attachment to Samantha. Either that or he had been secretly attracted to her while she was unavailable. Whatever the case, Stony had tender feelings for the widow.

"Better that you weren't the one who brought Phil down

with bullets," he said perceptively. "You and Sam don't need that standing between you."

Stony glanced up sharply and Jack flung up his hand. "I've known you too long not to see right through you."

"That obvious?" Stony mumbled. "Hell."

"I approve and I know you'll treat Sam with the courtesy and respect she deserves." Jack knew Stony was sensitive to women who had been physically and emotionally abused. When Stony was six years old, he had been placed in the orphanage after watching his mother die from internal injuries caused by a brutal attack. "And you deserve someone like her. Someone who appreciates a kind, considerate man."

Stony smirked teasingly. "Just because Pru tried her hand at matchmaking for you doesn't mean you get to do it for me. Stay out of this, thank you very much."

"Fine, fumble around with your courtship," Jack replied. "But you'll be damn sorry when someone else comes to call on Samantha while you're being overly cautious."

Jack heard the loud whistle, signaling the train's departure. He felt his stomach drop to his boots. Emptiness overwhelmed him so he called to Amelia Thorton and asked for his own stack of pancakes, hoping to fill the gaping hole inside him.

It didn't help so he drank his lunch and supper, determined to drown the tormenting emotions in a bottle. He hoped to be oblivious to the ache in his chest by the time Pru reached her destination and returned to the life her family expected of her. He still didn't understand why she felt she had to leave. Did she still feel guilty about disrupting his life? Did she believe she really had become the curse of his existence?

Well, it wasn't true. She had become the light of his life. The light went out when the train pulled away from the depot and headed to Missouri.

Jack decided he needed a motivating purpose. He would rebuild the house that was in ashes. He would return to his quiet, secluded life…and pretend his heart hadn't left for Saint Louis on the morning train.

Two days later, Jack rolled over on his pallet on the ground and groaned miserably. His head felt like an overly ripe melon. His mouth was as dry as cotton. And forget about trying to string together a thought. He'd never endured a hangover that compared to the one that had him in its vise grip this particular morning.

Creaking and clattering sounds drew his attention. He levered himself up on a wobbly elbow and pried open one bloodshot eye. The morning sun smacked him in the face and nearly blinded him. He groaned in agony, grabbed his aching head and fought the wave of nausea that threatened to engulf him.

Jack frowned curiously when he saw Stony leading a procession of men on horseback. Several wagons, heaping with lumber, brought up the rear. When Jack crawled to his hands and knees to greet his unexpected guests, the world tilted sideways, nearly throwing him off balance. It required a few moments of deep breathing to steady himself. Although his head hurt like a son of a bitch, he managed to stagger to his feet.

Stony halted his horse in front of Jack, gave him the once-over and said, "You look worse than you did last night."

"Thanks for making me feel better about myself," Jack

grumbled as he raked his hand through his disheveled hair. "What the hell is going on?"

Stony dismounted and handed Jack the letter Horatio Perkins had left. Jack's bloodshot eyes popped from their sockets when he read:

To Stony Mason,

Please see to it that Jack McCavett is compensated fully and immediately for the expenses he incurred and the trouble he faced to ensure my daughter's safety during her darkest hours. I deposited monetary compensation in his name at the bank and made arrangements with the proprietor of the lumberyard to rebuild the home lost because of his association with my daughter. The house will be three times larger than the original.

"Good God!" Jack cried in disbelief.
"I know. Keep reading," Stony prompted.

The same arrangements will apply to the barn, out-buildings and expanded corrals for the newly purchased herd of horses and cattle that will arrive in two weeks.

Although I cannot place a value on my daughter's life, I wish to acknowledge Jack McCavett's heroic efforts on Pru's behalf. Since I promised a reward for her safe return, I enclosed compensation. Also enclosed is the amount of money Pru claims she borrowed from McCavett.

I trust that the Perkins' debt to McCavett has been paid in full. Please extend my deepest appreciation.

Sincerely, Horatio Perkins

Stony stuffed a heaping pouch in the pocket of Jack's

wrinkled shirt. "In addition, I'm supposed to tell you that
Myrna Bates will be around at noon with a picnic lunch.
Kathryn Sykes will bring supper."

The waitress and the farmer's daughter, Jack thought
sourly. Pru wasn't even here and she was still parading
would-be brides past him. After getting to know Pru and
battling the myriad of feelings she unleashed inside him,
Jack wasn't sure he wanted to be around other women. Not
for a while at least. It would hurt too damn much. It would
stir up too many tormenting memories of what the woman
of his dreams looked like—and what she didn't look like.

"You look a little green around the gills, my friend."
Stony said in concern. "Are you going to be okay?"

"I'm fine. Perfect." Jack lurched toward the tree-lined
creek. "All I need is a bath to wake up." He honestly doubted
that would cure what really ailed him, but it was a start.

"I'm heading back to town." Stony called as he mounted
his horse. "I'm having lunch with Samantha."

"Good for you," Jack said as he wobbled away. "Give
her my regards."

Jack pulled off his clothes then cursed when he realized
he had blundered onto the site where he and Pru had first
made love after he released her from jail. The memories
were so thick they nearly suffocated him. He scooped up
his discarded garments, cursed sourly then trudged
upstream to a spot where the water was only ten inches
deep. Then he sprawled out and soaked himself from head
to toe. The cool water relieved the throbbing in his skull
but it didn't do a damn thing for the ache in his heart.

# Chapter Eighteen

Pru stared at her reflection in the bedroom mirror. "You have to tell him the truth. You can't live this lie. It's killing you day by day."

*You made a promise*, said the noble voice in her head. *You have to abide by it.*

Like a condemned prisoner heading for the gallows, Pru exited her room.

"You look divine as always," Edwin Donald praised as he watched her descend the staircase. "Breathtaking, too."

When she was within reach, he bowed over her hand then placed a kiss to her wrist. Pru stifled the shudder that inevitably assailed her when she and Edwin made physical contact. She couldn't imagine how she would respond if she had to share a marriage bed with him.

"Thank you, Edwin." *Jack, where are you and which potential bride did you choose? I miss you like crazy!* "It's nice of you to notice."

Edwin paid his respects to her father and Gram before the foursome ambled outside. Pru waited to be handed up into the carriage that would take them to another stuffy dinner party where she had to behave like the perfect lady who had been trussed up in the finest garments money could buy.

Since leaving Oklahoma Territory two months earlier, she'd only managed to sneak away from the house twice in her urchin's clothing to recapture the sense of freedom she had exchanged for Jack's prosperity. She could feel herself dying inside with each passing day, each pretentious gala affair she attended. The spark of her spirit was growing so dim that it had nearly been smothered, just as Gram had hoped.

Tonight, she suspected, would be the night when Gram officially announced her betrothal to Edwin. Then he would formally present her with a ring, while surrounded by a score of guests from the city's most elite circle.

Pru had played the role and attended all the functions at Gram's insistence. She had watched her father stand aside, studying her intently but saying nothing. She wondered if he was watching for signs that indicated she might bolt and run. As much as she would have liked to, she had made this bargain with her father and she couldn't call it off.

"What a wonderful evening for the Baxters' dinner party," Gram was saying when Pru got around to listening. "Don't you agree, dear?"

"Yes, Gram," she murmured tonelessly as Edwin assisted her into the carriage. *Kill me now,* Pru silently requested as she glanced skyward, wishing there were a lightning bolt overhead when she really needed it.

The clatter of a horseback rider thundering down the cobblestone street nabbed Pru's attention. She glanced up to see the rider race across the lawn then leap the fence.

"What the devil is the matter with that madman?"

Gram muttered in annoyance. "Oh, dear God! Of all the rotten luck!"

When Gram's voice hit a shrill pitch and she sputtered like a geyser, Pru took a closer look. Her mouth dropped open when she recognized Jack McCavett, dressed in the same stylish three-piece suit he'd worn when he rescued her from the stagecoach holdup. She was still gaping at him in disbelief when he skidded his winded steed to a halt beside the front gate. He bounded agilely from the saddle and strode quickly toward the carriage.

He nodded his dark head in the semblance of a greeting to Edwin, to her father and then to Gram. Then he said, "Prudence Elizabeth Perkins, as the deputy marshal from Paradise, Oklahoma Territory, I am here to notify you that you are being sued for breach of contract."

"What in God's name are you blathering about, you big dolt!" Gram demanded huffily. "I know for a fact that you were well-paid for your trouble. We are on our way to an engagement party. *Pru's* engagement party to be specific." She stabbed a bony finger in Edwin's direction. "Edwin has the ring and everything."

Jack couldn't take his eyes off Pru. Her face was ghostly white but she looked like a fairy princess in her silk and taffeta gown that probably cost more than he made in a month. She looked like an unattainable vision of poise and beauty and he nearly lost his nerve.

Then he remembered that he'd spent two hellish months without her and coming here was all that gave his miserable life hope and purpose.

"Edwin Donald?" Jack thrust out his hand. "Nice to meet you."

Edwin surveyed Jack's attire, which was nowhere near as costly and elegant as his tailor-made eveningwear. He stared pointedly at Jack's outstretched hand, as if he'd been offered a three-day-old dead fish. Then he flung his patrician nose in the air and struck an arrogant pose meant to belittle Jack.

"Why are you interrupting my evening and who the devil are you?" Edwin demanded haughtily.

Jack had felt slightly guilty about bursting Edwin's bubble. Until he actually met the conceited gent, who tried—unsuccessfully—to look down his nose at a man who was more than a head taller.

Cocky ass, thought Jack.

"The devil knows me as Jack McCavett and Pru knows me as her future husband."

Edwin's uppity manners abandoned him. *"What!"* he squawked like a plucked rooster.

"Afraid so, Eddie," Jack took great pleasure in confirming. "I made arrangements almost four months ago for a mail-order bride. I selected Pru from five other applicants. After I wired the money for her travel expenses, she came to Oklahoma Territory then changed her mind."

"Well then, there you go," said Edwin. "Apparently she came to her senses." He glanced sternly at Pru. "Are you going to tell this oaf to go away or shall I do it for you?"

Pru was still staring at Jack in shocked amazement. He noticed that all the scrapes and bruises she had suffered during her ordeals had healed. Except for a small, telltale white scar at the corner of her lush mouth. He had kissed the wound ever so gently the night before she had gone away and left him in tormented misery. He wanted to kiss that spot again—and several other places on her curvaceous body—but all these people were in his way.

In addition, Pru hadn't said one word since he'd shown up out of the blue like a lightning bolt. What if she wasn't glad to see him? What if she'd gotten on with her life while he was stuck in a quagmire of bittersweet memories?

Jack sucked in a deep breath of air before he lost his nerve. He dropped down on one knee, just as he had mentally rehearsed during the train ride to Saint Louis. "Prudence Elizabeth Perkins, I love—"

"Get up this instant!" Gram interrupted with a screech of outrage.

He ignored her and kept his focus on Pru. "I thought I wanted a quiet life and a dutiful wife who would work beside me on my homestead, one who would be grateful for a fresh new start, even if her new husband wasn't a prize catch."

"Dear God, will someone get this yammering idiot to shut up?" Gram howled.

Jack still paid her no attention. His gaze was trained on Pru's shiny blue eyes and heart-shaped lips. "You sent a troop of women for my approval as a replacement bride. I could have lived with each and every one of them—"

"Then go do it!" Gram snapped sarcastically. "Move to Utah and keep them all! I'll pay for your train tickets!"

"I could live with them, but you're the one I can't live *without,* Pru," he told her, putting his pride and his heart on the line. "Marry me. You can have all the independence and freedom you want while you support your worthwhile causes. You can work wherever you choose. Oscar Epperson at the newspaper office is begging to have you back. You can come and go from the ranch if you'll come home to me each night."

"This is the most absurd scene I have ever had the misfortune of witnessing," said Edwin. He grabbed Pru's hand to give her a jostling shake. "Step down from the carriage, dear—ouch!"

Jack reacted without even thinking. He slapped Edwin's hand away then bounded to his feet. "Never, *ever* lay a hand on her without her permission," he growled threateningly. "The last man who towed her away and struck her is pushing up daisies. I'm the one who made it necessary to plant him in the ground."

"I will have you arrested for accosting me," Edwin snapped as he shook the sting from his hand.

"Fine, have me arrested, but don't try to speak for Pru. She makes her own choices, Eddie. She is bright, witty and spirited. *She* decides whether to stay or to go. She has her own rights and privileges and I am here to see that no one stifles her ever again—*ooofff!*"

Jack staggered back when Pru launched herself from the carriage and slammed into his chest, forcing out his breath in a pained grunt. She wrapped her arms around his neck and her legs around his waist. He was half covered in lace petticoats and yards of expensive satin but he didn't mind one bit. Especially when she commenced covering his face and lips with smacking kisses and held on to him for dear life.

"Horatio!" Gram howled as she rammed the tip of her cane into her son's neck to spur him into action. "Do something!"

"I love you, Jack!" Pru shouted to the rooftops. "I need you to make my life complete. I don't belong here. I need to be with you in Paradise."

"Pru, for God's sake, you are making a spectacle of yourself," Gram sputtered.

"Prudence? What is wrong with you?" Edwin howled in shock. "You are a dignified lady and you best remember it!"

Gram glared at her son, who sat there saying and doing nothing. "Get this situation under control. I gave up the love of my life to fulfill my family duty and obligation. So must Pru. I have made the arrangements and I want this *jackass* arrested before he spoils our plans. If you won't stop him then I will!"

Gram raised her cane, prepared to smack Jack on the back of the head. Horatio latched onto the upraised cane and unclamped it from his mother's fist. "No one is going to do anything because it appears to me that Pru has made up her mind about whom and what she wants, Mother."

Gram crossed her arms beneath her bosom and fumed. "Who and what she wants should not be a consideration." She glared furiously at Jack.

Horatio turned his attention to Jack. There was a hint of a smile on his lips. "Quite frankly, I'm surprised it took you so long to come and get her, son."

"Son? *Son!*" Gram muttered as she jerked upright. "You cannot be seriously accepting him. You cannot—"

"Be still, Mother," Horatio interrupted. "I'm sorry you were forced to forsake love for family duty and that you and Papa were trapped in an arranged marriage. But I'm not going to do that to my daughter and see her unhappy." He half turned to smile fondly at Pru and Jack. "You two don't need my permission to marry but you have my blessing nonetheless."

Gram huffed and sputtered then sulked in the corner of the carriage.

Horatio grinned wryly at he focused his attention on

Jack. "I noticed the way you looked at my daughter during several telling moments while I was in Paradise. I'm not so old that I don't remember how it feels to love someone with all your heart."

Horatio stepped down to trace his forefinger over Pru's creamy cheek. "You have your mother's beauty and even more spirit than she did. She would be so proud of you. As I am. Be happy, Pru."

Pru's eyes misted over as she leaned over to press a kiss to her father's cheek. He had come to her defense when it mattered most. He was canceling their bargain and giving her the choice to live how she pleased, where she pleased, with the man she loved.

Pru looked into the ruggedly handsome face of the man she never thought she'd see again. "I wish I had married you the first time I had the chance," she told Jack. "Are you sure you love me? Are you sure you want me to be your wife? I don't even know how to cook or do laundry. I'm afraid I will always be crusading for women's rights and that I might put your reputation in jeopardy again."

He grinned broadly. "Someone has to fight for what's right. You can't leave the arrangements for all the rallies to Samantha, Roz, Molly and Amelia. And by the way, Molly and Amelia booted their abusive husbands from their homes. Their kindred sisters have united to make sure they don't lay a hand on their estranged wives. Also, Stony and Samantha are crazy about each other and intend to marry."

"Really? They will make a wonderful match," Pru replied.

Jack set Pru to her feet then pressed another kiss to her lips. "Now point me toward the justice of the peace then to the nearest hotel."

"For heaven's sake, jackass," Gram harrumphed. "Don't be so crude and obvious."

Jack ignored the old bat and offered Pru his arm. She eagerly accepted it then stuffed her foot into the stirrup. Jack boosted her up to sit astride the rented horse.

Gram commenced muttering about the impropriety of proper ladies riding astride, but Pru paid her no heed. When Jack swung up behind her, she nestled against him. That exhilarating feeling of freedom and pleasure that she had discovered in Paradise overwhelmed her as Jack curled his arm protectively around her waist to hold her in place.

She could have it both ways, she realized as they trotted down the street, serenaded by Gram's objections and Edwin's threats. Loving Jack didn't restrict her in the least. It gave her wings so she could fly. She couldn't wait to speak her vows so Jack would belong to her forevermore. She was eager to become the special woman Jack McCavett chose as his wife, not just a random name he'd selected from the half-dozen females who had responded to his ad for a mail-order bride.

"Misgivings? Second thoughts?" Jack asked as he reined to a halt at the downtown office where Pru had directed him.

"No. You?" she questioned.

He dismounted then set her to her feet. "Not a single reservation. I even delayed in furnishing and decorating the new house because I needed you to share the task with me."

"Oh, Jack," she said, choked up by his comment.

"I want the house to be *our* home," he assured her. "As for asking you to marry me, it's the smartest thing I've done since I turned in my law-enforcement badge."

She glanced up at him and frowned. "I thought you said you were a deputy marshal in Paradise these days."

He grinned wryly. "I lied. So shoot me."

Her blue eyes twinkled with love and amusement. "I'd rather marry you."

"I'd rather you marry me, too," he whispered adoringly.

And so she did.

\* \* \* \* \*

## THE ROYAL HOUSE OF NIROLI
*Always passionate, always proud*

The richest royal family in the world—united by
blood and passion, torn apart by deceit and desire

Nestled in the azure blue of the Mediterranean Sea, the majestic
island of Niroli has prospered for centuries. The Fierezza men
have worn the crown with passion and pride since ancient
times. But now, as the king's health declines, and his two sons
have been tragically killed, the crown is in jeopardy.

The clock is ticking—a new heir must be found before the
king is forced to abdicate. By royal decree the internation-
ally scattered members of the Fierezza family are summoned
to claim their destiny. But any person who takes the throne
must do so according to The Rules of the Royal House of
Niroli. Soon secrets and rivalries emerge as the descendents
of this ancient royal line vie for position and power. Only a
true Fierezza can become ruler—a person dedicated to their
country, their people...and their eternal love!

*Each month starting in July 2007,
Harlequin Presents is delighted to bring you
an exciting installment from*
THE ROYAL HOUSE OF NIROLI,
*in which you can follow the epic search
for the true Nirolian king.
Eight heirs, eight romances, eight fantastic stories!*

Here's your chance to enjoy a sneak preview of the
first book delivered to you by royal decree...

FIVE minutes later she was standing immobile in front of the study's window, her original purpose of coming in forgotten, as she stared in shocked horror at the envelope she was holding. Waves of heat followed by icy chill surged through her body. She could hardly see the address now through her blurred vision, but the crest on its left-hand front corner stood out, its *royal* crest, followed by the address: *HRH Prince Marco of Niroli...*

She didn't hear Marco's key in the apartment door, she didn't even hear him calling out her name. Her shock was so great that nothing could penetrate it. It encased her in a kind of bubble, which only concentrated the torment of what she was suffering and branded it on her brain so that it could never be forgotten. It was only finally pierced by the sudden opening of the study door as Marco walked in.

"Welcome home, *Your Highness*. I suppose I ought to curtsy." She waited, praying that he would laugh and tell her that she had got it all wrong, that the envelope she was holding, addressing him as Prince Marco of Niroli, was some silly mistake. But like a tiny candle flame shivering vulnerably in the dark, her hope trembled fearfully. And then the look in Marco's eyes extinguished it as cruelly as a hand placed callously over a dying person's face to stem their last breath.

"Give that to me," he demanded, taking the envelope from her.

"It's too late, Marco," Emily told him brokenly. "I know the truth now…." She dug her teeth in her lower lip to try to force back her own pain.

"You had no right to go through my desk," Marco shot back at her furiously, full of loathing at being caught off-guard and forced into a position in which he was in the wrong, making him determined to find something he could accuse Emily of. "I trusted you…."

Emily could hardly believe what she was hearing. "No, you didn't trust me, Marco, and you didn't trust me because you knew that I couldn't trust you. And you knew that because you're a liar, and liars don't trust people because they know that they themselves cannot be trusted." She not only felt sick, she also felt as though she could hardly breathe. "You are Prince Marco of Niroli…. How could you not tell me who you are and still live with me as intimately as we have lived together?" she demanded brokenly.

"Stop being so ridiculously dramatic," Marco demanded fiercely. "You are making too much of the situation."

"*Too much?*" Emily almost screamed the words at him. "When were you going to tell me, Marco? Perhaps you just planned to walk away without telling me anything? After all, what do my feelings matter to you?"

"Of course they matter." Marco stopped her sharply. "And it was in part to protect them, and you, that I decided not to inform you when my grandfather first announced that he intended to step down from the throne and hand it on to me."

"To protect me?" Emily nearly choked on her fury. "Hand on the throne? No wonder you told me when you first took me to bed that all you wanted was sex. You *knew* that was the only kind of relationship there could ever be between us! You *knew* that one day you would be Niroli's king. No doubt you are expected to marry a princess. Is she picked out for you already, your *royal* bride?"

* * * * *

*Look for*
*THE FUTURE KING'S PREGNANT MISTRESS*
*by Penny Jordan in July 2007,*
*from Harlequin Presents,*
*available wherever books are sold.*

# SPECIAL EDITION™

### Look for six new
### MONTANA MAVERICKS
### stories, beginning in July with

# THE MAN WHO HAD EVERYTHING

## by *CHRISTINE RIMMER*

When Grant Clifton decided to sell the
family ranch, he knew it would devastate
Stephanie Julen, the caretaker who'd always been
like a little sister to him. He wanted a new start,
but how could he tell her that she and her mother
would have to leave...especially now that he was
head over heels in love with her?

# MONTANA
# MAVERICKS

**Dreaming big—and winning hearts—in Big Sky Country**

# Do you know
# a real-life heroine?

## Nominate her for the Harlequin More Than Words award.

---

Each year Harlequin Enterprises honors five ordinary women for their extraordinary commitment to their community.

Each recipient of the Harlequin More Than Words award receives a $10,000 donation from Harlequin to advance the work of her chosen charity. And five of Harlequin's most acclaimed authors donate their time and creative talents to writing a novella inspired by the award recipients. The More Than Words anthology is published annually in October and all proceeds benefit causes of concern to women.

HARLEQUIN

*More Than Words*™

**For more details or to nominate
a woman you know please visit**
**www.HarlequinMoreThanWords.com**

MTW2007

Silhouette®

# Desire

# THE GARRISONS
A brand-new family saga begins with

# THE CEO'S
# SCANDALOUS AFFAIR
## BY ROXANNE ST. CLAIRE

Eldest son Parker Garrison is preoccupied running
his Miami hotel empire and dealing with his recently
deceased father's secret second family. Since he has
little time to date, taking his superefficient assistant
to a charity event should have been a simple plan.
Until passion takes them beyond business.

Don't miss any of the six exciting titles in
THE GARRISONS continuity, beginning in July.
Only from Silhouette Desire.

# THE CEO'S
# SCANDALOUS AFFAIR
#1807

*Available July 2007.*

**THE ROYAL HOUSE OF NIROLI**

Always passionate, always proud.

**The richest royal family in the world—
a family united by blood and passion,
torn apart by deceit and desire.**

Step into the glamorous, enticing world of the
Nirolian Royal Family. As the king ails he must find an
heir…each month an exciting new installment follows
the epic search for the true Nirolian king. Eight heirs,
eight romances, eight fantastic stories!

It's time for playboy prince Marco Fierezza to
claim his rightful place…on the throne of Niroli!
Emily loves Marco, but she has no idea he's a royal
prince! What will this king-in-waiting do when he
discovers his mistress is pregnant?

# THE FUTURE KING'S PREGNANT MISTRESS

## by Penny Jordan

(#2643)

**On sale July 2007.**

# REQUEST YOUR FREE BOOKS!

## Harlequin® Historical
### Historical Romantic Adventure!

## 2 FREE NOVELS PLUS 2 **FREE GIFTS!**

**YES!** Please send me 2 FREE Harlequin® Historical novels and my 2 FREE gifts. After receiving them, if I don't wish to receive any more books, I can return the shipping statement marked "cancel." If I don't cancel, I will receive 6 brand-new novels every month and be billed just $4.69 per book in the U.S., or $5.24 per book in Canada, plus 25¢ shipping and handling per book and applicable taxes, if any*. That's a savings of close to 15% off the cover price! I understand that accepting the 2 free books and gifts places me under no obligation to buy anything. I can always return a shipment and cancel at any time. Even if I never buy another book from Harlequin, the two free books and gifts are mine to keep forever.

246 HDN EEWW    349 HDN EEW9

Name _____ (PLEASE PRINT) _____

Address _____ Apt. # _____

City _____ State/Prov. _____ Zip/Postal Code _____

Signature (if under 18, a parent or guardian must sign)

### Mail to the **Harlequin Reader Service®**:
**IN U.S.A.:** P.O. Box 1867, Buffalo, NY 14240-1867
**IN CANADA:** P.O. Box 609, Fort Erie, Ontario L2A 5X3

Not valid to current Harlequin Historical subscribers.

**Want to try two free books from another line?**
**Call 1-800-873-8635 or visit www.morefreebooks.com.**

* Terms and prices subject to change without notice. NY residents add applicable sales tax. Canadian residents will be charged applicable provincial taxes and GST. This offer is limited to one order per household. All orders subject to approval. Credit or debit balances in a customer's account(s) may be offset by any other outstanding balance owed by or to the customer. Please allow 4 to 6 weeks for delivery.

**Your Privacy:** Harlequin is committed to protecting your privacy. Our Privacy Policy is available online at www.eHarlequin.com or upon request from the Reader Service. From time to time we make our lists of customers available to reputable firms who may have a product or service of interest to you. If you would prefer we not share your name and address, please check here. ☐

HH07

# HARLEQUIN®

# *Mediterranean* NIGHTS™

*Experience the glamour and elegance of cruising the high seas with a new 12-book series....*

## MEDITERRANEAN NIGHTS

**Coming in July 2007...**

# SCENT OF A WOMAN

*by*

## Joanne Rock

When Danielle Chevalier is invited to an exclusive conference aboard *Alexandra's Dream,* she knows it will mean good things for her struggling fragrance company. But her dreams get a setback when she meets Adam Burns, a representative from a large American conglomerate.

Danielle is charmed by the brusque American—until she finds out he means to compete with her bid for the opportunity that will save her family business!

**www.eHarlequin.com**    HM38961

# COMING NEXT MONTH FROM

# HARLEQUIN®
# HISTORICAL

- **SEDUCTION OF AN ENGLISH BEAUTY**
  by **Miranda Jarrett**
  **(Regency)**
  No self-respecting Italian rakehell could ignore the lush beauty he
  spots on a hotel balcony, but no sweet English rose would succumb
  to passionate seduction...right?

- **THE STRANGER**
  by **Elizabeth Lane**
  **(Western)**
  Haunted by his past, he has never stopped wondering what
  happened to Laura. Will Caleb's secrets deny them a future
  together?

- **UNTAMED COWBOY**
  by **Pam Crooks**
  **(Western)**
  Riding the trail, Penn McClure only wants to satisfy his wild need
  for revenge—yet his heart may not escape unscathed!

- **THE ROMAN'S VIRGIN MISTRESS**
  by **Michelle Styles**
  **(Roman)**
  Beautiful Silvana Junia has a reputation for scandalous, outrageous
  behavior. Still, when she agrees to become Fortis's mistress, she
  has no idea of the consequences....

HHCNM0607